The Best American Erotica 1999

EDITED BY

Susie Bright

Touchstone
Published by
Simon & Schuster

TOUCHSTONE
Rockefeller Center
1230 Avenue of the Americas
New York, NY 10020

TOUCHSTONE and colophon are registered trademarks
of Simon & Schuster Inc.

Designed by Barbara M. Bachman

Manufactured in the United States of America

1   3   5   7   9   10   8   6   4   2

ISBN 0-684-84395-1

Acknowledgments

Thank you to my usual suspects, Jon Bailiff, Bill Bright, and my managers Joanie Shoemaker and Jo-Lynne Worley, for all their time and attention to this volume. They have been invaluable every year to this series. I'd also like to thank my assistant, Kirstin Broome, who helped immeasurably.

This book is dedicated to
the memory of author and poet
Kathy Acker
(1947–1997).

"We are dreaming of sex,

of thieves, murderers, firebrands,

of huge thighs opening to us like this night."

Contents

A Special Note
. . . and a New
Publication Date

Dear Readers,

This year, for the first time, *The Best American Erotica* series is coming out in February. Since we started the series in 1993, we traditionally published in October, but we are glad to have this new debut date. It will allow us to have the current year on our book cover for eleven months instead of three!

This volume, which would have been called *BAE 1998* on our old schedule, is now the newly titled *BAE 1999*. We have not skipped a volume in our series, but rather adapted the title to fit our new calendar.

What you have in your hands are the favorite stories I have collected for the past year and a half since I delivered the 1997 edition. Enjoy them all, and every moment of satisfaction and inspiration they provide!

Clits Up,
Susie Bright

Introduction

I'm the woman who loves mail too much. In porno parlance, I'd say I have a big blue box with a red flag that begs to be stuffed. Bills do not count. Flyers offering me 4.9 percent interest for six seconds or season-end catalogs for ladies' cotton underwear also do not count. I hate that trash.

What I like, and fortunately what I get nearly every day, is a letter from a stranger telling me what he or she thinks of my work. Sometimes it's one of those reader surveys tucked at the end of this volume. Other times people have the urge to go beyond those tiny sheets and send me a full page of opinion.

I bask in their praise. I also seem to soak neck-deep in their criticism until I turn pruney. I am driven to hear my critics without flinching, to have the fortitude to say, "You're absolutely right, and I'm going to change this." Yet I do have rebellious moments when I want to turn the tables, and say, "Oh, shut up." I guess this introduction is one of *those* moments.

The number one peeve in my complaint box is, "Why aren't there more stories in *The Best American Erotica* that get me off?"

I've written down the entire list of demands I've received on this count, including "No more stories about gays," "No more stories about weirdos," "Lay off the S/M," "More lesbo sex but drop the fags," "No yucky blood," "Can the fatties," and "Please, no more men with big throbbing thighs."

I have also noted the reader outrage that certain types of sex are not well enough represented in *The Best American Erotica*, to wit: "normal heterosexuals" (I'd like to see Exhibit A on this one), "normal intercourse," "lesbians who are really lesbians" (panty check?), and "men with extra-large penises" (who's measuring?).

Pleasing everyone has been hopeless, and yet on some entirely serendipitous occasions, a simultaneous pleasure. I would say the most popular story I ran in the last edition was certainly not about "normal intercourse," but it was the hands-down crowd favorite: "She Gets Her Ass Fucked Good." I couldn't pass up a story with a name like that either, and it was a thrill for me to finally find authors with the proud butt-sense to write a story where a woman thrives on anal sex instead of being disgusted.

In *The Best American Erotica* edition the year before that, "The Hit," by Aaron Travis, was the favorite. It's got blood, S/M, nasty gunplay, and an all-male cast, and it is also one of the best erotic crime stories I've ever read. I wondered, after I stopped screaming at its climax, "Will this be too much for *BAE*?" But I've learned over the years that if a sex story is so riveting you can't put it down, it doesn't matter what the content is, the reader will be captivated. It turned out "The Hit" was the most frequently praised story in that year's collection, and I'm certain that none of the fans who wrote me have experienced anything "normal" in real life like the Mafia hit job that author Travis described.

One of the first stories I ever published, early in my erotica career, was a story called "Rubenesque," by Magenta Michaels. People still write me about this story ten years after I edited it. In it, a woman with an ample figure and, in particular, queen-size thighs, finds herself at a literary luncheon where she gets eaten out underneath her heavy tablecloth by one of the hotel workmen. Now, this whole business of under-the-counter cunnilingus is not new, but this character's voluptuous innocence was so poignantly and sensually described that the story was irresistible—to the slim as well as the fat.

I never tell people ahead of time what the "content" of my erotic collections will be. If I tell you I have fifteen heterosexuals, nine and a half lesbians, six men who may or may not be gay, and a partridge in a dildo harness, what does that tell you about whether it's hot or not? Likewise, I could testify to the number of come shots and detail the positions—but who's to say any particular cock and clit will make music together? The best kind of sex writing takes me on an adventure I'd never dream of myself, and at the same time, gets me exactly where I live.

I also like to be selfish sometimes, and it's taken a hell of a long time to admit it. I think the worst personal criticism I ever heard as a child was, "You're nothing but the worst sort of selfish." I wanted the first slice of every birthday cake, and mourned for my toys and books when I was supposed to be doing the laundry. All of these were likely to get me branded with the big "S."

Now that I'm a mother myself, as much as I vowed I would never use that label on my daughter, it has come to haunt me—the innocent audacity with which children will tell you just exactly what they want—and that, by the way, they want it *now*. How can they be such thoughtless little pigs!

In due time, I learned as an adult all the vile niceties about how to say what you want . . . without really saying it. When that failed to make an impression, I blamed my-self for daring to have a preference in the first place. It was the burden of my first years as a lover that I never revealed what would make me have an orgasm, I never touched my clit or asked for it to be touched. I wanted someone to just look into my eyes and turn on the magic. To say out loud how I wanted to get fucked would have been so humiliat-ing!—that is, until finally I got so frustrated (or was it just old enough?) that I blurted it out.

I had no idea that it was a turn-on to tell my lovers what aroused me—now *that* was magic. The way they reacted to my trust and confidence could easily be the most pas-sionate part of our time together. I simultaneously realized that being chastened for my fantasies by a lover was worse than a cold shower for ruining any chance we had for erotic chemistry.

I actually have two sets of ideas about erotic self-interest. If someone tells me in bed that they like it missionary style, I'm thrilled to know the details and I'm more than ready to pray and play. It's good for people to know what makes them come alive, and I envy those who know themselves without apologies.

But outside the bedroom negotiation, if that same self-ish little brat tells me that I'm supposed to make an an-thology of *The Best American Erotica* out of their strict formula—well, I'm afraid that's where you have to learn to share. When erotic fantasy becomes literature, there has to be a spirit of generosity and adventure to keep the artistic momentum alive. This is a group experience.

The Best American Erotica isn't one of those handy stroke zines or Special Prosecutor Reports where all the juicy parts are labeled by page: "Cigar fantasies, pp. 5–7." When I was a kid, exploring my first erotica, this is what I was familiar with. It was so exciting to read something forbidden in my repertoire that I couldn't read enough, and I followed the signs and page numbers to all my favorite taboos. Until, one day, to my amazement, I realized that the same page number over and over again was not enough—there had to be something in the writing to elevate me past the expected. I wanted to be surprised.

The Best American Erotica, I'll confess, truly does have an agenda. It isn't a dial-an-orgasm collection. The stories have to pass the wet test, but they don't aim for the broadest common denominator—if there even is one in human sexuality. This whole business of defining what is "average," or worse, "normal," in erotic fantasy is a losers' game. We may have plastic surgery to make everyone's noses and tits look the same, but psychologically our erotic profile is unique, and there's no messing with it.

Instead, I like my *Best American Erotica* stories to be a portrait of the times we live in. I have daydreams of aliens discovering *The Best American Erotica* collection a thousand years from now and saying, "So this is what turned the earthlings on." I hope they have more tolerance and curiosity than the critics who write to me now and say, "If this is sex in America, then I'm a duck."

The doubters might as well start quacking—or get out of the house more often. You better believe this is sex in America—and if we weren't so pruney from our own long soak in censorship and shaming, that fact would be perfectly obvious.

Susie Bright
Valentine's Day, 1999

ELISE D'HAENE
From Licking Our Wounds

I just had a pitiful orgasm. It doesn't even qualify as full-fledged. Let's just call it an *org*. It was fast, less than a minute to cum, and before the first beat of the clitoral tom-tom sounded, tears were pouring down my cheeks. Emotional cumming. The ache was loss and as soon as I conjured up a picture of your sweet, sweet face and those moony eyes, well, all was lost. My vagina misses you too, like my heart, and both of us spilled forth, gushed tears and wet cum like two blubbering babies hungry for a nipple. What's that song say? I'm a whimpering simpering child, romance fini, and all that shit.

I had to try again, and since necessity *is* the mother of invention, I pulled out the electric toothbrush (you took the vibrator) to shudder speedily across my clitoris; not the bristles, but the smooth blue side of the toothbrush.

Nothing happened. My vagina packed up and left no forwarding address.

"I just can't stand the pain no longer," she said, as she boarded the bus and headed nowhere in particular.

Cup, I tried all my best material. You sucking me, engaged in serious mouth-to-clit resuscitation as your fingers skitter and slide all over and I beg you to enter me and wear me like a glove. Didn't even get wet. Dry as chalk and sore like slamming your palm on hot cement trying to break a fall from a bike that's too big. Shouldn't have been riding it in the first place.

Now, Cup, I'm lying here—alone. My DKNY black skirt is pushed up around my waist, my DKNY black tights scrunched at my ankles, an electric toothbrush dangling like a sorry limp cock between my legs, and I'm screaming in my head, "Mona! Come back little Mona, please come back."

I remember the first time I told you that I named my vagina Mona, because it sounded like sorrow, like the word melancholy, and you laughed and then asked me to come up with a name for yours, and without missing a beat, I said, "How about Lizzie, as in Borden?"

After you squeezed my inner thigh until I apologized, you said, "Amelia, I'll call her Amelia."

Sure enough, you and Amelia have flown away and disappeared and my Mona's taken flight too, and I'm lying in a wrinkled heap, in my funeral outfit, fresh from another memorial service, and I don't know where to turn.

The only thing I want is your head buried between my legs.

I call Christie and tell her there is no way I can show up tonight to pass out meals to dying people. She made that noise I so cherished when we were lovers: Fuck you meets I'm disappointed meets you're so pathetic. Of course, she's secretly thrilled that you're gone, Cup, and thinks I deserve every excruciating moment of anguish that's coming to me.

After she discharged that noise, she says, "It's important to keep commitments, Maria, at least it's important to *some* people."

(Fuck you.) "I wish I had your strength, Christie," I say.

"I gotta go now, the dogs are threatening to eat me unless I take them for a walk. Bye."

Molly and Sadie are sleeping peacefully on either side of me, unaware that I've used them, shamelessly, to get away from Christie Madigan, whom I've come to refer to simply as "the Vatican." She has that awful effect on me, that quavering air of superiority. Her spiritual plane is soaring; mine hasn't even left the runway.

Christie was my first real relationship. Two years of dried flowers, lazy cats, antique quilts, oatmeal, and home-made bread. We lived in a wood cottage in Silverlake. It was cozy. We shared hushed quiet orgasms, tender and loving. We cuddled a lot.

After a year, I started having fantasies of squatting on the antique quilt and taking a shit. The only music I would listen to was Billie Holiday and Janis Joplin. I worshiped Sylvia Plath and I wanted my life to be a loaded gun, not a loaf of rosemary bread. I hated myself for hating it. I felt there was something bad inside of me for wanting to escape lazy cats, pots of dried flowers, and fruit tea. This was B.C., before you, Cup. Before death too.

I strip off my funeral gear and put a T-shirt on sans underwear. Theoretically, one wears undergarments to protect one's private areas. My privates have gone public, so what's the use?

At the memorial service today, I was thinking how insensitive you are, Cup, for not being there to pay your respects. It occurred to me, though, that you probably don't know that Eduardo is dead, and I can't call you because I don't know where you are. Then I realized that Eduardo belonged to Christie's circle, and that you hardly know him, and I hadn't even seen him for over a year, and then it all came crashing down. The only reason I wanted you there today was for me, not him, just so I could hold your hand, and after the service we could come home and go to bed, and forget, for at least those moments, forget that friends are dying, one by one.

Your departure, Cup, is one thing. As for Mona's leave of absence, I don't know what I'll do. I feel as if I've lost a vital organ and there's no one around with a donor card offering me a transplant.

I reach over to the bedside table and grab a book from a pile of yard sale paperbacks I bought. Wouldn't you know it, *Portnoy's Complaint,* the book that began this long whine:

I'm twelve years old and poring through the pages of the latest paperback I've swiped from my older brother Joseph. Technically, I steal them, if Mom finds out, but actually, Joseph puts the books he's done reading in a pile for me at the back of his closet. We have an agreement.

Today I'm reading *Portnoy's Complaint.* I'm halfway through it, and I still don't know what the complaint is. I don't really understand half of the books Joseph reads, I just stuff the words into my brain.

I'm lying in bed in the middle of a sunny Saturday afternoon. It's hard to find peace and quiet in the house. Noise is constant. Outside, in the backyard, I can hear the high-pitched ting of the ball as it's kicked into the air by my little sister Beth. She squeals and Paul is yelling at her, "Run the bases, stupid." They have a regular weekend game of combat kickball with our neighbors, the O'Briens. They have ten kids in their family, we have seven. Mr. O'Brien and my dad work at the same auto plant.

So, I'm reading away: *"While here is a honey of a girl, with the softest, pinkest, most touching nipples I have ever drawn between my lips, only she won't go down on me."* I stop. Contemplate the words. *Go down on me.* Suddenly I find I'm staring at my bedpost. The sleek, shiny wood ball. I put the book down and climb on top, just like getting up on my brother's bike. I bounce a little and swivel and pretend I'm Annette Funicello on the *Mickey Mouse Club* riding her horse.

I gyrate and wriggle and feel the most joyous pleasure imaginable. I'm stunned and wonder, does everybody know about bedposts?

When I climb down, I put my hand between my legs, and I have a big wet spot on my white painter's pants. Did I pee without knowing? I unzip to investigate and scoop up with my fingers a substance that's gooey and sticky and in my twelve-year-old mind I figure this was where Elmer's glue comes from.

I go back to the page: *". . . it is her pleasure while being boffed to have one or the other of my forefingers lodged snugly up her anus."* I stop, again, and dreamily gaze at the bedpost. Boffed? I'll have to ask Joseph what that means.

My mother flings open my bedroom door. I slam my legs shut and my face heats up red. She has a basket of laundry in her arms which she drops to the floor. "Maria, fold these clothes for me."

"Sure, Mom," I grunt, as I carefully cover up the book with my hands and tightly squeeze my legs.

"What's that you're reading?" She grabs it from my lap. "Joseph!" she screams.

"He's not home, Mom, I stole it from his room."

She glares at me. "I've told you a hundred times, Maria,

you are not allowed to read grown-up books." She swats my leg. "Now fold those, and then go outside and play with your brothers and sisters. Go have fun!"

"Okay," I mumble, knowing I have just discovered the most fun thing ever.

She begins to leave and then turns suddenly. "I'm doing a load of whites, take those off so I can wash them, they're filthy." She's pointing at my pants.

I panic. The wet spot! The Camel nonfilter hidden in my pocket that I also stole from Joseph! "No, Mom!" I bark, "I just washed 'em!"

She eyes me suspiciously. There's a tense pause. "You kids," she whines, and then leaves.

I love my white painter's pants. They have these little loops on the side where I rest my thumb and pretend to be a cowboy. All these pockets and secret side compartments where I slip my stolen cigarettes and matches. I never get caught. I'm a bookworm, not a brat. I don't get into much trouble, except for stealing Joseph's books. Mostly, I do what I'm told.

I begin taking a lot of baths. All objects, including the bedpost, come to life. Umbrella handles. Shampoo bottles. My little brother's plastic football with the ridges. I am a bookworm, who takes a lot of baths and does what I'm told.

When I was a child, I played like a child, I thought like a child. Then there came a day when I left behind my childish ways. This developmental hurdle was ushered in by Helen Gurley Brown and *Cosmopolitan* magazine.

I'm fourteen and in my parents' bathroom and I'm rummaging through my mom's toiletries. It's become a peculiar habit of mine. I'm a scavenger of all her scents and smells.

The sweet aroma of the White Satin perfume my dad gives her every Christmas. The pink bars of Dove soap she buys only for herself. (We kids get plain old Ivory or whatever is on sale.) The box of Calgon blue bath beads, called Midnight Luxury. And, my favorite, Pond's cold cream. My mom's nighttime smell. She used to leave slight traces of it on my cheek or forehead when she'd come into my bedroom, bend over me, and whisper, "Night punkin." I'm too old for that now.

I unscrew the lid and inhale deeply, dip my finger into the white oily goop, and spread it on my cheek, just like her, then wipe it off carefully with a tissue.

I reach way, way back in their bathroom cupboard, the top one where my mother puts her stuff to keep it away from us kids. I reach past my mom's makeup bag and her Estée Lauder's gala collection of ten different colored lipsticks, past a basket filled with rose-shaped soaps. Then I push aside the pile of musty old towels we got after Grandma died. That's where I found the magazine, hidden where a kid's arm shouldn't be able to reach, unless that kid is me and I've already learned how to balance myself, one leg on the bathtub and one leg on the toilet, in order to snoop.

One of the magazine subscription cards is sticking out like a bookmark. Page forty-six. "Sexual Advice for the Seventies Woman," by Dr. Mark Goodman. He has a Ph.D. in exercise physiology and works as a consultant to media and television on maximizing sexual appeal. I'm fourteen. I want to maximize anything about me, except my thighs, especially my breasts and sex appeal! The doctor is all smiles, he has dark wavy hair, nice long sideburns, a thick moustache and beard, and big sensitive eyes just like Cat Stevens.

It was just one word that caught my eye. On page forty-six, in *Cosmo* magazine, one word that absolutely changed the entire course of my life. There was no fork on this path that diverged in the wood. No pondering, this way or that. I had chanced upon a one-way road. Mark was describing, in detail, *cunnilingus*. Up till now it was just me rubbing this little spot that felt good. Now, I had a picture in my head, a scene involving another person.

I hesitate. I think of school—the nuns. Suddenly Sister Rose pops out like toast, in her long black habit, right in my parents' bathroom.

"Leggo of my eggo!" I scream.

"You are turning your back against God and all that is sacred," she roars, pointing that ruler right at my crotch.

Then I hear Cat Stevens' voice, so sweet, so truthful, *"Morning has broken, like the first morning, blackbird has spoken, like the first bird . . ."*

Ponds cold cream beckons from the cupboard. I stare at Mark's face, his inviting smile, and Sister Rose dissolves like bath beads.

I read: *"A woman's clitoris can be described as her little nub of joy. It is a man's responsibility to understand what I call the woman's clitoral personality."* I stop breathing. My eyes bulge. Just a little pitter pats between my legs.

"Place your hands securely around her buttocks, grasp and pull her toward you, and tease playfully with the tip of your tongue."

I'm so moved at this point that my legs are starting to shudder, so I slowly make my way over to the toilet to sit down. I'm gripping the *Cosmo* like I've never gripped the written word before. Mark discusses the clockwise rotation of the tongue interspersed with *sucking!*

My bell-bottom jeans mysteriously fall to the floor. My J.C. Penney white cotton briefs for girls creep down to my knees. I have a dollop of Pond's on my index finger.

I close my eyes tight. (If I don't see myself do this, then God won't see me either.) The Pond's stings slightly on my clit, my fingers twirl and twirl on my little nub of joy. In my fantasy, the tongue spins around and around. I'm making noises, brand new ones, ones I've never heard before.

Quickly, I reach over to the sink and turn on the faucet to drown out my moans.

I'm breathing so deep my belly extends like a balloon as those lips suck and suck so delicately.

"Sweet the rain's new fall, sunlit from heaven . . ."

My mind is like a movie screen. I'm lying, splayed across my bed, my butt is being held firmly, the lips come toward me, I raise my supine head in order to see—to reach my hands out to grasp my made-up lover, and it isn't Dr. Goodman, or Cat Stevens, or the bedpost. It's the model on the cover of the magazine, her name is Cindy, and she has long dark hair and she's wearing a black negligee and her lips are slightly pink from Estée Lauder's Cimarron Rose.

I'm lost, swirling and swooning in my parents' bathroom in Pond's Now-Warm Cream.

I leap off the toilet, startled and bleary. Those lips in my mind weren't surrounded by a moustache or beard or even stubble. They were all hers, soft and full, slightly glossed with a touch of rose. I knew this was trouble, with a capital T that rhymes with P that stands for *pink*—lips.

I grab some tissues and wipe myself. I flush the evidence down the toilet. I flush twice, just to be sure. This sensation washes over me: on the one hand a feeling of such satisfaction, like putting that last piece into a puzzle, and at the same time, a desire to toss the puzzle into the air and start over.

I gaze at the cover. Cindy's poutier and bustier than she was in my mind. I stuff the magazine back where it belongs, hidden under my grandma's musty towels.

When I emerge from my parents' bathroom, into their bedroom, it feels as if I have new eyeballs. My little brother Fitz is sitting on their bed watching *Romper Room*.

"Are you a good dooby?" he asks, holding my mom's hand mirror toward me.

I don't answer. I ruffle my fingers through his hair and turn the mirror toward him. "You are, Fitzy," I say. "You're my good dooby."

I hop up on the bed with him and he curls into my lap. When *Captain Kangaroo* comes on, Fitzy is silent and wide-eyed, he sucks his thumb and giggles when Mr. Green Jeans appears. I fall asleep during the storytelling, and wake up with Fitz pulling my hair, needing to go potty. I take him downstairs, to the kids' bathroom.

He sits unsteady on the edge of the toilet, his little boy stomach poofs out as he strains to make himself go.

I'm thinking, as I sit on the floor, hugging my knees to my chest, that Fitzy and I are both crossing over into new territory. We're expanding. Our bones and skin, our eyes, what we see and hear, and most importantly, what we know and understand. New shapes and words and sensations adding to the old, and there's no turning back.

Perched on the toilet, his legs dangling above the floor, Fitzy begins to hum, *"Row, row, row your boat,"* high and sweet, like a girl, and then points to me.

"Gently down the stream," I sing, *"Merrily, merrily, merrily, merrily, life is but a dream."*

A dream, Cup. If only I'd wake up and find you asleep next to me and an eager Mona tucked safely between my legs.

My forefinger is lodged snugly between the pages of *Portnoy's Complaint* when the doorbell rings. Unlike Mr. Portnoy, there's no spare anus around to lodge into. I open the book slowly and I'm punched by two big bold words: "WHACKING OFF." Shit, Mona.

I hear the door open and I assume it's Christie, here to keep herself company and continue pestering me like a reporter from *Hard Copy* about why you left, Cup.

"I'm in the bedroom," I yell, figuring Molly and Sadie will do their ferocious dog-being if it's a stranger.

I have the book draped over my eyes and a wet washcloth over my groin and still no underwear. I moan as I lift the book so that Christie will know just how badly I'm feeling, and staring quizzically at the washcloth on my groin is Peter.

"Peter?" I say, "If I knew you were coming I'd have baked a cake."

He hands me one of the wrapped meals from Angel Food. "Someone died," he says, "so we had an extra." He bounces down on the bed. "You're tragic!"

I unwrap my meal. Chicken breast, green beans, sweet potato, and a brownie. "What are you doing here?" I ask.

"I came to cheer you up."

"I don't need cheering up." I start to pick at the beans one by one and pop them into my mouth.

Peter grunts. "Look, girl, you've got to forget that old

snack, she's gone! Live like I do," he says, then grabs the brownie from my plate.

"Good idea, Peter. I think I'll drive over to Griffith Park, climb through the bushes. Suck off some guy, then call it a night. No names, no phone numbers, no sticky sheets."

"Women," he snorts. "Look, Mia, here's my motto: What's too painful to remember, I simply choose to forget."

"I feel better, Peter, thank you."

"You do?" He smiles widely.

"Yes, I've already forgotten that you're here. I don't know who you are. Now go home. I'll call you tomorrow."

He turns at the door for one last look at me. "Tragic," he says in dismay, "but I love you."

ANNE TOURNEY
How to Come on a Bus

First, find a man who's been at a party all night. He should look haggard and battleworn so that no one is surprised when he lies down in the back seat (the very last seat, where the engine shakes you like a ten-ton vibrator) with his face in your lap. Gaze indifferently out the window as you wriggle your skirt waistward and spread your thighs. You should be wearing underwear because (1) the fabric will ride up your crotch, causing a delightful friction between your cunt lips, and (2) the bus may be involved in an accident. Cover your lover's head demurely with your skirt as he begins to circle your clit with his tongue. Do not shriek or moan as the bus rockets over a pothole and his teeth clamp down on your pussy. Do not pant or salivate excessively when he slips a hand under your thighs and pulls your sticky panties out of your twat in order to fuck you with two fingers. Pretend to study the fare information on your bus schedule if you find it necessary to grind your teeth. Lift your ass slightly so that you can settle down on his hand and open your legs a few inches more (don't sprawl, or people will think your mother raised you wrong). Whenever the bus turns a corner, squeeze his fingers as tightly as you can with your cunt muscles and rock back and forth on the heel of his hand. Your traveling companion should recognize this undulation as a signal to lick you harder. If he begins to snarl or grunt as he does so, pat his head and gasp, "Don't worry, Daddy, we're almost at the hospital." Yank the bellrope as hard as you can as you feel yourself peaking. You may indulge in one more ass-lift, just to give his teeth and lips full access to your pussy as the vehicle shudders to a halt; then let your juices flood your fellow passenger's mouth. At this point you may scream, "Stop! Stop! Stop!" The other passengers might turn around and glance at you curiously. The bus driver might swear at you. But their unpredictable reactions won't matter, because you'll be using alternate transportation on the trip home (a vertical fuck in the train toilet will seem blissfully easy by comparison).

KELLY McQUAIN
Je t'aime, 'Batman,' je t'adore

To Bob Kane and Donald Barthelme

>:Rob00062

I can't hide the truth anymore. I love Batman—his furrowed brow, his chiseled jaw, his Bat emblem emblazoned atop pectorals hard as marble. I love his sculpted stomach, his running-back thighs and gymnast calves, the impressive bump of the safety cup sewn into his shorts.

These feelings grow as wild as I do—in the past year I've shot up a good six inches, the *Gotham Gazette* now dubbing me the "Teen Wonder" instead of "Boy Wonder." Why is life so confusing? I long for simpler days, when fighting the Joker, Penguin, and Riddler was enough, when each fisted blow produced an explosive *BAM!* or *POW!* that I could almost see.

Yesterday, Alfred caught me preening in the mirror, trying to master a hustler's roguish come-on. He pretended to be dusting, but I could feel his eyes undressing me. Alfred's old, has only five hairs on his head, but still I got a chubber simply from being desired by a man. But I have standards. I want a superhero.

. . .

>:Rob00063

Last night in the Bat Cave, as I sat typing this computer journal, Bruce crept up so quietly I was nearly discovered. Damn his Bela Lugosi moves! I hit the exit key just as his gloved hand clamped down on my shoulder.

Whirling around, I experienced familiar breathlessness upon seeing the width of his shoulders, his tapered waist. "Just finishing my French homework!" I lied, glad my mask was on so that he couldn't see my eyes.

"Good," Bruce said, adjusting his cowl. "Let's patrol before it gets late. Tomorrow's a school day."

"Sure." (I wished he hadn't reminded me. At school, everyone teases me for being his ward, calling me "pretty boy" and "millionaire jailbait." I can't fight back, can't flaunt my Bat-training. Even my French teacher arches an eyebrow, his slimy mind imagining naughty scenarios Bruce puts me through each night. If only it were true!)

As Bruce revved the Batmobile, I flung my yellow cape around my shoulders. Over the past months the hemline has crept up my calves, reminding me of the frilly shoulder piece the ringmaster wore back in my circus days. My red tunic feels snug as well, and my green shorts never more skimpy. But I like how these old clothes show off the muscles thickening my boyish limbs. Only drawback is the difficulty in concealing the Bat-boners that pop up with increasing frequency, so I've taken to wearing my utility belt lower on my hips, like a gunslinger's holster, like I'm ready to shoot.

Hidden hydraulics rumbled as the faux cave wall rose before us. I leapt over the Batmobile's fin, sliding into shotgun. Bruce shot me a look that said "Ever hear of a door?"

He pressed the turbos, and in a roar of flame we rocketed toward Gotham City.

Dark woods flashed by. I tried not to stare as Bruce's powerful hand gripped the gearshift. We turned off the old logging road onto the Gotham Expressway, and the familiar peaks and spires of the city loomed before us.

"Stay alert, chum," Bruce said, patting my knee.

I bit my lip. Suddenly the Bat-signal cut a golden swath across the sky. Skidding through a maze of streets, Bruce pulled up beside Police Headquarters—completely disregarding a conspicuous fire hydrant. It thrilled me how easily he took the law into his hands.

Commissioner Gordon greeted us in his office. "Working out a bit?" he asked, seizing me in a neck hold and rubbing my head.

"You'll wreck my mousse!" I cried.

The Commissioner laughed and let go, his fingers tweaking the nape of my neck. He directed Bruce's gaze toward what appeared, to the untrained eye, to be an ordinary piece of mail. "From the Joker," Gordon announced. "That madcap menace broke out of Arkham Asylum again. Sent me this birthday card."

"Your birthday?" asked Bruce. "I didn't know. Robin usually keeps better track of such things." He shot me a wicked glance.

"That's just it," said the Commissioner, lighting his pipe. "My birthday was months ago."

Bruce picked up the card with a pair of Bat-tweezers. "Obviously that crazed sociopath is taunting us with clues to whatever crime he's hatching."

"Well, duh," I said.

"Don't give me any lip," Bruce glared. He studied the card. I slunk up beside him, breathing deep his intoxicating perspiration, resting my head against his hard shoulder.

"Robin. Do you mind?"

"Sorry," I said, lifting my head. I concentrated on the card. In the Joker's messy handwriting an inscription read, *Sorry—no present! But you'll soon have a GRAND time OPENING your front page to discover what I have in STORE!* As Bruce read aloud, the madman's usual trademark—a Joker from a deck of playing cards—fell onto the desktop.

Bruce rubbed his chin. "A card within a card. Anything else?"

"Well," said Gordon. "I had the lab boys look it over. It's a Hallmark."

I cracked my knuckles, imagining the Joker's jaw. "At least he cares to send the best."

Bruce frowned. "A Hallmark," he continued. "That, combined with the Joker's peculiar emphasis on the words *grand* and *opening,* can only mean one thing. He's going to rob the Hallmark card store at the brand new Gotham Shopping Plaza."

"A brilliant deduction!" cried the Commissioner. "Should I send a patrol to check it out?"

"No," said Bruce. "The Joker's slippery—he's already struck once today; he'll let us stew a while before hitting again."

"Your insight astounds me," croaked Gordon. Bruce's chest swelled at the compliment. He shook hands with the Commissioner and ordered me to gather the evidence. From my utility belt I extracted a Bat-baggy. It pained me to recall the countless hours I had spent stenciling bats onto endless, ordinary Ziploc bags.

Outside in the Batmobile I asked, "Why do villains insist on sending us clues? Don't they know we'll figure them out?"

"Ah," said Bruce. "You have much to learn. Criminal minds are compelled to throw such crumbs. Sometimes I think they want to be found out, to be punished, to feel the rock-hard fist of the law pounding their flesh."

"Holy Freud," I muttered.

Bruce pushed the pedal to the floor; the Bat-speedometer shot up several notches as we ricocheted through Crime Alley. My partner's enthusiasm fired my own hot tremors emanating from the epicenter of my crotch. I fanned myself with my cape.

The Batmobile skidded to a halt as Bruce spotted a purse snatcher. In one savage motion he pitched himself onto the hoodlum. He was hard on crime. I loved it.

I began to rise, but froze when I noticed my Bat-chubber had created an embarrassing pup tent in my shorts. While Bruce delivered the old one-two, I pulled my aching python free. He whirled to kick the lawbreaker in the abdomen. My prick thrashed with a life of its own! As the dark knight delivered the final blow, I shot a huge wad beneath the dashboard.

Maybe Bruce would think it was gum.

I watched my partner loom over the criminal, cast in a light I had never before noticed. Always a still-waters type, he seldom showed emotion—not even Catwoman wagging her tail could get a rise out of him. This pent-up fury spent on a common hoodlum, this primal release—what did it mean? Was it a crumb he threw my way, a desperate clue I was meant to decipher? I stuffed my limp pee-pee back in my shorts.

Bruce glanced my way. "Don't just sit there," he panted. "Throw me your Bat-cuffs."

>:Rob00064

I can't believe what I'm reduced to.

Yesterday, coming from the shower, I saw Alfred gathering our uniforms to throw in the Bat-washer, so I filched Bruce's cape and took it to my room. Shutting the door, I dropped my towel and admired myself in the armoire's mirror. I ran my hands over my nipples, down my chest, toward my crotch. How could someone not want this virgin skin, these limbs plump with young muscle? Pretty boy. Pretty bird. If Bruce had any sense, he'd lock me in a cage so that only he could ravish me. Doesn't he notice the Riddler salivating as he takes me hostage, the Joker catching his breath as I bend to retrieve my Batarang? No. He's as blind as the proverbial bat.

Naked on my bed, I whipped the blue cape in the air. As it parachuted over me, I imagined Bruce's dark eyes and muscled torso swooping down—a vampire mad with bloodlust. His finned gloves gouged me, his belt buckle ground my pelvis. My costume ripped as his fingers gripped my ass and his Bat-cock pierced my Bat-hole. I wanted him to need me like he needed Gotham's criminals—locked in a battle not of good or evil, but of desires rampant in us both. I wanted to be more than just the boy behind the mask.

Pulling out, Bruce whacked my face with his billy club of flesh until I cried, "Excessive force!"

"Eat my fat worm, little bird!" he grunted. "Chew that Bat-boner!"

I did, and I liked it.

Suddenly Bruce's seed pelted the back of my throat like a hail of bullets. I gripped my own cock, a thousand Bat-signals exploding as I came. Tears eddied in the eyes of my mask as Bruce nuzzled my cheek, grateful. . . .

"Excuse me, Master Dick," said Alfred, barging in and cutting short my reverie. I bolted up, covered my crotch. "Have you seen—excuse me, but why is Master Bruce's cape in here?" He averted his eyes from my compromising position.

"It's not what you think! I was cold! I needed a blanket!"

"'The lady doth protest too much,'" replied Alfred, shutting the door.

>:Rob00065

I paused outside of Bruce's study. Desire warmed me at the sight of my partner relaxing in his favorite chair, reading the newspaper—handsome in his smoking jacket, a silk cravat knotted at his throat. From a vial in my pocket I poured several colorless, odorless drops of liquid into the snifter of brandy I had brought for him—a concoction derived from the Bat-computer's catalog of Poison Ivy's Spanish-fly recipes. Bruce looked up as I entered the room. "Alfred thought you might enjoy a drink," I lied.

He folded his paper in half. Our fingertips brushed as he took the glass. "Thank you," he said grimly.

My pulse quickened as the brandy wetted his lips. Before he could take a full sip, the Bat-phone rang. Bruce rose, crossed to his desk, switched on the speakerphone. Commissioner Gordon's voice rattled the air: "The Joker's swiped a wrecking crane from the site of the new convention center!"

"Holy demolition," I said unenthusiastically.

Bruce's voice sank to the dramatic register of the Bat-man. "That's lowbrow even for him; there must be a greater scheme!" I stared at the glass in his hand, willing Bruce to take that first swallow. "Robin and I will head to the Plaza to see if that madman strikes there as expected."

Hanging up, Bruce flashed the crisp stretch of pearly whites that passed for his smile. He dumped his drink in a houseplant then flung the empty snifter into the fireplace. I wanted to scream!

"Ready for a little action, old chum?" he asked.

Anytime, anyplace, I nearly confessed.

Bruce pressed a secret button and a bookcase slid aside to reveal the entrance to the Bat Cave. He leapt through the gloomy portal. Sliding down the Bat-pole after him made me yearn all the more. It felt bittersweet having my legs wrapped around something long and hard, but cold, just like Bruce.

On the way to Gotham Plaza I broached a delicate subject.

"I think it's time I received an allowance." I wanted to update my costume with a new mask or a rakish scarf—anything to get Bruce to notice me.

His eyes narrowed, becoming more angular than usual. "You don't need an allowance," he said coldly.

"Everybody else—"

"'Everybody else' hasn't devoted their lives to battling crime," he intoned.

"It's not fair!" My voice broke like the waves in Gotham Harbor. "I know crime doesn't pay, but crime fighting should be worth something!"

Bruce's arm shot out, seizing my collar. "Look, mister," he growled, "we've got a job to do! Financial compensation is not our motivation." He shook me like a rag doll, producing a strange stirring in my utility belt.

"At least give me a cut of the Bat-merchandising," I pleaded.

"I will not tolerate insubordination!" His spittle stung my cheeks with each word: "If you're going to behave like a child, you should wait in the car." He shoved me against my seat.

Pulling into the Plaza parking lot, Bruce cut the engine and we coasted to a stop. A van, marked Clown Catering, was parked near the employee entrance. Bruce leapt out and raced toward the mall. I pressed the button for the Bat Wet Bar and snuck a cocktail as Bruce launched a Bat-rope to the roof, then scaled the building. His cape caught the wind, lifting from his shoulders. I sighed at the movement of his back, the tremor of muscle and tendon as he pulled himself over the rooftop and disappeared.

Sipping my drink, I scanned the deserted parking lot. Banners announcing grand-opening sales fluttered in the breeze. Suddenly a terrific crash came from the back of the mall near the card store. Cinder blocks crumbled as a section of the wall gave way. The Joker's heinous laughter pierced the air. Through the dust came a menacing wrecking crane, driven by none other than the Clown Prince of Crime!

"Holy wanton destruction of private property!" I cried as Bruce leapt from the ruined facade. The Joker whirled the crane's iron ball through the air, shattering the wall above Bruce's head. With inhuman agility the caped crusader dodged the debris. The wrecking crane turned, thundering toward the Batmobile, the iron ball swinging back as the Joker aimed my way. I dropped my cocktail and launched a Bat-rope to the mall roof, leaping clear as the

Joker smashed the Batmobile to smithereens. He whirled toward Bruce once more. "You might have a lot of balls, Batman," he taunted, "but mine's bigger!"

Bruce double-flipped into the air as the ball crashed toward him. Avoiding the blow, he grabbed onto the cable as it swung back around.

"Curses!" screamed the Joker, locking the crane controls in a head-on collision with the crumbling plaza wall. He leapt toward his getaway van.

Bruce glanced up. "Quick, Robin, throw me your Bat-rope!" The wrecking crane volleyed toward destruction.

"Maybe this is a good time to reconsider that allowance," I said woozily. Being cruel turned me on.

"The rope, Robin! The rope!"

"Is that in my job description? Do I even have a job description?"

"I'M NOT KIDDING!"

"All right, all right." I threw him my rope, and he began climbing up. "But you're probably violating child-labor laws."

Bruce vaulted the building's cornice, grabbed me, and shoved me down. Blood surged toward my groin at such manhandling. "Punish me if you must," I said, hoping he'd beat my ass with his utility belt.

From below, the Joker's laughter echoed in our ears as he escaped.

"You rotten whelp!" screamed Bruce.

He shook me by the scruff of my neck. I loved it.

A terrific shock jolted us apart as the crane plowed into the Plaza. The roof crumbled like cardboard; I plummeted toward doom like a wounded bird. Would Bruce clutch my lifeless body to his? Would he shed a tear? At the last sec-

ond, his gloved hand seized my wrist. I dangled for life—
the closest to climax I got all night.

Bruce pulled me up, held me close. Sniffing, he asked,
"Have you been drinking?"

>:Rob00066

Bruce punishes me by patrolling alone—still mad that
we had to bus it home. No sign of the Joker, so Bruce
busies himself poring over the birthday card, searching for
more clues. I go mad from neglect, frittering away hours
on the Soloflex, using the Bat-computer to hack in and
change my French grade. This evening I shaved my legs,
deciding that if I'm going to wear those damn shorts I have
to do something about this embarrassing bikini line. Dark
curly hairs have begun to trickle down my inner thighs. If
I'm to win Bruce over, I have to look hot.

In desperation, I sought Alfred's advice. "You've known
Bruce longer than I have," I said as we cleared the dinner
table. "What's the bug up his Bat-butt?"

The butler fixed me with a knowing wink. "His idio-
syncrasies are getting to you, are they?" He smiled. "It's
true, he's always been rather complex. Take him at any
level of social intercourse: he's a man possessed of fearful
strengths and endearing weaknesses; a careful strategist
but impetuous risk-taker; a gregarious host yet reticent
with his feelings; a bon-vivant but a street brawler; a non-
conformist yet a supporter of moral absolutes; an appreci-
ator of both abstract and realistic art—"

"You're saying he's schizoid?"

"Not exactly—what were Walt Whitman's words of wis-
dom?" Alfred's British accent cut through the tongue

twister with laser precision. "Ah, yes. 'I am vast, I contain multitudes.'"

>:Rob00067

Today while Bruce was at the Wayne Foundation, I peeked in his desk and came across an application for Andover. He's planning to ship me to boarding school! A small notebook was filled with forgeries of my signature. I cried over an ad addressed to the *Gotham Gazette: SWM seeks subordinate younger WM partner for nite-time activities . . .*

I mustn't lose him! I used to spend nights worrying—what if he were shot or crippled? Or sprayed with acid and disfigured like Two-Face? What if he got testicular cancer—a real possibility the way he keeps his balls knotted up. Would I still love him? Of course.

I've seen other boys develop crushes on mentor figures—coaches, teachers, Catholic priests—but our relationship penetrates deeper. If Bruce has taught me anything, it's the courage to face our darkest parts. But ever since his parents died, Bruce has locked everything up! There was no comforting stranger for him like there was for me. I must show him the way out. Now, before he sends me away.

>:Rob00068

The Bat Cave is very quiet. I study Bruce's shoulders as he hunches over his crime-analysis equipment. His head does not turn, but he knows I am here. There's still a chance.

Unfastening my cape, I throw it on the Bat-trampoline. The prospect of our joined flesh sends shivers through my body. What will happen after we touch? Will Bruce still send me away? Will he be jealous and obsessed, tortured by the memory of our union—an empty shell, drifting from one sidekick to the next, looking for the silky texture of my skin in their inadequate flesh? I pull off my gloves and kick off my shoes.

"Fascinating," Bruce says, still not turning. "The Bat-spectrograph has isolated seven different monofilaments on the card sent to the Commissioner."

I remove my tunic and drop it on the floor, catching a glimpse of myself in the polished instruments above Bruce's shoulder. Will you be regretful, maudlin—nights spent in endless self-flagellation, days spent reciting countless Hail Marys?

"Five of them are used in textile production around Gotham City."

I remove my shorts and stand naked, growing hard, waiting. I must confess my love. Say it fast, blurt it out so that we can pretend we didn't hear it if the words are too painful.

"Another matches the Commissioner's wool sweater."

Finally, I remove my mask. "I love you," I whisper.

Bruce freezes. He does not turn, he does not speak.

I am doomed.

>:Rob00069

Bruce, unable to fathom the Joker's next move, has given me the cold shoulder for days. He was studying plans for a new Batmobile when I tried to engage in small talk.

"So, the Joker knocked over a card store—"

"Quiet, Robin—wait! That's it! The Joker knocked over a store of cards. And tomorrow, the Gotham Museum will display a rare collection of playing cards by Aubrey

Beardsley. The other night's crime was a metaphor of his real scheme. Good work, chum."

Redeemed, I accompanied Bruce into town on the Bat-cycle. Unfortunately, I had to ride in the little sidecar. "Holy humiliation!" I fumed, but after a while, the hypnotic vibrations of the motor lulled me into the usual sexual thoughts. My thighs tensed as yet another Bat-boner popped up, my shorts stretched so tight I could make out each engorged vein.

At the Museum, Bruce leapt off the Bat-cycle, whisked a Bat-rope into the air, and scaled the building. In my condition, I could barely scale fish. Still, I drew my cape around to disguise my chubber, then clambered up. Looking down, I noticed my green slipper tarnished by feces from an uncurbed dog. Faint brown footprints trailed up the side of the museum. "Holy shit!" I yelled.

Bruce flashed an icy glare. "Don't swear, Robin. It reflects poorly on our image." He made his way across the rooftop, dropping through a skylight in the east wing. I lingered, scraping my shoe.

Suddenly, a dark figure pounced from the shadows, knocking me against the wall of an access stair. Dazed, I looked up to find the Joker grinning more hideously than usual. "Ah! The Boy Wonder—oops!—Teen Blunder. Say, is that a Batarang in your pocket or are you happy to see me?"

My face blushed as red as my tunic.

The Joker grabbed my throat in an iron grip. "Your partner may stop my henchmen below, but you're my ticket out of here! One move and I'll break your neck!" Being insane gave him the strength of ten.

He pulled me to him, slipped his hand down the back of my shorts. "I know your desires," he whispered, "the fierce longing to tangle with Batman." He pressed a chalky finger against my ass. "But you'll never occupy his attention like I do." He ground his fist into me. "You're just not bad enough." I strained against him, thinking of Bruce. There was a wildness in the madman's probing that curled my toes.

"Ahh, my little finger puppet," cooed the Joker, slipping a digit inside me. "It's a shame I must destroy you." Any protest stuck in my throat as my Bat-boner tore at my shorts.

Suddenly Bruce burst through the access door, unconscious hoodlums slung over each arm. "Holy full house!" I cried as he threw them in a heap on the rooftop.

"Let the boy go," he scowled. Maybe Bruce did care, after all.

"One step closer and I snap his neck," warned the Joker.

"All right, take it easy," replied Bruce. He lowered his arms and his cape slid down his shoulders. Our foppish foe dragged me toward the roof's edge. "Let me get rid of Robin," the Joker prissed. "He's just baggage! It's you and I who are meant for each other." He plunged another finger in me, nearly driving me mad.

"Whoa, nelly!" I cried. I could tell the Joker was trying to distract Bruce so that he could hurl a lethal round of razor-edged playing cards, but I wasn't about to free his hand. I clamped my ass cheeks harder.

His fingers floundered inside of me like a trout caught in a net. "Face it," he leered at my partner, "you don't give a damn about the kid's plight." He squeezed my throat tighter with his other arm. Oxygen deprivation intensified my rush. "So pathetic, it reminds me of a poem," chortled the Joker, clearing his throat.

"There once was a boy who was sobbin'
Cause his dick was so hard it was throbbin'

He felt sad to be slighted
For his Love, unrequited,
Wouldn't bugger the hell out of Robin!"

Suddenly Bruce's hand flashed in a streak of midnight blue. Light glinted off whirling metal as his Batarang coursed through the air, cracking hard against the Joker's elbow.

"Ack!" the clown cried, "My funny bone!" With his other hand still tangled in my shorts, I easily walloped the Joker's face until there was nothing left but bruises and battered flesh. Bruce watched but said nothing. Perhaps it was just the sight of my ridiculous, mangled shorts, but his scowl softened, seemed to give in.

While Bruce secured the criminals for the police, I headed back to the Bat-cycle, happy to find a rusty nail had punctured the sidecar's front tire.

Fate had finally dealt a hand in my favor. We left the sidecar behind when we rode home. I sat behind Bruce, my arms circling his waist, my weary head resting between his shoulder blades. With my ear pressed against his back, I heard the tumble of his inner workings unlocking like a safe. His cape whipped the air, surrounding me like a dark flower. I inhaled his sturdy scent, reached down and released my straining boner, resting it against the soft cloth of Bruce's shorts. As Gotham fell behind us, I worked my shaft snugly beneath his utility belt and rocked against him like a baby. If he noticed, he did not say anything. Once or twice a light sound escaped his lips—a murmur of pleasure? We turned onto the logging road, each bump offering new levels of sensation. The friction built to a fever pitch. The woods whizzed by. The cave entrance loomed before us.

And like all good heroes, I came just in the nick of time.

RICHARD COLLINS

The Two Gentlemen of Verona

Before settling in Ankara I lived for several
years in Bucharest, among ghosts, in a house that was built
at the beginning of the century for a rich man's mistress.
Since the house was designed for pleasure, I could imagine
how the large, high-ceilinged rooms once echoed with
sumptuous entertainments, chamber music, and lavish
dishes to fill the men's mouths with something other than
their own titles, careers, and fortunes. These men—with
names like Brancoveanu, Cantacuzino, Paraschivescu, and
Zaremba—were mostly rich and married, their waistcoats
like brand-new tapestries to match their coats of arms. The
women were chosen for their eyes (like chips of stained
glass or fallen sky, I've heard it said) or their laughter, as
bright as it was careless and intoxicating. At dinner the
men spoke guttural French or facile German of an Aus-
trian flavor, and drank the legendary Murfatlar wines from
the region on the Black Sea where the men had vineyards
and a summer residence, and where the grapes grew fat
and purple like the nipples of hardy women in the autumn
of their sexuality.

After dinner they spoke Romanian for the benefit of the
feminine company and sipped imported liqueurs in the
bright Byzantine colors of wet mosaics. At three A.M., or
thereabouts, the men would drip the liqueurs onto the

women's tongues. Drops of *vishinata* made from the sour cherry would descend into their soft warm mouths, like molten rubies into rose petals. (I can see her now, the mistress of the house, intelligent and darkly beautiful, petulant and pleasure-loving, but perhaps tainted with the sadness of her understanding.) If the liqueur overflowed her lip, forming a rivulet like a stream of blood that gathered in the cleft of her chin, or cascaded onto her breast white as meringue, the men would gather to lick and savor the sweet sticky flesh of the lucky girl, as though she were the *chef d'oeuvre* of the night, the intended dessert, and climax of the evening. And her lover, as host, would have to allow the liberties, because it would be a breach of hospitality to deny his guests any pleasure that presented itself so irresistibly. But of course the entertainment did not stop there. The evening had just begun. And so it went, the measured pleasures of the early evening dispersing in a swirl of petticoats and unlaced bodices, torn trousers, and flesh nicked by eager teeth. The sweetness of the man-made liqueurs mixed with the saltiness of blood and semen. At dawn the musicians would pack their instruments into the dawn, arm in arm with the husbands returning to their wives—who had slept well or not at all, according to the size of their husbands' inheritance, the number of anniversaries they had celebrated, and if they were lucky, the vigor of the young men who had just left their beds—leaving the mistress of the house alone in the large echoing rooms to find her own way to the sole bedroom to await the return of her "uncle."

You might ask how I know all this. I lived there, as I said, among ghosts. I have seen the mistress of the house very clearly on the staircase and at the window. At times, late at night or very early in the morning, I have heard the music, and I have caught a whiff of the perfumes of men and women in the midst of their pleasure. And I have heard the door close with the dawn.

And besides, Bucharest has not changed all that much.

These mistress mansions have suffered decay over the years, through age, neglect, and abuse. When the Communists took power they confiscated the houses from the heirs of the rich and carved them into dismal rooms, so many square meters per person. After the Revolution of 1989, the new government evicted the Gypsies and the goats (these too, like the women's perfumes, I can still smell in the hallways) and offered the houses to foreign embassies for exorbitant rents in hard currency. Now the mistress mansions house diplomats. I was one.

My predecessor, the former Cultural Affairs Officer at the Embassy, thought the house too large for a bachelor and asked for a modern apartment. I, however, found the house to be just about the right size for the receptions I was required to host from time to time. What's more, I found it only fitting that I should be quartered and pampered like a mistress living off the fat of Uncle Sam (whose love handles made it easy for me to cling to my patriotism). Fitting too because, like her—she became clearer to me with every week I lived in the house, especially in those gauzy hours between dusk and dawn when she, still bearing the fragrance of those orgies, would wander the halls, lonely in their aftermath, her bruised flesh a warm lamp evaporating the milky perfume of her debauched loneliness—like her, I was forbidden the free use of the house for my personal satisfactions. That is, my uncle, like hers, put certain restrictions on my use of the bedroom.

The State Department's "nonfraternization policy" forbade me to have anything but platonic cultural exchanges with the Romanian women who came my way. Not that I was celibate. Like the rich man's mistress, perhaps, I took my pleasure where I could find it. (A note slipped into the violinist's talented fingers would soon have him back playing vibrato on her orgy-taut nerves.) There was the thirsty, long-throated Irish nurse who melted the icicles of February. There was the eager Peace Corps volunteer who still sends me postcards with exotic stamps, and more than one Iberian-eyed secretary fresh from the peninsula and working for this or that "friendly" embassy. But Romanian women were off limits, which of course made them all the more delicious.

To keep my job I had to watch my step. Embassy gossip is particularly nasty. Those of us who could not get close to the natives followed the affairs of those who could with the sharp eye of a spy or voyeur. My friend Joe Bierce, for example, being unattached to any embassy, was observed by us with Puritan fascination. Anywhere else my interest in his love life would have been called disinterested, friendly, supportive. It was more like an aesthetic interest. I considered my voyeuristic tendencies as a legitimate extension of my duties concerning "cultural affairs."

One night I was hosting a reception for a group of American musicians on tour. Cocktails, followed by a little concert of chamber music and a stand-up dinner with wine, Murfatlar of course, followed by brandy and liqueurs. It was a mixed crowd of expatriates and natives, and expatriates "gone native," as they say. My colleagues from the embassy were whining about the tortures of living in Bucharest (a "super-hardship" post at the time), waxing nostalgic about their last post, speculating about where they might end up next

("God preserve me from Chisinau!"), or bragging that they were on their way to Kuala Lumpur, Johannesburg, or Moscow. Unless they happened to be cornered by some native for whom their duties in the political or economic section dictated that they switch on their Interested Smiles, their own careers (or the ruin of someone else's) were the sole topic of their conversation.

Joe Bierce had been trying to get them to talk about something else. Having left America several years ago, Joe hungered for any news of America that could not be obtained from CNN. But he had now given up on them and turned his attention to the Maker's Mark that he was gulping in large tumblers without ice. He was lingering at the edge of a group of Romanians when one of them said something about how the Americans had sold them out to Stalin at Yalta.

"Yalta, Schmalta," Joe said. "You Romanians. *The saddest thing about oppression is that it makes its victims unfit for anything but to be oppressed. In the end they turn out to be fairly energetic oppressors.*"

I recognized his remark for the deliberate provocation that it was. The Romanians naturally took offense. They answered him in tones of mortal injury, shrugging their shoulders, bunching their cheap suits around their thick necks, and holding out the palms of their hands, each a Christ displaying his national stigmata. Joe leaned against the fireplace, cigarette in hand, and grinned. He loved this kind of uproar. So did I, though I was not allowed to show it. It's why I invited him to these gatherings.

Joe had lived abroad long enough not to think it romantic. Not that he had gone native, on the contrary. For me, Joe

Bierce represented what is best in America—or at least used to be—namely, making his own way, making do, doing what he had to do, without complaint or compromise, and without trying to coerce others to do likewise. He had complete faith in what he called "the unimprovability of the species." In the eyes of some, I suppose, that made him a cynic. To me, Joe was sheer idealist, in the All-American grain. He knew precisely what compromises it sometimes takes to get things done, yet he personally declined to compromise, with the result that he seldom did anything. He could never, for example, have done my job, as he well knew. He wasn't cynical enough. "You're a moral ironist," he once told me. I've turned that phrase over in my mind more than once, and I've decided he was right. But at the time I only bristled and said, "Is that another of your names for a diplomat?"

On another occasion, we were having cognac and cigars in my study, a habit of ours on cold winter nights when the wind was howling down from off the Russian steppes. We were on the subject of women and the State Department's nonfraternization policy, when he told me, "Nobody's going to legislate the morality of my dick." That sort of attitude, I told him, would get him nowhere in the Foreign Service. "Perfect," he said. "That's just where I want to go—nowhere."

It was an empty boast. His wife had left him the year before. What troubled him most about this crisis was not the banality of her having left him for another man, but that the man she left him for was a diplomat—my predecessor in fact. "I don't blame her for leaving me," he had said in self-disgust. "If I was her, I'd have left me too—only sooner. But, my god, with a *doormat?*" Ever since then, he had legislated the behavior of his dick himself by conducting his own anti-nonfraternization campaign. "I only sleep with women from unfriendly embassies," he said. But that too was an empty boast. I suspected that he was not sleeping with anyone at all, out of a self-imposed vow of chastity, abstinence, atonement, or ascetic procrastination.

It was at the reception that I discovered that he had broken his vows.

Amid the uproar over Joe's undiplomatic comment about Yalta, one of the Romanians, a pretty girl, spoke up in Joe's defense.

"I think Domnul Bierce know us better than we know us," she said.

I recognized her as the date of the young British lecturer in art history, a closet Marxist whom I sometimes invited to these gatherings to fill out the quota of English speakers. But he must have recognized her for the work of art that she was, for she had the fine facial features of a Verrocchio boy. And magnificent hair—long spiraling corkscrews that almost obscured her androgynous features.

"Verona!" said her date. "How could you say such a thing about your people?"

His slumming North London accent showed he wanted to be "of the people," but this came thinly through a fine set of teeth that I happened to know came from Surrey and the genes of a father who lectured at Oxford and a mother who was a Member of Parliament.

Verona's comment had renewed the shoulder-shrugging, stigmata-displaying uproar of her fellow countrymen. She ignored them, and her date even more pointedly, to risk a more intimate smile at Joe from beneath that cascade of bronze corkscrews before turning away to refresh her glass of Maker's Mark. Where had I seen that smile? In the Louvre? Da Vinci's *John the Baptist*?

Joe scowled at her. She was ruining his fun. The last thing he wanted was someone to agree with him, certainly not a pretty temptress. Joe found his empty glass on the mantel. He looked around for the bottle, but she was filling his glass from the bottle she was holding before he could object. He proposed a toast: "Here's to woman," he said in a loud, boorish voice. *"Would that we could fall into her arms without falling into her hands, because when God makes a beautiful woman, the devil opens a new register."*

But she had already turned away, leaving Joe to nurse his bourbon-soaked misogyny alone. This new topic put Joe back in the good graces of the Romanian men. But I could tell he had been stung. For the rest of the evening he kept stealing glances in Verona's direction. Later, I noticed him working his way through the crowd toward her, like a young Romeo drawn to his Juliet, or a rusty blade to a shiny new magnet. It took close to half an hour for him to brush elbows with her, but in my role as voyeur I'd grown sensitive to the most subtle gravitations of sexual allure. When he reached her, he whispered something in her ear. Was he renewing the battle of wits? She pretended not to have heard. Soon afterward, she left with her young professor of art. Joe pretended not to notice.

As the other guests were leaving, I asked Joe if he'd stay for a nightcap. "Exactly what I intended to do," he replied. He disappeared into the study, where he would make himself at home, pouring himself a drink and settling into one of the two leather armchairs, the sole pieces of furniture I moved about with in those days. I still have them. My sentimental attachments are few but permanent.

I politely booted the last lingering bore out the door, exchanged my shoes for soft leather slippers, and joined Joe in the study. I settled into the other chair, a sighing leather throne whose soft, feminine contours were well acquainted with my after-hours, off-duty slouch. I'd just stretched my legs, let my slippers fall to the floor, and tasted the first sip of Armagnac, a better brand than I'd served the horde, when the doorbell rang.

"Damn," I said, stepping back into my slippers.

"Somebody must've forgot something," said Joe with a grin. "Or remembered something. The proverbial comeback."

At the door—or rather *framed* in the door—I was astonished to see Verona, the young professor's date, his work of art, without the young professor. The porch light shone on her like the dim lamp attached to a gilt picture frame. The snow, glinting as it fell, provided an appropriate background against the dark canvas of the night.

"My name is Verona," she said, looking up at me through those bronze corkscrews.

"I know," I said. I would have invited her in, but the way she said it made me pause. It was shameless, like an offer or a dare. Yet the way she held her head down, looking up through those dizzying spirals of wild hair, gave her the chaste air of an ambiguous Florentine boy.

"May I come in?"

"Have you forgotten someth . . . ?" I was going to ask if she'd left something behind, a pair of gloves or her slingshot, but then came Joe's voice from the other room.

"Let her in," he said. "I grant you diplomatic immunity. She's with me."

I stepped aside and Verona swept in toward Joe's voice. I glanced out into the darkened street. Only the snowfall. I closed and locked the door. What was Joe up to? Didn't he know I could lose my job—or at least my post— if I didn't get her out of the house soon to prevent, as they say, an appearance of impropriety?

When I got back to the study, she was in Joe's arms. They enwrapped her narrow waist, his hands clutching the cheap fancy fabric of her dress, causing the hem to rise. I glimpsed the smooth white flesh of her thighs above the black stockings, which were not encumbered by the scaffolding of a garter belt. Her creamy thighs were thicker than one would have imagined near her crotch, and looked hard and strong as a nutcracker. He turned her around to face me and held the slight Aphroditic bulge of her belly cupped in his hands, making the tight dress shine.

"This is Verona," he said.

"We've met," I said. "And so have you, it seems. I thought you'd sworn off women, Joe. What was all that charade tonight at the reception?"

"Shall I tell him?" Joe said to Verona, running his hands along her sides. She put her hands on his and leaned back against him. She let her hands leave his only long enough to caress certain parts of her body that he was not attending to.

"Mmm, I don't know," she said. "Isn't it better to show?"

"Right," he said. "Okay, it's show-and-tell time."

I sat down in the leather armchair and found my glass where I'd left it. I raised it to my lips. The cognac went down smoothly, smooth as amber beads, smooth as their hands over the smooth curves of her waist and hips, and now and then over her breasts. Their hands might have been the hands of islanders gently coaxing ripe tropical juices from her body, of pineapples or coconuts, so that something stronger and smoother and sweeter than any liqueur might be distilled, drop by drop from the dark petals of the secret flower between her legs.

"It was a dark and stormy night," Joe began. "And the flowers were glistening in the garden. . . ."

"Skip that," said Verona, directing one of his hands below. "Go to the good part."

"You're absolutely right," Joe said to Verona. "That's all just *litter-cheer*. But it did happen to be a dark and stormy night, the first night I took you home. We'd been fooling around in the taxi and we were both dying for it, especially you."

"Especially *you*, you mean!" she said. "'Just give it a little suck,' you said. When my head go down, the taxi driver bump his head on the ceiling trying to see us in the mirror and almost wreck us."

"Almost wrecked *me*, you mean! Anyway, there we are, going up the stairs to my apartment in the dark—someone had stolen the lightbulbs again—with our fingers in various orifices not our own, that shall remain unmentioned but are easily shown."

Somehow Verona's dress had come unzipped in back and it was slipping inch by inch down her shoulders. She didn't appear to be wearing a bra, and her movements threatened to shift the dress at any moment to expose a nipple. I found myself in a state of anticipation for the chance viewing of just one of them, please. Would her nipples be broad, round, and brown, with slightly concave aureoles, like diminutive sombreros? Or would they be sharpened cones, red and petulant as devils' tongues? Would they be hard as tiny matchstick heads? Or inverted, willing to be coaxed and coddled? Or would each nipple, as her cleavage promised, be another mouthful, a little breast upon a breast?

Joe must have read my eyes.

"That's one of the wonderful things about Verona," he said. "She was meant to be naked. I think somewhere in her family tree—breadfruit or coconut tree—she's Polynesian in her molten core. Her breasts don't look large in a dress, do they? And they're not. But their shape is perfect, just made to hold in your hand, the nipple nuzzling the palm of your hand like a koala bear."

The dress slipped away. But instead of a nipple, there was a bra. A black strapless affair that created the supernatural cleavage above. Verona stepped out of her dress, which she caught on the tip of her shoe and kicked onto the desk. Behind the desk was a window, and its shade, I suddenly realized, was up. Anyone happening by the window . . . I should have told them to stop this little game, but her panties were a white cotton V, trimmed at the sides with a fine fringe of just the right luxuriance of excess pubic hair. My mouth was dry.

Joe was caressing her shoulders, dipping his fingers into the soft depressions around her collarbone and armpits, nibbling at her neck. Now and then a word would bubble to the surface: "then she . . . then I . . . her ass . . . into my pants . . . and . . . bit it . . . lifted her up . . . sitting on my shoulders . . . horsey-back . . . but . . . ass-backwards . . . riding . . . so that . . . her cunt was in my mouth . . . sucked . . . sucked . . . screamed. . . ."

"And I come like that," said Verona brightly. "It was

foarte ciudat." The Romanian words sounded like chew-dot, but meant "very strange." It was.

"Yes, *very strange,*" said Joe. "As I chewed your little dot."

"Then you throw me on the bed," said Verona.

"I eased you down gently on the bed," Joe corrected her.

"I fall on the bed," said Verona. "Hard."

"I was," said Joe. "Hard, that is." Unzipping his pants behind her with one hand, he lowered her white V with the other, just low enough to allow him to slip his unlegislated dick in from behind and yet still feel the slight constriction of the waistband. "Am," he added. "Hard. But all good things must come in the end."

As he slid up inside her, she bent forward slightly at the waist to make his entry more comfortable for them both. She closed her eyes for the first time and opened her mouth, breathing hard, puffing and blowing, as though she would have liked to blow out his candle, or burn it at both ends. She was blowing my candle, though, into a flame, halfway across the room.

"I think that's meant for you," said Joe, his breathing slightly constricted from the pleasure he was taking in Verona.

I must have looked uncomprehending, or merely stupid. I felt like I was in a trance.

"Her mouth," he said, with an upward tilt of his chin. "Trust me. She's very articulate."

I glanced at the window. The soft light from the floor lamp cast a reflection on the glass, making it impossible to see if anyone was watching. Only the reflection of Joe and Verona peered back from another angle, in a darker version of their performance. I was still unable to move from my chair.

"Are you sure it's . . ." I said.

Verona didn't open her eyes. She only nodded her head quickly and opened her mouth again. As though to emphasize that she was ready for anything, she placed her hands over her breasts above the cups of the bra and pulled the material down, revealing what I had most wanted to be hiding there: two extra mouthfuls, two little swollen breasts at the tips of her breasts. Exquisite nipples. Then she held them out toward me and squeezed them, italicizing each pink swell.

Joe was moving against her in warm undulating strokes. Every time he pushed her from behind, she moved a small step forward, toward me. Her thumbs were passing over her nipples, flicking them like a Bic, then adjusting them like fine-tuning knobs. Her bra now encircled her waist like a fallen black tiara. Her black bra and white panties were, I noticed, like her stockings, of a finer workmanship and quality, far more expensive than her dress, which was of a cheap party-dress fabric. The extra care she'd taken for what was usually unseen endeared her to me. I don't know why. Was it the premeditation of seduction? Or the modesty of self-absorption? It didn't matter. It struck me as sensuously innocent. Like the ambiguities of her appearance, part feminine siren, and part Renaissance castrato.

Joe gave another heroic thrust from behind, and Verona took another giant step forward, planting her feet in a sturdy A. Now she was almost on top of me. Her eyes were still closed. She bit her lower lip, and I could see her teeth, slightly crooked, like smooth white pebbles in a hot, sulfurous spring, so rich with iron it was scarlet. Joe gave her another good prod and Verona gave a little cry as she let go of her breasts and grasped the armrests of my chair, her fingers deep in the soft leather.

I reached out—full of the fear of being seen through the window, of being fired in the morning as I arrived at the Embassy, whisked off in a military guard, and transported to Washington for disciplinary actions I'd rather not think about—and touched her shoulder, ready to withdraw my hand if she flinched. But Verona was not in any condition to flinch. She was malleable as clay in Joe's hands—and now in mine. She purred at my touch and rolled her head on her neck like a cat. I touched her hair, running my fingers into the thick, fragrant mane that I had seen until then only in paintings and had only dreamed of touching. It was softer than I ever imagined, not like copper or bronze at all. For the first time in my life, I had grasped the meaning of art. I held out my hands, palms upward like a beggar for alms, and let her nipples touch them in the center, then traced my life-line, heart-line, head-line, and fate-line with each pink volcano. She pressed her breasts into my hands. They were softer than I had ever imagined. Hot and feverish, and, most strangely, downed with light furze. I was exploring a volcano in the Sandwich Islands, picking heather from the lava slopes.

One of her hands found my thigh and squeezed. From there it went directly to my belt, which was soon sprung, like a window shade, along with buttons and zipper. "Oh no," I said aloud. Like a blind newborn she knew, even with her eyes closed, where to grope to find what she needed, something to lick sweet and hard, something to suck swollen as that first full tit, thick with milk. My cock, my legislated cock.

Joe kept up his end of the bargain, rolling his hips against her gently, dipping his hands into her panties to curl his fingers in the thick dark promise of her hair. As he rubbed with one finger, then two, stiffening and quickening their pace as he felt her clitoris stiffen and quicken, I almost thought I saw sparks fly. But then all flames were doused as I felt Verona's hot mouth slide down and still further down my newly freed cock, my now unlegislated cock.

"Do you feel that?" said Joe, his disembodied voice relishing my experience like a vivid memory, which I'm sure it was. "How her tongue laps and swirls like a whirlpool, how her cheeks are sucked in? Feel how her mouth contracts? Doesn't it feel just like she's sucking a spool of waxed thread from your gut into hers? That's exactly how her cunt feels, all hot and suckysmooth, when she's coming. Like she's going . . . to turn herself . . . outside-in . . . and you . . . with her. Like . . . right . . . now!"

Verona began to moan, her knees were shaking, her shoulders trembling. One of her fingernails broke off as it entered the leather armrest, trickling blood. I was afraid she was going into convulsions. I started to get up. Her head came down like a hammer. Then I forgot to worry. Her moaning set up such a vibration around my cock, that even if she wasn't bobbing her head and sucking with such vigor, with such an expert pause at the bottom of her stroke, and another, longer, kissing pause at the top, I would have come through the sheer vibrato and pizzicato of her sonic fellatio.

I began to moan too as I tried to keep it back, to keep

the last whipping tail-end of white thread inside me. But it couldn't be done. I'm afraid I let out a throaty hurrah that must have wakened the spirits of all the house's dead mistresses. I imagined their breasts exploding out of their bodices and their pale fleshy hips bursting their girdles as they rushed to join us from the shadows of the paneled study. That did it. Out it came with a force that snapped my eyes open and shut several times. I saw Joe's grin, as in a flickering stereoscope, above the lunar landscape of Verona's back a mist of ghostly sweat glowing there and, I imagined, rising in steam from the surface of her overheated body.

He seemed to pause, holding his cock at the root to give it extra polish and rigidity. He lay it on her back like a swan's neck, then smearing the moist tip of it between her buttocks, he grinned at me again as he placed it against the smaller hole. He put one hand on her shoulder to pull her forward to embed the whole purple bulb of the head. Then, having thus carefully set it, like a screw, he put both hands on her shoulders and gripping them, pulled, driving it all the way home.

It wasn't a procedure I would have recommended. He must have known what he was doing, though, because at that moment her muffled outcry reversed direction to become a vacuum pump that sucked me suddenly dry. Her finger had disappeared up to the knuckle in the stuffing of the chair, the leather fitting snugly around it, as I imagined her mouth fit me, or her nether hole fit Joe.

She swallowed everything I had, and only gagged a little, for which I'll be eternally grateful. Never have I known such an articulate mouth. Nor such an accommodating body.

The aftermath I expected to be filled with embarrassment, if not shame. Or awkwardness, at the very least. I imagined the three of us would part with a kind of tenderness, and sadness that it could never be repeated, glad that it had been, but guilty for having once experienced such paradise. The rest would be atonement. Mere life again.

It wasn't like that at all. As Verona finally collapsed to her knees in front of me—it had only been Joe holding her up until then, hoisting her on his petard—she lay her cheek against my crotch and nuzzled me. Sounds of half-conscious satisfaction escaped her throat after bubbling up from a deep spring of contentment, as though she had just had a long sauna, a rubdown, a good meal. Shame would have been as foreign to her as to a kitten soliciting promiscuous scratches behind her ear from a roomful of cat-lovers, or to a cannibal licking her lips.

She rolled my swollen meat in her hands, rubbing it dry in her hair. When she looked up at me, there were little rubbery pearl-white beads and ivory streamers adorning her bronze locks. Her eyes were sleepy.

"Thanks," she said. She was looking at me but she was talking to Joe.

"My pleasure," said Joe, staring at the sculptured ceiling. He was lying flat on his back on the carpet, where he had fallen like a warrior at the end of the gentle three-way battle, one hand still caressing her warm buttocks with lazy appreciative motions. He had, miraculously, his drink in his other hand.

"I suppose I should be the one to say thank you," I offered.

"That would be nice," said Joe.

"Very diplomatic," said Verona.

"Not really," said Joe. "You know, he could lose his job over this kind of behavior."

I was playing with the corkscrews of Verona's hair. It may seem sentimental to say so, but I consider it my moment of sublimest freedom.

Then I said, "Nobody's going to legislate the behavior of my cock."

Joe chuckled. "Amen."

"What does that mean," said Verona, raising her head a little. "Legislate the behavior of my cock?"

"Not *your* cock," said Joe. "*His* cock. Your cock behavior is just fine."

"His cock then. What does it mean?" she persisted.

"It means he's in love," said Joe.

"With me?" said Verona, a little surprised.

"With life," I said. "Thanks to you." I raised a handful of Verona's hair, damp and fragrant with my own admission of something important. I held it to my nostrils and took a deep and much needed breath of fresh air.

Perhaps I should end this story here, the story of my erotic epiphany. But that strikes me as somehow false. As though it were just *litter-cheer,* as Joe would say. My erotic epiphany, which was really just an echo of Joe, an empty boast of a glimpse of paradise at the time, has become reality. Our *égoïsme à trois* drew to its dramatic climax, as we knew it must, but not before we repeated our fugue in the coming months, reveled in its variations well into spring, in combinations of threes, twos, and ones. None of us knew, until then, how many permutations could be worked out of that simple but holy number, three. It continued into summer and into fall. We had our lovers' tiffs and blisses. More than our fair share perhaps, but that's what comes of the multiplication of pleasure.

One day Joe went back to America "to convert the natives," he said. I left the Foreign Service to teach at this small college in the Turkish capital. We live, Verona and I, near the quarter where the merchants still deal in the long goat-hair that gave the city its former, more sensuous name, Angora. I can hear Verona in the other room. She is chasing our child, a daughter, who is on a naked rampage through the house, shrieking something obscene in Turkish (God knows where she picks it up), her hair trailing behind her in glorious long blonde spiraling corkscrews. Her name is Juliette.

MICHAEL THOMAS FORD
Jack

When Jack finally arrives, I am sitting in the hotel bar sipping a drink and surreptitiously listening to a handsome young man with black hair and blue eyes as he tries to convince another man who is not his lover to come back to his room and make love. I know the man being pursued, who has honeyed skin and hair the color of mahogany, does not belong to this one because I saw the black-haired man check in with another earlier in the morning, saw them kissing on the landing when his lover left to conduct some business. Now, the one with the blue eyes is whispering the things he would like to do on this sticky afternoon, and I am becoming aroused by what I can hear of the furtive conversation. I am just wondering what he would look like with the other's cock up his ass, how his mouth would open as he took the man's prick between his lips, when I see Jack in the big mirror behind the bar, descending the staircase into the almost empty lobby.

She is late, and I have been sitting in the lazy late-day Louisiana heat for almost an hour waiting for her, thinking about her until my cunt has begun to moisten and I can feel the dampness between my legs. I am wearing a thin white dress, and I wonder if it will stain. The tall glass of iced tea I am holding is nearly empty now, and small beads of sweat roll down the smooth sides to collect along my fingers. I can feel the warm dampness at the back of my neck where my hair is pulled up into the elaborate design that Jack likes so much, and I raise my wet hand to cool my flushed skin. The feeling is electric as I trace the line of my neck down to the small space between my breasts, all the while watching Jack move gracefully across the floor toward me.

Seeing me watching, Jack makes her way across the dark wood floor slowly, showing off for the handful of people, both men and women, whose eyes turn to look at her. When she is halfway across, she stops to speak with a woman seated on the low sofa that faces the check-in desk. The woman is short, heavy, and blonde, the opposite of my Japanese features, my birdlike thinness and the blackness of my hair, and I know that Jack finds her attractive. She checked into the hotel this morning while we sat on the veranda eating our breakfast of peaches and buttery scones. She was accompanied by a stern-looking man, and Jack remarked, "I'd like to make love to her." She does this to make me jealous, knowing that it makes me want her even more than I usually do, which is already almost unbearable at times. I see her give the woman a small kiss on her rosy cheek, her eyes looking at my reflection in the mirror so that she can take in my reaction.

Even though I return to my drink and the conversation of the young men next to me, I feel when she is standing behind me. It is as though my heart is drawn to her, forcing my eyes up to stare at her reflection in the mirror. When I look at her face pictured in the watery glass, she is smiling slightly. Her bright blue eyes look back at me intently, daring me not to smile back. We stay locked like this for a few moments until I give in, my lips rising up in a pouty greeting. It is only then that she touches me.

"Hello," she says, her breath warm on my bare shoulders. Her voice is mellow, like a note drawn from an oboe and hanging still in the air. I feel her hand slip against my waist as she presses in closer. She smells of aftershave, a light bay scent that mingles sweetly with the sweat rising on her skin from the afternoon heat. "Have you been waiting long?"

"No," I lie, settling back against her so that my back is resting against her chest. She knows exactly how long I've been waiting and wants me to be angry. I study her again in the mirror. She is wearing a white linen shirt, buttoned to the neck and perfectly pressed with tiny gold links at the cuffs, and white trousers held up by brown leather braces that button inside the waistband. Her short brown hair has been oiled back so that it lies flat against her head, a few stray hairs dipping down in front over her left eye in a curl. She is the most beautiful man I have ever seen, her skin smooth as cream, and she knows it. It is her power over me, the fact that I want her so much.

"Who is she?" I ask.

Jack's eyes light up as she realizes that I have begun playing the game she has devised, have in fact been playing it all along. She moves onto the tall chair next to me, sitting with one hand on my knee, her fingers pressing points of heat into my skin. I look down and see that she is wearing brown leather shoes, brightly polished and neatly tied. "Her name is Sara," she says as she motions the waiter over and orders an iced tea for herself and another for me. "She's here with her husband, a banker of some kind. She asked us to join them for dinner."

"You said no, of course," I say, knowing full well that she has in fact done just the opposite.

Jack sips from her tea, pulling a leaf of mint from the glass and biting a piece off. She leans in and kisses me softly on the mouth, her tongue teasing me momentarily and leaving behind the fresh taste of the mint. "I said that six would be fine for us," she says.

A few minutes after the appointed time, Jack and I enter the dining room. It is crowded with people escaping from the oppressive heat, taking some comfort from the slowly circling overhead fans and glasses of gin. I see to one side the dark-haired man I'd watched in the bar earlier sitting with his lover. Several tables away is the mahogany-haired man, with a pretty woman I take to be his wife. The idea of these two men spending their afternoon in one another's arms (while the lover sat in a stuffy room doing business and the wife looked through the local stores for some small item to bring home to the waiting children) makes me laugh, and I make a note to tell Jack about it later, when we are alone. My arm is tucked neatly into Jack's, and as I catch a glimpse of our reflections in the full-length mirrors that flank the entranceway, I can't help but think that we look like characters from a Fitzgerald novel, me in my simple white dress with my hair swept up into impossible curls and Jack in her spotless linen.

Sara and her husband are seated at a far table nearest to the windows. She sees us standing at the doorway and waves awkwardly. I can tell by the way she drops her head when we wave back that she has already fallen in love with Jack. As we make our way through the maze of tables, I begin to think of all the possibilities for the evening, and wonder which ones will come to pass.

Coming up beside the table, Jack stops next to Sara. "Hello," she says, "I'm sorry we're late."

Sara's husband, a balding man in his late forties with absolutely nothing distinguishable about him, rises clumsily, pushing a recently discarded newspaper to the side of the table. He is wearing a badly fitting suit of heavy material, and his skin is waxy. I take an instant dislike to him, but smile pleasantly.

"Not at all," he says, obviously annoyed that his wife has invited strangers to dinner. "I'm Stewart Oliver. I believe you already know my wife."

Jack takes Sara's hand and kisses it lightly, and I see Stewart flinch. "We certainly did," she says before turning back to Stewart. "I'm Jack Thomas, and this is my wife, Lily."

Stewart takes my hand and shakes it harshly, his skin moist and unpleasant. Summoned by a wave from Jack, a waiter arrives and drinks are ordered all around. They arrive quickly, and I drink slowly, enjoying the taste of the gin and tonic on my throat while I listen to the conversation, adding some words when I am required to. Stewart, we learn, is involved in international banking, and Jack is asking him questions about his work.

Sara is silent, watching the men talk, and I am able to look at her more closely. She is quite heavy, wearing a billowy white dress that hides rather than shows off her fullness. Her face is wide and open, and she has exquisite green eyes. Her blonde hair is done in small waves close to her head, and her fingers clutch anxiously at the thin strand of pearls encircling her neck.

"Your necklace is very beautiful," I say to her across the table, and she starts as if my voice has frightened her.

"Oh," she stammers, "thank you." She is embarrassed and takes several sips of her drink quickly. *Later,* I think to myself, *later we will learn much about one another.*

Jack has ordered oysters and they arrive on a bed of crushed ice. "You must try an oyster," Jack tells Sara as she lifts one from its elegantly curled shell and brings it to her lips. "It's said that the taste of oysters incites people to the most carnal of desires."

Sara puts her hand on Jack's wrist, the delicate pink nails resting lightly on her skin as she tries to protest. "No," she says faintly. "I don't think I'd like it." But Jack is insistent and holds the silvery oyster in front of Sara's mouth as she looks into her eyes. After a moment, her lips part slightly, and Jack feeds her the oyster, watching her face as she tastes for the first time the deliciously sweet saltiness of its flesh on her tongue. Her throat ripples as she swallows, and she smiles at Jack.

"See," Jack says, "I knew you'd like it." Sara's cheeks flush as she reaches for her drink.

The remainder of the dinner goes by quickly. Because Jack and Stewart are talking, I say very little, instead enjoying the delicious food and listening to the mingled voices around me, inventing possibilities for the faces I see. At one point, Jack leans over to me. "I want to fill her cunt with berries and watch you eat them out one by one," she whispers, and then goes back to discussing bonds with Stewart.

Dinner ends when Stewart glances at his watch and says that he must go meet his client. This is Jack's cue. She turns to Sara. "Why don't you come up to our room for a drink," she says. "We can keep you company until Stewart is finished."

Sara looks at Stewart, who is worrying over the bill and doesn't hear a word that's been said. "I'd like that," she says simply. She is slightly drunk on the wine we have been drinking and her face is flushed.

Finished looking at the bill, Stewart says his goodbyes and departs, leaving us in the lobby. Offering an arm each to Sara and me, Jack leads the way up the staircase to our room. She makes some joke as we reach the landing, and Sara bursts into a shower of laughter as Jack leads her to our door and opens it. Inside, the room is bathed in the purple shadows of a dusk rapidly settling into the blueness of a summer night. The tall windows are open and the long white curtains are moving with the small breaths of wind that come in from the garden. Jack has turned on one of the table lamps and warm golden light pools across the enormous bed that occupies the center of the room.

Sara is still giggling as Jack ushers her into the room and shuts the door behind her. As soon as the door is locked, Jack presses her against the wall and kisses her hard on the mouth, pinning her arms to her sides. Taken by surprise, Sara gives in to her, letting Jack's tongue enter her mouth as she restrains her. When Jack pulls away, Sara looks across the room to where I am sitting on the bed.

"But what about Lily," she says, her voice almost a whisper.

Jack laughs. "Lily doesn't mind," she says, taking Sara's hand and leading her over to me. "In fact, I think she finds you quite as delicious as I do, don't you Lily?"

Sara sits nervously on the bed next to me. She holds her hands in her lap, avoiding my face as I study hers. *Yes,* I think, *I want her very much*. She looks like I did the first time I was with Jack, the first time I learned what love-making could be. Jack has poured herself a whisky and is sitting in one of the big armchairs, a large overstuffed affair covered in the darkest scarlet velvet. She has undone one of the buttons on her shirt and is watching us, one hand resting on the arm of the chair, the other rubbing her crotch slowly.

Sara looks at me nervously. "I've never done this before," she says. "I'm not sure that I know how."

Jack laughs, the sound rolling through the thick air. "Don't worry," she says. "Lily will show you how."

Standing up, I unhook my dress and let it fall to my feet. Underneath I am wearing nothing, and I see Sara's eyes fall to my small, dark bush, a thin black line between my legs. I pull the pins from my hair and let it fall carelessly over my shoulders and to my waist. I stand quietly, my hands clasped lightly behind my back and my weight thrown slightly onto one hip, the way Jack likes to view me when we are alone. At times like this I feel like the pleasure women my grandmother used to speak of, the beautiful women trained to make love to emperors and generals in the times when Japan was less tame than it is now. I remember also her stories, told far less often and in a whispered voice, of the empresses and fierce warrior women who also partook of these forbidden pleasures. It was these women that haunted my dreams, their faces I saw when I entered myself with trembling fingers and stroked myself in my darkened bedroom, shuddering and crying as I came.

Sara stares at me, taking in every inch of my body but keeping her hands resting in her lap. I see her pause at my small breasts, lingering on the nipples that have become erect as a result of my thoughts. Moving toward her, I stop when I can feel her breath fluttering across the skin of my belly. She is breathing quickly, nervously, and I enjoy knowing that she has never done this before, that I am her first. Leaning down, I kiss her, feeling the stiffness of her mouth as I run my tongue across her lips and taste the wine she had been drinking with her dinner. I push my tongue harder against her, and her lips open to me slightly, allowing me inside. *She gives in too easily,* I think.

I kiss her for several minutes, then Jack's voice breaks the magic. "Undress her," she says. "I want to see her naked."

I take Sara's hands and lift her from the bed so that she is standing. Moving behind her, I undo the buttons holding her dress closed and push it down her body so that it puddles at her feet. Her heaviness hangs on her like extra cloth, the fullness of her skin sensuous as folds of silk. She is wearing blue silk panties and a matching bra, and her skin is white as moths' wings against the darkness. I look over at Jack and see that she is pleased.

"I want to see her breasts," she says.

I fumble with the catch of Sara's bra, my fingers clumsy as I try to unhook the stubborn clasp. Finally I get it to relinquish its hold and slip the thin straps from her shoulders. Her breasts are large, the nipples surprisingly small and pink. I want to take one in my mouth, but wait for Jack's permission.

"Come over here and suck my dick," Jack growls, obviously aroused by the sight of her tits. Sara starts to walk over to Jack, but she stops her with a motion of her hand. "On your knees," she says. I watch, enthralled, as Sara gets down on her hands and knees and crawls across the floor toward Jack, her breasts swinging gracefully beneath her. Her ass shifts heavily as she moves slowly across the carpet, her large thighs brushing against one another. When she reaches the chair, she kneels obediently before

Jack, waiting for her order. Jack places her hand under Sara's chin, drawing her face up to look into hers. "Take my cock out," she says.

Sara runs her hands up Jack's legs, stopping when she reaches the buttons of her pants. Slowly she unbuttons them and pulls the material apart. As she does, the dildo that Jack has been wearing all evening comes into view. I watch Sara's face collapse in surprise as it dawns on her that what she has been worshiping all night is another woman.

"Suck it, bitch," Jack says before she has time to think about what is happening. She grabs Sara's hair and pushes her forward, sinking a couple of inches of prick into her soft throat. Sara resists, pushing at Jack's legs, but Jack is stronger, and Sara is not really fighting. She quickly ceases her protestations and begins to work her lips all over the big cock that rises from between Jack's thighs.

"That's right," Jack murmurs as Sara pushes another few inches into her throat. "I knew you were a cocksucker the first time I saw you. Suck me really well and I just might fuck that pretty ass of yours later."

I stand watching Sara blow Jack, her neck and back arching as she works her way up and down the big dick. I am still holding Sara's bra, and I finger the softness of the cups where her breasts had been encased. I feel my cunt begin to moisten as I imagine sticking my tongue into her asshole, my fingers into her pussy. I want to play with myself, but it is not yet my turn. I can only watch while Sara pleasures Jack.

Finally, Jack pulls her cock away from Sara's mouth. She leans forward hungrily, trying to take it back in, but Jack pushes her away roughly. "No more," she snaps. "Go lie down on the bed."

Confused, Sara gets up and comes back to the bed like
a child that has been slapped by its mother. I want to tell
her that it is all part of the game, that it is all right, but she
has to learn it for herself. She lies down on the soft white
spread and I look at Jack. "The ropes," she says.

I go to Jack's brown leather traveling bag and find the
two lengths of soft silk rope she carries with her whenever
we go away. I am more than familiar with how they feel
wrapped around a wrist or ankle, sometimes even a throat,
and I envy Sara. I try to hand the ropes to Jack, but she
waves me away. "You do it," she says. "Tie her."

I am surprised. Jack has never before allowed me to use
the ropes, or any of her toys, except on myself. I experience
a thrill of excitement as I realize that I am to take on a new
role in tonight's game. I grip the ropes in my hand tightly,
for the first time thinking of what can be done with them
rather than what can be done by them. It is an electric feeling, and I silently thank Jack for this unexpected pleasure.

Going to Sara, I take one of her wrists and wrap the
rope around it firmly, making sure that it is neither too
tight nor too loose, the way Jack usually checks my bonds.
Her eyes are closed, and she makes no attempt to resist me
as I fasten the ends to the frame of the antique iron bed-
stead. Soon both of her arms are stretched above her and
her legs are squeezed neatly together.

I look at Jack, but she is only drinking her whisky and
stroking her cock, giving me no instruction. Getting onto
the bed, I lean over Sara and put one of her tender nipples
in my mouth. She inhales sharply and her body rises up as
I bite down gently on it. I feel her mound scrape against
my belly where I am straddling her and push her back
down by lowering myself on top of her. Her ample flesh is
soft and yielding, and I feel as though I am resting on a bed

of flowers when I smell the scent of lemon water that rises from her skin.

Biting her nipple more forcefully, I take her other breast in my hand and squeeze it, working the nipple with my fingers until she is writhing and crying out for me to stop. I do so momentarily, letting her catch her breath before resuming my assault on her tender buds. I know Jack is watching and I want to put on a good show for her.

I look over to see what she is doing. She has shed her clothes and is sitting in the chair naked. With her thin, athletic body and small, perfect breasts she looks like a beautiful golden boy watching us make love, her hand rising and falling along the length of her cock. She is twisting the small silver ring in her left nipple slowly as she jerks off, and her eyes are centered on me as I sit atop Sara's prostrate form.

Moving down Sara's body, I spread her legs with my knee, forcing them apart. I feel dampness on my leg and realize that she is steadily leaking a stream of stickiness through her panties. Gripping the waistband, I pull the front down so that her reddish blonde swatch comes into view. The pinkness of her lips is visible at the center where I have forced her thighs apart, like the leaves of a summer poppy opening up.

Bowing my head, I run just the tip of my tongue over her bush, dipping into her warm folds momentarily. Sara cries out as she feels me begin to enter her, and I know that no one has ever done this to her, has ever really made love to her. *She has no idea how beautiful she is,* I think as I drink in her juices, smearing my chin with them.

Pulling away, I yank her panties down her thighs and legs so that she is completely open to me. By now they are drenched with her cunt juice. I hold them to her face so that she can smell her own desire, know what pleasure lies inside of her. She breathes in her own scent and I feel her body stiffen. Bringing the material to her lips, I push it into her mouth and she sucks at it eagerly.

I leave her like this as I go back to her pussy. Her legs are spread wide, and I resist the temptation to go back to eating her. Instead, I slip a finger into her quickly so that her whole body lifts off the bed in an attempt to get away from me. I am amazed at how hot she is inside, as though her heart is pumping fire through her veins. Another finger joins the first, and I pump her slowly, spreading her wider as she relaxes. I watch her eyes as I fuck her with my hand.

She is about to come when I pull my hand back out and lick her from my fingers, relishing the taste of her. Her chest is heaving as she lingers on the edge of her orgasm, unable to move the single step she needs to bring it all crashing down around her. I like seeing her at this moment, but I know I cannot keep her there forever. There is much more to do.

Pulling the panties from her mouth, I listen to the soft moans that escape from her throat. She licks her lips thirstily, and I am happy to oblige her. Crawling up her body, I crouch over her face, my cunt hanging just above her mouth. "Drink," I say simply, and she obeys, straining against the ropes as she reaches upward to lick my pussy. I feel her tongue pushing inside me, and I know she is licking up the sweetness that runs from my center so easily.

She sucks at me as though she has not drunk in a week, her teeth pulling at my soft lips, her tongue probing for my clit. I lower myself slightly so that her mouth and nose are consumed by my cunt, grinding myself on her face and forcing her tongue straight up me. She works feverishly, pleasuring me until I begin to shake from the combination of having to remain still so long and the rhythm of her mouth working my insides.

Before I can come, Jack moves onto the bed behind me and pulls me back forcefully, away from Sara's mouth. "That's enough, you two," she says as she positions me between Sara's spread legs and takes up a position behind me. "I've been watching you two play. Now I'm in charge." She pulls my hands behind me and snaps a pair of leather constraints around my wrists. I am off balance now, perched on the bed, and cannot resist when she pushes my head down into Sara's steaming crotch. She takes up the discarded panties and puts them back in Sara's mouth.

She presses the tip of her cock against my ass, and I push my face deeper into Sara's sopping pussy as I brace myself for what I know will come next. I feel her hands on my mounds and shiver at the touch. She massages me for a few minutes, enjoying the sight of my face buried in Sara's thighs. Then she raises her hand and brings it back down with a stinging smack, making me jump with pain.

Just as the last ripple of fire under my skin begins to dissolve, Jack moves her cockhead down to tickle my cunt. I am so worked up that I don't even care that she hasn't lubed it. The dildo slides in between my waiting lips, parting them easily as she enters me. This cock is a new one, thicker than any prick she has ever used on me, and I welcome its width. As inch after inch slides into me, I feel trickles of wetness begin to slip down my thighs.

"You're one horny bitch tonight," Jack says, pleased. "Could it be because I let you have a little taste of being the master? I see I'm going to have to fuck you extra hard to bring you back to your place."

She pushes deeper and deeper into me, opening me up more than I have ever been opened. She is almost completely in when she suddenly pulls out again, leaving me unbearably empty. I look back at her to see why she has stopped, and she slaps my face. "Your cunt is too easy," she snarls. "You're too loose tonight to please me. Perhaps I shouldn't have let you have so much fun."

She moves the head of the dildo back to my asshole and starts to press against it. She has never fucked my ass with something so large, and I am not sure I can take it. I tense, waiting to feel the big prick tear me open. Jack notices that I have paused and forces my head back down between Sara's legs. "Keep working," she orders.

She begins to push in, and I groan as the huge head penetrates my asshole. I am amazed at how I stretch around her cock, at how I take it as though it has always been a part of her. When I feel pain, I dissolve it by slamming my tongue deeper into Sara's hole, as though my mouth has become an extension of Jack's prick. Finally, I feel the leather straps of the harness pressing against my skin, and I know Jack is all the way in. Her hands are on my shoulders, digging into my skin, and I feel completely filled by her. I clamp my ass around the length of her tool and slide along it as much as I can.

"Much better," she says. "Nice and tight the way Daddy likes it. A boy's ass should always fit his daddy's prick. A loose hole is a waste of time."

Jack fucks me in slow strokes at first, just fast enough so that I cannot get completely used to the size of her dick. I work out my frustrations on Sara's pussy, licking her clit until I feel her start to shake, then pulling away. By the way Sara is pushing herself into my mouth, I know she must be worked up to the point where she feels her body will shatter into a million pieces if I touch her again, and I want to keep her there until I am ready. The pain of needing is a lesson Jack has taught me well, and I want to show her that I appreciate her teaching.

Jack is fucking only the first few inches of my ass, her cock teasing me mercilessly as she massages the most tender part of me in quick thrusts. Sometimes she pulls all the way out, and I whimper for her to fill me, my cries muffled by Sara's pussy in my mouth. But she takes her time, working me up to where she wants me, to where she knows I can't wait any longer. I know she is also getting close because her nails are biting into my skin. I imagine the way the cock must feel pressing against her clit.

I am aching with the need to come when she finally slides the entire length of herself back into me, causing me to lose my breath. I feel my cunt begin to spasm as my walls grip her shaft, trying to keep it locked inside me. She rips it away, pulling back out in one long movement that starts the flood roaring through my body. By the time she begins to fuck me wildly, her body bucking against me, I am coming uncontrollably, my whole body shuddering as she continues to beat at my asshole.

Jack pulls out of me and pushes me off of the bed so that I fall to the floor and land on the soft oriental carpet upon which the bed rests. My body is still shaking as my orgasm rages through me, and I can only lie there as wave after wave crashes through my bones. When the intensity begins to subside, I bring myself to my knees and look up at Jack, my arms still held behind me.

She has positioned herself between Sara's legs. A used condom has been thrown onto the floor next to me, the thin skin fouled from my shit. Jack has rolled a fresh one onto her cock and is in the process of sliding it into Sara's cunt. I watch as she pumps the entire thing into the waiting hole at once, pushing Sara's big legs back with her strong hands.

Jack has removed the panties from Sara's mouth, and she is crying out loudly as Jack begins to fuck her brutally, the dildo entering and retreating in quick bursts. A steady stream of filth is pouring from Jack's mouth, and Sara is wallowing in it. "You slut," Jack says, gripping Sara's pearls in her hand as she pummels her cunt. "You like me fucking you like this, don't you? You like me using your hole, like me sticking my cock up your pussy like I'm fucking a whore."

Sara moans out a string of "yeses," her head thrashing from side to side as Jack brings her to the breaking point. Her lipstick has smeared over her face like drops of blood, and she is crying. Then Jack pumps her cock once more into her, and Sara cries out a long, agonized wail as her desire tears its way through her throat. She pulls her head back, and the strand of pearls breaks, sending the small, white drops scattering over her skin and onto the floor, where they come to rest at my feet.

Jack is coming as well, her eyes closed. I see her chest heave several times as she rides along with Sara, sharing her pleasure. Then she pulls out of Sara's thighs and gets off the bed, her cock slick and wet as it hangs between her legs. Helping me to stand, she unsnaps the restraints and kisses me deeply for the first time since the game has begun. It signals the end, and I know that now I am kissing not Jack but my equally beloved Eliza.

On the bed, Sara is breathing softly. Eliza and I go to her, untying the ropes at her wrists and lying on either side of her, softly stroking her skin and kissing her face as she cries with joy.

A. M. HOMES

From The End of Alice

She writes: *Sometimes I have the weirdest dreams. . . .*

Boys. Boys from before, ghosts, come back to visit her. One in particular, sixth grade. The tag end of the elementary years, a four-foot-eight-inch transplant from Minnesota. First noticed when she caught his eyes on the figures at the bottom of her page, copying answers to the math test. In the coatroom, her thick whisper threatening to turn him in had him fast begging for mercy, for leniency, for her pardon. She offered closely supervised parole. He accepted.

When he felt her up, all he got were the puffy protrusions that promised greater future swellings, and when she felt him down, all she found was the narrow little nightstick that might with patience grow to a cop's thick billy club. Like that they played, equals, bald in all the same places.

And perhaps in the guise of making new friends faster, perhaps not knowing the disillusion it would cause—one so willingly makes excuses for the young—at the first boy/girl parties of their lives, before her very eyes, he took up with other girls. All of them, one right after another, if only for a single kiss, a five-minute ride on the swings. She often caught him, lips pressed to the evening's hostess, to the girl whose desk abutted hers, the one with the blondest hair, biggest boobs, him and whomever, rustling in the bushes beyond the patio. Hers was the divorced heart, but she carried on, sure—or nearly sure—that none of the others did the things she did with him. On the floor of her mother's walk-in closet, she gagged his mouth with a suede Dior belt; behind the cinder-block retaining wall, she employed a railroad tie to hold his legs spread. Deep in the furnace room, hidden among the spare tires and Flexible Flyers, she repetitiously wrapped him with kite string and extra electrical cords, tying him to the hot-water heater, his puny ass burning a bright and cheery pink as heat seeped through the thin insulation. She pushed him past his limit, drove his sweet *Schwanstück* backward and forward, slamming him from drive to reverse. Stripped, she slid her naked body over his, sweeping the rubbery tips of her tits across his fine and sensitive skin from neck to nuts, making him twist and turn, trying to pull away from the heater, the heater itself making a groaning sound and him begging, "Put it in, put it in." She'd pull away, smile, take herself in hand, and do a little dance around that furnace room, hairless body, narrow hips pumping the oily air until finally with the smallest shudder she'd stand suddenly stone still, like someone struck dead. And when she recovered, she'd go to him, pull his underwear up over it and put her mouth down on it, sucking him off, the thick BVDs a kind of prophylactic cheesecloth. In the end, she'd untie him, turn him round, and spit onto his hot buns, licking his bright red ass, soothing the sore flesh with the water of her tongue. And he'd thank her profusely, bowing to her honor, "Thank you, thank you, thank you." She'd shrug it off, moving on to the next thing—the teaching of luxury, of smoke and drink. She'd hand him a Winston filched from the cleaning lady, a stolen bottle of her father's whisky, bartered marijuana in a corncob pipe. Days and nights they spent together, inseparable. "Sweet," both sets of parents said about the twinness of their children, so charmed. Playmates.

Slowly, steadily, he fell in love, never losing the fear that she would turn on him, direct her anger at the five inches of difference between them and once and for all take it from him—though there is no way he could have told me this, I can swear it is true, remembering it from my own experience, from my grandmother's helper girl who once came at me with a paring knife. If you don't believe me, I invite you to my room, where I am free to raise my shirt, lower my pants, and show the white scar it made, tracing down from just below the inverted stump of my umbilicus, through the matted down, and on into the nether regions stopping not a breath away from the veiny cord that is my manhood. Scarred forever.

Summer. Her boy went to camp—the recurrence of this theme being explanation for her worry about the new boy being lost to those woods. There was a long, slow goodbye in the trunk of his father's Ford—the tire jack like an extra member nearly taking her up the ass—followed two weeks later by a strange late-afternoon phone call and her mother coming quietly into the den, whispering, "Lightning on a ballfield." And the girl, being the closest companion, the best friend, was offered his toys, his collections—buffalo nickels and tumbled rocks—his cassettes and stereo as parting gifts.

THOMAS S. ROCHE
Up for a Nickel

I **cruise the streets,** smelling cheap tacos and junkie vomit, searching the faces of whores. Searching. I drink rusty water at the Darkside; some of the old guys remember me from the neighborhood, but no one gets my name right. I slip down 20th and pay a visit to Mama Lamia the Palm Reader in her curio shop, stalking the shadows among shrunken heads, ritual daggers, voodoo dolls. *No shit, Jakey, you ain't a little boy no more. . . .* She has to be fifty years old, but she never stops coming on to us young bucks. No one's ever been sure if she's Cuban or Haitian or Puerto Rican or what. *You're nice and big, Jake . . . where you been?* "Listen, Mama Lamia, I need a little heat, could you help me out?" *Sounds like you got enough heat of your own, pretty boy . . . was it hard time?* I smile. "Hard as it gets, Mama. You know what I mean. Some hardware." *Foreign or domestic?* "Either one." *Preferred caliber?* "Thirty-eight'll do, short barrel if you got it, nothing too heavy." *How about .38 special? Detective Special?* "Better still, I always wanted to be a detective."

Mama L. takes me into the back room, hands me the piece. It's a simple weapon, black as death, nothing pretty, but it'll do the job if it comes down to it and the job needs doing. Mama L. lets me check it out, roll the cylinders, check the action. The grip and trigger are wrapped with that porous tape that won't take prints. Nice touch. Mama L. carries only the best. "How much?" *I could set you up for a dollar, with one of those shoulder holsters like in the pictures and a nice box of shells.* "A dollar? Damn, Mama, where'd you get this piece?" *Took it off my thirty-sixth husband when I took a cleaver to his head last night, okay, Jake?* I should know better than to ask Mama Lamia dumb-ass questions. I give her two fifties, strap on the holster, slip the gun into it. I put my old jacket on over the rig.

She pushes me up against the back counter, her hand groping my crotch. She kisses me hard and I let her tongue sink into my mouth. It feels good after these years and she knows it, she feels me getting hard. She puts her hand down my pants and feels my cock, stiff.

Slot number thirty-seven's open, Jake, care to step up to the plate? "Thanks, Mama, I've got some business to transact." With a glance down her arm: *Sure looks that way.* She takes her hand out of my pants, straightens her hair. *That business gets transacted, or not, you come back here and let Mama Lamia show you a little business of her own, complimentary. You take good care of yourself, Jakey. I don't want a pretty boy like you to end up with central air conditioning, if you know what I mean.* "Thanks, I'll be careful. Listen, Mama L., I'm looking for a girl from the neighborhood. You remember her—Consuela? Connie? Sweet girl, half Puerto Rican?" *Jake, she's not . . .* "Yeah, yeah, Mama L., I know, I know. I know. Where is she?" *She's got some powerful relatives who don't like her much, Jake. You know her mama was . . .* "Yeah, I know all about that, Mama, I know all about it." *I hope you're not—* "I'm not, Mama. I would never hurt this girl, I just want to talk to her. Just tell me where she is."

Mama Lamia thinks about it a long time, slips her hand into the Windbreaker, pats the butt of the .38. *All right. The Uptown. You know the place?* "I know it. She still dancing?" *Uh-huh, that's what I hear. Dances under the name Banana Flambé.* "Banana Flambé? Oh Jesus Christ." *I know. But I hear it's a good act.* "She have a guy?" Lamia shakes her head this time. *No.*

"Thanks." I kiss her on the lips. *Watch your back, pretty boy. You know what they're saying.* "What's that, Mama?" *They're saying you whacked that guy upstate. Jimmy decides he thinks it's true, things could get ugly.* "Don't you worry about me and Jimmy, Mama L. I didn't whack nobody. Yet."

I drop by one of those discount stores on the main drag. I get myself a dark suit and some new wingtips. I head back and get a room at the Ambassador. I set the .38, loaded, on the edge of the sink as I shave my beard into a Van Dyke. I want to look good for her. I wonder if Connie will recognize me right away or if she'll have to think about it, remember how I looked, remember who I was, what I meant to her once upon a time. I put on a black tie and slick my hair back. Day burns slow and steady into evening. I sit down at the tiny table, cheap wingtips propped on the windowsill, watching the world through the open window and the jail-cell matrix of the fire escape. I light an unfiltered Pall Mall and watch things go blood red, shit brown, gray, dark gray, black. I get up and put on my hat.

The guy at the counter says Banana Flambé doesn't hit the stage until after midnight. I get myself a nice dinner up the street, sit there reading the paper, looking for word about the body. Nothing. Have a drink, have two, feeling the bulge of the .38, keeping my eyes out for trouble. They can do me in public and never get taken for it. It just ain't fair.

I'll tell you what ain't fair. I mean, I'm up for a nickel and I don't open my goddamn trap to tell the fucking pigs Jimmy Silver's fucking shoe size, for Christ's sake. So the parole board, they hear about how I'm an uncooperative prisoner, no matter how many times I scrub the fucking floor of my cell. Five fucking years. Who ever heard of serving five years on a nickel? And what's the word I get from Jimmy Silver's people inside? Jimmy can't associate with me, I'm too hot. All because I went up on a drug violation.

So Jimmy let me rot, and he never once said so much as thank you, Jake, for doing your time and keeping your fucking mouth shut.

That doesn't bother me half so much as it will if the cops get an ID on that body. I killed a made man without getting an okay from his boss first. Not only that, but Jimmy and Frank shared blood. I'm fucked.

The only thing that kept me alive through five years in the joint was that the body was never found. So what? Fucking goddamn lousy timing for them to find it now—if I hadn't been up for a nickel I could have driven up and taken care of the body when I heard they were building that housing development right where I'd whacked him. I could have kept it under wraps, just like it had been for five years. Jimmy never knew what happened to his brother that night, and if it wasn't for me serving the whole goddamn nickel he never would have known.

Too fucking late now. Now Jimmy will figure out what

happened, figure out who did his half-brother, and there's some sort of poetic justice in that.

Frank. Fucking prick. That son of a bitch deserved to die for what he did to Connie. It still made my trigger finger itchy thinking about how she must have felt—

So I did him, wearing the hat of the pale rider, as the bringer of divine retribution, but funny thing, I don't think Jimmy will see me as the hand of God. How could that son of a bitch let his brother treat a beautiful, innocent girl like that and think he can get away with it—

Easy, I tell myself. *Nobody knows a fucking thing—yet.*

I finish my second drink and walk up the street to the Uptown.

It's close to two when she takes the stage. They have one of those silver balls that flickers multicolored lights all over the room. Connie appears up there in a gentle caress of half-dark and the mist from the smoke machines. She wears a thin silky thing of a tiny white slip-dress, virgin pale contrasting with her rich light brown skin, as always. Her eyes are painted dark, so moist and sad. Her black hair spills over the gown and past the swell of her breasts.

She enacts her erotic *danse macabre,* the badly recorded music a tragic Latin dirge, every verse another button coming undone. She looks down and sees me and doesn't miss a movement of her intricate dance, even though I know she recognizes me right off. She wriggles out of the slip as the song grinds to a halt, and it seems to hover after her in the smoky darkness as the spotlight follows the subtle curve of her back. She looks back just in time to vanish into darkness, looking over her shoulder, her eyes glowing sadness, with a purse on her blood red lips. The spotlight illuminates just enough of that beautiful ass, bare except for the tiny G-string, to bring a thundering round of applause and a hail of bills onto the stage. She floats back out like a seductive ghost, smiles and licks her lips, clutches her white slip in front of her, arches her back just so as she bends down to pick up the bills, so that each movement shows off the swell of her breasts. Then she's gone.

She spots me coming back. Big guy tries to stand in front of me, puts his arms up like logs blocking my path. Connie touches him on the shoulder.

"It's okay, Louie. Let him come back."

"The other dancers ain't gonna like that—"

"Look, just forget it, Louie. Jake, give the guy a tip." I slip him a five. He backs off. "Jake, close your eyes."

She pulls me backstage, holding my hand, kneading my fingers gently. "Keep them closed," she tells me as she takes me into her dressing room. She turns me toward a wall and I hear her fidgeting around as she changes clothes. I smoke a cig, wondering what she looks like getting into her clothes—I want to see that more than I want to see her taking them off. I smoke another cig. It's taking a real long time, but I didn't expect anything different from Connie. "All right," she says. "You can open your eyes now." She presents herself to me, raising her arms. She's changed into a tiny red minidress that comes down over her shoulders, and carries a handbag that matches the red perfectly. She's got a rhinestone choker on and her lipstick's a darker shade than before. Her long earrings match her necklace. Her black hair's pulled up in a bun, just a few strands dancing around the curves of her neck and shoulders. She looks beautiful. "We'll go out the back. Do you have a car?"

"Afraid not," I tell her.

She smiles at me. "All right then, we'll walk. It's a nice night out. I think the only place left is the Darkside."

I shrug. "Sounds about right."

"You think about me while I was gone, baby?"

"All the time, Jake."

"Then how come you didn't come visit me?"

"Jake, don't start. You know the answer to that."

"Yeah, I do. It was Jimmy?"

"Mmmm-hmmmmmm."

"Things going okay for you? You making money?"

"I get by."

The waitress comes with our drinks. Whisky sour for me, Brandy Alexander for Connie. I tip the waitress five bucks and ask her to bring us an ashtray. Connie lights a thin, exotic cigarette and sips her Brandy Alexander, leaving an inviting lipstick kiss around the tip of the straw. I take a drink, hear the ice cubes clattering.

"How's your drink?"

"Fine, Jake. I like them here. Nice and weak. I can't be too careful." She laughed.

"You got a man?"

"I got someone I see."

"Cop?"

"Night shift at the airport. Graveyard."

"Union man."

"Yeah, sort of."

"Look, baby, I can't get you out of my head. I want you so bad, but you know I'm hot right now."

"I know that, Jake. Word on the street is they're digging up Frank's body. Word is you did him."

I stand up. "Who the fuck told you that?"

"Don't pull that shit, Jake. I'm just telling you what you already know. I figure you did him because of what he did to me. I always wondered who had gotten him. I figured it was you. Now I know."

The waitress floats by with the ashtray, puts it down, and slips away, looking nervous. I sit down and light a cigarette with shaky hands. Connie leans close, touching my arm. "Jake. Jake, listen to me. Thank you for what you did. You have to hear that, Jake. I know it's wrong, but I'll always be grateful."

"You're welcome, but I didn't do nothing."

"Yeah. Well, thanks anyway."

"I need to get out of town, Connie."

Her rich brown eyes fill mine, spicy perfume clogging my nostrils, seducing my mind. "Jake, come up with me. I've got a place near here."

"Connie, I need the money."

She pulls me close. Her tongue snakes into my mouth and she drops her hand down, under the table, scratching my cock through wool trousers with her sharp fingernails. She begins to knead it and squeeze. "Come on," she whispers. "We'll talk later."

Barely in the door to Connie's place, and the door's slammed and she's on her knees. She gets my cock out, starts sucking on the shaft while she works my balls. I don't know where the condom comes from, but she's got it in her mouth and is rolling it down over my cock. Then she swallows my prick like it was nothing, taking the whole thing down her throat. Then she lets it slip out of her mouth and rubs it over her face as she pulls her dress down over her small tits. She slips up just enough to rub the head of my rubber-clad prick over her tits, over the pierced nipples, then pushes her tits together and wraps them around my cock as she works it up and down. Then I'm down her throat again, but she knows I'm coming close, she knows my body better than she knows her own even after all these fucking years. She stands up slowly, locking my eyes in hers. She goes over to the window.

The neon lights outside flash on-off-on-off: LIQUORS, BEER, CIGARETTES. NAKED GIRLS. OBJETS D'ART. ALL NUDE FEMALE MODERN BURLESQUE. WRESTLING.

Consuela pulls her skimpy dress down to her waist, then shimmies out of it like a snake. Her slight round ass wriggles back out of her panties—the shimmer of her thighs as she spreads them slightly, leaning forward over the windowsill with her hand slipped over her crotch.

"No hands below the waist," she tells me.

I know it. It's Connie's rule, ever since . . .

I come up behind her and crouch down just a little so that I can get the head in between her smooth, light brown cheeks. I fit the head into her tight little hole and start to work it slow, taking my time, opening her up. Then I'm in, just with the head, and she lets out a luscious little gasp. I slide it home. She pushes back against me, putting her head back and turning her face toward me. She reaches back with one hand and touches my cheek, stroking it oh so lightly with her fingertips. Her tongue slips in and out of my mouth as I fuck her from behind. The night air is cool on my face and belly. Connie lets out a little whimper as I do her. For Christ's sake, I can't believe how bad I want to reach down and grab it with my hand. I guess it comes from the time in the joint, you know, it wasn't like this before. It probably wouldn't do much for her, but I just want to touch it, caress it, taste every bit of her. With her free hand she grips the windowsill, holding herself steady. She whispers my name as I let myself go inside her. Then I whisper hers.

Connie takes a moment to go use the can. She comes out naked except for a frilly pink robe with pink fur down each side, framing her luscious tits. She takes me in her arms, the robe bunched between her legs. We tumble down onto the bed, laughing like old times, rolling about. Connie curls up with me, one hand spread across her crotch in the dark. I light up a Pall Mall and Connie takes a drag or two. In the flare of the cherry, I can see her eyes forming big moist pools. A single tear drizzles out of one eye. If she's anything like she used to be, Connie spends about half her life weeping.

"The money," I tell her. "I've got to get out of town."

There's a key in the lock. I'm off the bed in a second, the rubber leaking come and dripping Connie's spit. I get my pants buckled and get down in a crouch, hiding in the dark, the .38 in my hand. I pull back the hammer and Connie looks at me, horrified. She sits up, clutching a pillow in her lap. The door opens.

A kid comes in the room, he can't be more than fifteen. He doesn't see me at first. He takes a look at Connie, disheveled and half-clothed. The guy's wearing airport blues, smoking a big fat stogie, but he's definitely not more than fifteen, sixteen years old. Okay, I've got it figured. This is the guy Connie's living with. She always did have a weakness for younger men. He turns and sees me. I drop my hand to my side, still holding the .38 but out of sight. I stand up. "What the fuck is this?" says the guy, and his voice is as high as they get. He starts at me and I bring up the .38. He stops. Then I get it. She almost had me taken, the chick has practically no tits and this thin sleazy moustache. And that fucking cigar, it's bigger than my dick by a couple inches. She's not a bad-looking dame, though. She turns to Connie and looks like she's about to hit her. I grip the butt of the .38. Connie stands up, clutching the robe together in front of her. "Please, Mickey, take it easy. He's just a trick. Just a trick I brought back here after the show."

Mickey looks at me, her eyes stone butch rage. She takes the cigar out of her mouth. "I told you not to fucking bring them here," she growls.

"I know," Connie says, wriggling up against the dyke. "I just brought him here because it was so late. I didn't think you'd come home early, I figured it'd be okay, he just wanted a quick one and he was paying. I thought you'd be at work."

"I moved to first graveyard shift, Consuela, don't you fucking remember?"

"Oh, Mickey, I'm so sorry, I was gone when you left for work today, remember—look, he's just a trick, I didn't think you'd be here."

Mickey stares at me, shaking the cigar like an accusing finger. "Get the fuck out." She seems like an okay broad, but I just stand there smiling for a second, floored by the whole weird scene. I take time to light a Pall Mall and then slip the .38 into its holster. Mickey's watching me, and if she's even a little afraid of me now that she knows I've got a gun, she doesn't give me a fucking hint. She's got balls, I'll give the girl that. I peel a Franklin out of my roll. I reach over and tuck it into Mickey's breast pocket. "You got a hell of a woman there. You treat that whore right.

She gives some damn good head." I blow Connie a kiss. I straighten my tie on the way out and then stop to pick up my hat from where it fell by the door when Connie pounced on me. I look back at Connie and wink at her. She's crying, but then, like I said a minute ago, she cries about half the time. The dyke watches me leave, her face carved out of rock.

I open my pants, pull off the used condom, and toss it into the growing pile of matching condoms in the alley. I go out into the fog.

The sewer grates are steaming like hell's ready to pay a visit. I know I can't sleep. I wander through the street-level clouds looking for something to keep me awake. Connie has her dyke, and that's the way things are. I'm not jealous. I'm happy for her. I mean, I'm up for a nickel, and Jimmy orders Connie not to visit me, with good reason. So that's the end of it. Five years later, she's found herself a dyke to keep her warm. No big deal, no one gets blamed by me. I just don't want to sleep alone—yet.

There on the corner of Tenth there's this cute Filipino girl turning tricks. She has this tight white minidress that shows everything. I like the way she looks and we trade a few jokes. I take her back to the hotel with me and do her long and slow from behind on the single bed with a half a tube of K-Y and one hand slid down between her legs, the other playing with her tiny breasts. I kiss her neck and then her mouth as I enter her from behind; she's got this stud piercing the center of her lower lip. It feels pretty bizarre and I kind of like it. She does good work for fifty bucks, and she's really cute, with nice tits. But she doesn't match Connie. Maybe it's because she lets me touch her. Maybe I'm just still in love or some such bullshit. Either way, I give her the fifty bucks and an extra twenty for staying till morning. And I can finally get to sleep when she takes off around dawn leaving cheap perfume on the pillow.

I wonder if the dyke has weekends off. It looks like they're just getting out of bed, or maybe getting back in. I crouch on the fire escape just outside their apartment. Mickey and Connie are going at it.

I want a cigarette, real bad, but I'm too close to their window, which is open. They might smell the smoke and look out the window, and see me crouching there in the midday shadows. Then again, they're pretty distracted. Connie's down on her knees, wearing just her red slip and a pair of black lace-top fishnet stay-ups, and the dyke's standing over her, one of those weird contraptions hanging out of her jockeys, looks like she's got a strap or something underneath. Connie's going at it like it's a real cock, her mouth and tongue drawing wet swirling patterns up to the thick flesh-colored head and then back down to the balls again, which look unbelievably real. Connie moves her mouth up and gets her lips stretched around the head of Mickey's schlong, which is no small job, believe me. Then, with what looks like only a faint effort, Connie chokes the whole unbelievable shaft gradually down her throat until her lips are wrapped around the base. I shake my head, suppressing the urge to applaud.

Mickey rocks her hips in time with Connie's ministrations. Connie lets the cock slip out of her mouth, then rubs it between her firm tits. It looks like Mickey's ready to get down to business. Connie looks up at her man and nods.

Connie lays facedown on the bed and lifts her red slip up over her ass, spreading her legs wide and sliding her fingers up and down in her crotch. Mickey gets up behind Connie and puts the head in, bringing a breathy moan from Connie. She teases the girl for a long time, just the head pushed in. Then, inch by inch, she gives Connie the whole schlong, making the girl's full lips part wide, showing her white teeth as she whimpers, "More . . . more . . . more . . . ," with every tiny squirming movement of Mickey's hips. She's loud enough that I can hear everything. I don't know if maybe Connie's putting on a good act to try to pay the dyke back for that scene last night, but either way it seems to be working. The dyke presses her meat home and gives Connie a long, hard bang on the bed, making her clutch the dirty sheets and choke and sob as she gets fucked.

Mickey lets go, I'm not sure if it's an act for Connie's sake or if she really gets off on this. But it sure sounds real, like she's shooting long streams of jizz up inside Connie's lush body.

Then Mickey curses, loud. "I'm gonna be fucking late," it sounds like she says. I shrink deeper into the shadows as Mickey races around getting on a fresh pair of jockeys and some blue jeans and a work shirt.

It takes a long time for the dyke to get ready, and I risk a cigarette, hiding back on the edge of the fire escape in the darkness between the buildings. I don't move until I finally hear the sound of a motorcycle far below and see Mickey pulling away on a Harley, wearing a backward baseball cap and a black leather backpack, with a big bunch of white roses hanging out. I go back to Connie's window.

It's still open a crack to let in the humid summer breeze. I lift it up, nice and easy, and slip inside.

Connie's still lying on the bed, sprawled on her back. It looks like she's taking a little nap. She's got the sheets tangled around her body, bunched up between her legs. The slip's hanging off her body, revealing her delicate curves. I was always a pretty good second-story man, though I suppose you could say it's part of my moral code not to break in on girlfriends. But I guess Connie counts as an ex. I'm real quiet as I come up to the bed.

Like I said, she's still got her red slip on, but one strap's hanging over her shoulder and one beautiful soft brown tit is winking at me. One long leg hangs over the edge of the bed, the torn black fishnet stocking, a lace-top stay-up, bunched almost to her knee.

Connie's eyes flutter open, and she gives a little gasp.

She moves to cover herself up. "Jake," she says, a little surprised. "What are you doing here?"

"What do you think?" I ask her.

Connie squirms over to the edge of the bed, just a little.

"Come here and show me," she says, parting her lips and reaching out with one long-nailed hand.

I could never say no to her. I come over to the edge of the bed and she gets herself laid out on her back so that her head hangs over at just the right angle. Her lips part, her tongue flickering out eagerly. She works my zipper down with her fingers and gets her lips pressed around my shaft. I don't know where it comes from, but there's a condom in her mouth again, and I don't even know it's going on until after she's got half of my rubber-sheathed prick in her mouth. Then she starts taking it down her throat. That angle she's at, on her back with her head hanging over the edge of the bed, means that it goes down easy, smooth, gentle, without a hint of hesitation. Connie always was real good at this. Connie starts to whimper, low in her throat, as she swallows me.

"Connie," I make myself say, "I need the money."

She moves back, easing my cock out of her mouth. She rubs it all over her face, smearing her spittle across her cheeks and messing her makeup. She looks somehow sexier with her mascara and lipstick all wet and gloppy over her face. "Business first," she whispers. "Then pleasure."

With that she takes me down again, working my cock down her throat, pumping it in and out. I reach down and touch her breasts, squeezing the pierced nipples. I play with them as she works my cock in and out of her throat. Next thing I know she's getting me off right in her mouth and then I'm falling forward, stretching out on the bed with her.

"Where'd your dude go?" I ask her.

"Tomorrow's Mother's Day, remember? She went to her old man's place upstate."

I wonder about that for a minute as I light a Pall Mall. Then I let it go. I look into Connie's beautiful brown eyes and kiss the soft pink lips with their red mouth painted on and skewed about a half-revolution across her chin and cheeks.

"I need the money," I tell Connie. "I've got to get out of town."

Connie's eyes get all watery, glistening with lush pain.

"You did him for me," she says.

"I didn't 'do' anyone," I tell her.

"You gave me that .22 that day, about a week before you went up the river. With the money from that airport heist. You told me to hide them both and get rid of the gun when it was safe."

"Connie, I need the money. Some people are after me. They don't want to talk."

Her rouged cheeks are streaked with black lines. "Jimmy. He's going to kill you because you did his brother. Where did you shoot him? I have to know. Tell me where you shot him."

"Connie?"

"Please, Jake, I have to know how he died."

I look at her.

"Back of the head, all eight shots," I tell her. "With a twenty-two caliber, they take a lot of lead to die, even at that range." I'm speaking in a flat voice, like it's nothing, which it's not. "He and I went up the highway to do some gambling, maybe catch a few whores. We'd just made a big score at the airport and I had to go up the river on that late-night charge in a week. I knew what he did to you. I was just stringing him along. No one knew where we'd gone. We were drinking the whole way, talking like we were buddies. Frank had to take a piss. I pulled off the road and said I had to take one, too. Ba-da-bing."

Connie looks very sad. "I hated Frank for what he did. I'm glad he's dead."

"Look, I'm sorry. I should have okayed it with you first." I kiss Connie, hoping that will make her stop crying, not that it ever did before. "I'm going to get whacked if I can't hit the road before Tuesday. Maybe even then." I take a deep breath, telling myself this is the last time I'll ask her. "Where's the money?" I ask, knowing the answer.

Connie takes my wrist, draws my hand to her face, kisses the fingertips with sticky lipstick-disaster lips. Slowly, she spreads her legs as she guides my hand down between her parted thighs. She presses my fingertips into her crotch, and I feel the slick wetness of her cunt, the full lips, the exquisitely sculpted clitoris, the smear of lube that's dribbled down from where Mickey had fucked her ass. Gently, Connie prods my finger and I press it into her tight cunt. She gives a little gasp as I do, like her cunt's real tender. My eyes are the ones full of tears, this time.

"It's still itchy," she tells me. "And it hurts a little. But it's the best money can buy. I did it about six months ago. I'm sorry, Jake. I'm sorry. I knew you'd be back, but I just had this chance to be happy, is all . . . and I couldn't say no."

"Oh, Connie," I whisper sadly.

Then she kisses me, climbs gently on top of me, her body soft and open and her legs spread facing me for the first time ever. She nuzzles my ear and tells me softly, "You get to be the first, lover, my very first, just like I'm a sweet little virgin. Let's pretend I'm sixteen or something, and we're both doing this for the first time . . . you can be my boyfriend, Jake." And so she gets off the bed and floats across the room to the lingerie drawer, slips out of the stained red slip, and puts on a new clean white one. "Take off your clothes, Jake."

I get off the bed and undress, leaving my clothes in a pile on the floor, and the two of us embrace in the slanted light from the window. We climb into bed together and make out for a long, long time, like we really are sixteen or something and horny as can be, and when we finally do it I know for sure it's for the first time ever.

It feels different than anything I've ever done, like I'm a virgin, too, which maybe I am, technically. But Connie's weeping as I finish off inside her. She tells me, over and over again, "I'm sorry, Jake, I'm sorry, I'm sorry...I shouldn't have taken that money..." And even though I know Jimmy is going to whack me, smear my brains like succulent marmalade, I tell Connie, "It's okay, shhhhhh—shhhh, little girl, it's okay, it's okay, don't worry..." I can't get the thought out of my head, of what it's going to be like, when they finally come for me.

What's the fucking point in running? Hiding? It doesn't seem to matter anymore. I've still got the room at the Ambassador. I'm drinking pretty heavy. I keep looking at the .38, wondering if it wouldn't be smarter to kill myself. Instead, when I hear the footsteps on the stairs, I empty the .38 and toss it out the window, into the garbage heap below with all the shells.

But they don't bust the door down. Something's really fucked up—they knock. Maybe it's the landlord. I answer the door in my underwear, not really giving a shit if it is Jimmy, not caring if he does it or if he sends one of his men, if they give it to me in the face or the back of the head. Who gives a rat's ass anymore? But instead of one of those anonymous mob revolvers with porous tape on the grip and trigger, I see a different kind of silver, a shield.

The cop says my name.

"Maybe," I tell him.

He tells me his name and department—Sergeant Fitz, Homicide. "We'd like you to come down to the police station."

My ears are ringing. I know what it means. My whole body goes numb. I wonder how he'll do me in the joint. Piano wire? Hung in my jail cell?

"Just let me get my pants on," I tell the pig. I look out the window as I get my black suit on. Someone's rummaging around in the garbage heap in the alley.

They show me pictures of her, stretched out across the bed with two holes in her chest, wearing the white slip pulled down and soaked with blood. She's got a strange look of peace on her face, one of her sad, lush pouts on her soft pink lips. Her arms are stretched out like she's on some kind of obscene cross. The rusty little .22 that did Frank Chambers is clutched in one of her tiny hands. I told her to get rid of that fucking thing when she could. I sit there, numb, I can't even feel a goddamn thing.

"You know her, Jake?"

"Can I have a cigarette?"

They get me one, a fucking Marlboro Light, for God's sake. I light it and blow smoke.

"Yeah," I say. "I know her."

"What's her name?"

"Connie," I say. "Consuela Rodriguez."

"Born Conrad Jesus Rodriguez Chambers," says the pig, reciting all of Connie's erstwhile names like a list of offenses. "Mama was Maria Consuela Rodriguez, a pretty Puerto Rican whore, just like her son turned out to be." The pigs laugh all around the room. "Mama OD'ed about six years ago in a shooting gallery in the Heights. His daddy was Rick Chambers, consigliere to the gods. With a taste for fresh PR whore-meat." Fitz is grinning, pushing me as far as he can push me. "Can't blame him, can you? Rick Chambers later started his own family, you wouldn't know anything about that, would you, Jake? Nah, I didn't think so. Anyway, Conrad changed his name early last year, legally speaking. We understand he was a fruit for a whole lot of years, turning tricks out by the wharf. Taking it up the ass, I guess. But then they say guys give pretty good head—you wouldn't know anything about that, would you, Jake? We think he was killed in some sort of lover's quarrel. He had been down to the station to talk to some detectives the day before, saying some things about certain people in his life, saying that maybe his girlfriend wanted him dead. She was one of those women who likes to slap guys around. You wouldn't know anything about that, would you, Jake?"

"Afraid not," I say. I can't stop crying, but I'm not making a sound, just wet tears filling my eyes so I can't see straight. "Did you ask her brother? Jimmy Silver? Silver Chambers, that is? Rick Chambers, Connie's old man, he married Martha Silver Chambers after Paul Silver got whacked, and adopted Martha's boy Jimmy. Sure as fuck you must know Jimmy Silver, right? I mean, they pay you to do *something* over here, don't they?" I'm looking right at Fitz, knowing I'm going too fucking far.

Fitz looks at me like he's going to smack me. Then he does. He hits me pretty fucking hard, my head rings through the hangover fog, and I taste blood through the day-old whisky coming up my throat. I swallow.

"We think she was killed in some sort of, you know, love triangle," he said. "So maybe you could tell me, Jake. What was your relationship with Conrad?"

I close my eyes. "We were lovers."

The pigs all mutter under their breath, saying shit about faggots and pansy-perverts.

"Seems she had another lover, do you know anything about that?"

"I think she was seeing some woman."

"A woman?" More chuckles from the pigs. "You know this dyke's name?"

"Mickey something."

"Michelle Dubois. Works up at the airport. Smokes big cigars."

"Sure. I never knew her."

"Do you think Michelle might have wanted Conrad dead? Might have been some sort of lover's quarrel? Some sort of sick—"

"Consuela confessed, didn't she?" I say. "She confessed to something, didn't she? Told you she had the murder weapon? And you fuckers sent her home, knowing she'd be whacked, leaked the information to Jimmy, fucking had her snuffed, all because it's easier and pays better than getting off your asses to prosecute her." I stop all of a sudden. I'm killing myself and I know it.

The cop is stone-faced. He acts like he hasn't heard me at all, which is lucky for me.

When he does answer, he speaks very slowly, as if talking to a child. "Do you think this Michelle might have wanted her boyfriend dead? Some kind of lover's quarrel?"

Boyfriend?

I wait a long time, finish my cigarette, and snub it out before answering that one.

"I wouldn't know anything about that, Sergeant. But Michelle didn't seem like the violent type. Even if she *was* a union man."

Mickey comes to see me at the Ambassador. She's still packing, all dressed up with a bulky jacket. I know she has my .38 under there. It was her baseball cap I saw bent over the garbage heap the day the cops picked me up. I wonder if maybe she came to kill me, that day or today. She did and didn't, in that order. The cops are looking for her, they've got her and Connie's apartment staked out. She's been wearing the same clothes for days.

"I thought you did her," Michelle tells me, sitting on the edge of my bed. "Who else could get to her like that? But now I figure it wasn't you who killed her."

"It wasn't."

The .38's out of her pocket like a quick whisper of death, pressed hard in the hollow under my jaw. Mickey's in my face, her teeth set, her lips curled back under the thin moustache.

"But you know who did." She's all stone butch shit and I know if I had done Connie I'd be dead by now.

I stare her down, waiting long seconds before answering her. When she doesn't say anything, I know she's going to let me live.

"It was her brother," I say, the .38 pressing against my throat. "Her half-brother. The only one left. She was taking the fall to protect—"

Mickey still has the .38 under my chin. "That bastard raped her, didn't he?"

"Not Jimmy," I say. "Frank."

"Frank? Who the fuck is Frank?"

"It was a long time ago," I tell Michelle. "A long, long, long time ago. Frank's dead. Jimmy's the one who got Connie done like that."

"Where does he live?"

I look at her, cold. She doesn't deserve to die like that, but then again, neither do I. Neither does anyone, with a few distinct exceptions.

I stare at the dyke, wondering just how much she loved and wanted Connie, just how much she needed her around

to keep her warm in this city of fog and stone-cold bullshit, how much her stone-butch *cojones,* pencil-moustache
bravado, and stuffed-jean swagger are worth when it
comes time to pull the trigger. Wonder what will happen if
the whole fucking world gets blown up by one bullet from
a .38, in the forehead of a scumbag who would murder his
own sister for supposedly doing something that should
have gotten done a lot more than five years ago.

I reach up and take the .38 out of Mickey's hand. "Tell
you what," I say to her. "I'll take you to where Jimmy
works. We're gonna go over there together."

Then I catch Mickey on the jaw with a good one, she's
out in a second, and I've got her stretched out on the bed.
I've got one phone call to make, before I go, to Sergeant
Fitz, telling him he was right, it was a lover's quarrel, but
it wasn't Mickey. I did Connie with a .38 special, two bullets in her chest from about three feet. Sounds from his
tone like I guessed right on the caliber and range. It's the
only way to save the dyke, and Connie loved this woman,
so I suppose I might as well, too, and this is my parting
gift.

"You killed Conrad Rodriguez. In a domestic dispute."

"That's right."

"And you're willing to sign a statement to that effect?"

"Well," I say, "I'll be a little busy for the next hour or
so. But if I'm still around after that . . . I'll sign George
Washington's autograph on your fucking grandmother's
ass, flatfoot."

I cradle the phone, pocket the .38, get the keys to
Mickey's bike out of the pouch of her airport blues. She's
waking up, but I'm gone before she knows what's happening. I figure her bike's probably in the alley. There it is,
parked up next to the garbage heap, Harley 883 Sportster,

beautiful. I fire it up and hit the clutch. Rubber spins and then I'm moving like hell. Mickey screams after me, hanging out the window of the Ambassador. Yelling for me to stop. "Put it on my tab," I mutter as I shift into third and lay down the rubber, skidding onto the main drag, screaming toward Jimmy's bar like a pale rider with the .38 heavy in my pocket and the bad taste of payback in my mouth. It's almost sunrise, Jimmy's always at work early, his muscle's gonna be light this time of day. The sky cracks open, spilling fire overhead, casting black skyscraper shadows along my path. Two in the chest. Birds rise in flocks as I pass, screaming death wails, announcing my approach. God put a lightning bolt in my hand, motherfucker, a lightning bolt in a .38 special. Blood is thicker than tears, you piece of shit. The city blends like nightmares into a soundless watercolor around me, painted in Connie's blood.

Jimmy's in his office, greeting me with a smile.

CECILIA TAN
Penetration

You think I'm going to tie you down and fuck you, don't you. You think I'm going to strap on a dildo, and do this intercourse thing, play butch boy for you, and let you scream and carry on, indulge your rape fantasies and all that good stuff, that stuff that gets you so hot, that makes you drip wet. . . . I can see you dripping now, from the way I grabbed you by the hair and forced you into the bonds, spread-eagled on your bed. Maybe it's the bed, especially, that makes you think we're going to fuck, and maybe it's all the hints you've been dropping me about the way you like it, the things you've done . . . you're a smooth bottom, practiced, you've been with badder bitches and butches than me. So if I'm going to give you what you want, I know, I've got to give you something you don't know you want. I'm going to start with my finger. I pull off my leather glove and toss it away, and work my index finger right between your wet lips, right into the hot spot, and into you it goes. I can see the look in your eyes— what, no foreplay? no clit action?—but as my finger slides as deep as it can go, your eyes close and you gasp with deep pleasure. Then two fingers. You don't need foreplay, you don't need lube, sweet thing, your cunt is hungry and I'm going to feed it. Next, I pull a dagger from my pocket.

It's not a dagger, it's a letter opener, but you don't know that. I see you gasp and flinch and squirm—you think I'm going to pretend to cut you, run the tip all over your flesh, across your nipples. . . . I see your eyes go wide as I dip it between your legs. Have you figured it out yet? I slide the dull metal into you, using the flat blade like a tongue depressor, to peer into the folds of your flesh. Your vagina convulses as you realize what I'm doing and you strain against your bonds, helpless to stop me. I know if you really want to stop me you'll say the word. But you're too interested, wondering what I'm going to do next. I pull a magic marker out of my pocket and write my name in flowing script across your belly, then cap the thing and hold you open with the fingers of one hand while I slide the hard plastic cylinder into you. Your legs are shaking as I move it in a wide circle . . . what are you thinking, darling? Have you ever put a magic marker up your cunt before? Is this something you used to do when you were a kid, under the sheets at night, terrified of being caught, but unable to stop your own lust—what did you turn to when your fingers weren't enough? The marker is not large, but it is hard and foreign, is that what's making you shake? The thought of this thing protruding out of your body, probing into places it was never intended to go? You almost laugh when you see the kielbasa, a thousand phallic puns half-remembered flicker across your face as your eyes take in the curve of sausage in my hand. No, I wouldn't, you think. But I will, and I do, rolling a condom onto the end for full phallic effect and pushing the thickness against your lips until they give way and then inching it inside. You whimper, a sweet sound. It feels big, I know it, I see you clenching and relaxing, trying to take it in—good girl. It's too soft to fuck you with so I settle for burying it a few inches deep and then leaning down to bite off the end. When my nose rubs your clit I stop my nibbling and pull the meat out of you, toss it away. Too late I realize I should have made you eat some of it, should have let you taste your own juice on it. No matter, there is more in store. The unlit end of a burning candle. You twitch as you feel the heat of the flame, although I'm the one who gets wax on her hands as I'm moving it from side to side inside you. A pair of black lacquer chopsticks, so thin you barely feel them at all, until I split them like a speculum and widen you side to side, top to bottom. I let you lick them when I'm done. What else can we stick into your cunt, my girl? I've used up the things that I brought with me, so I cast about your apartment looking for more. You've got dildos galore, but they don't interest me, cunt girl. I roll a condom over an Idaho potato I find in your fridge, cold and fat and wide, and I push the tip of it in as far as it will go. I fuck you with it until it is sliding in up to its widest point, and you are moaning and thrashing. Have you ever been fucked with something this big, cunt girl? You probably have, I don't kid myself after all the hints you gave me. Have you ever slept with a man? The potato is getting slick and hard to hold onto, but I'm shoving it with my palm into you now. I bet you have slept with men before, even if you haven't said anything about it to me. How could that hungry cunt resist? A pole of hard, hot flesh, that fits snug and twitches in response. I'd love to have one myself, love to have one to ram into you and feel your wetness on every nerve ending. But there's no use wishing for things I don't have, and what I have is you, wide open before me, your cunt is my cunt and I can put anything into it that I like. The potato slips out onto the floor and your head jerks up, your vagina gasping like a fish, so empty, so needy. A bottle of shampoo. The handle of a hairbrush. Pinking shears. Yours is the cunt that ate Tokyo. When I'm done with you there won't be a phallic object left in your apartment that doesn't smell like your desire. Everything will remind you of me. I am just beginning to wish I had a crusty baguette to go with the kielbasa when I decide maybe you've had enough. You sense the hesitation and look up, hope in your eyes. No, I'm still not going to fuck you. You realize it when I pack the harness back into my bag. You want to ask so bad, I see you holding back, you want to beg me for something, but you aren't sure whether you can abase yourself that way. Silly girl, you'll let me stick anything into your slit as long as you're tied up. Maybe next time, I'll sit and watch while I order you to stick things up into yourself: a flashlight, a fake rubber dog bone, the old standby: a cucumber. Maybe I'll take photographs of each of these things sticking out of your cunt to horrify my politically correct friends. You're biting your lip with impatience—I'm sorry, my sweet. I get this way sometimes. For now, what kind of a top do you think I am? Don't worry, I'll get you off. After all, I've brought a whole array of things to try on your clitoris: fur, sandpaper, chains, a nail file, macramé rope, a hairbrush, a braided thong, and when I run out of those I'm sure there are more things here I can try. I'm not tired, not in the least.

JACK MURNIGHAN

Watershed

That afternoon I had decided to stop kissing everybody. That was my master plan. To stop kissing Eleanor because it was starting to matter to her too much, to stop kissing Simone until she trusted me and wanted me back, and to stop secretly kissing her housemate Anna, too. Then it happened: a group of English Lolitas, who together could form the cast of any number of one-acts of the id, pranced into my life and asked me to give them poetry tutorials. There I was, Hylas leaning toward the depths, nymphs beckoning . . . sometimes, you know, we just can't choose.

I proposed we read Milton. Lisa wasn't part of the original group, but she'd heard about it through the grapevine and showed up for the first meeting. And despite the multitude of diversions, I noticed her immediately when she walked in the room. She was dressed more for a Russ Meyer casting than a poetry class: platinum blonde bob, two trapped glacial lagoons for eyes, eyelashes like a pair of flexing tarantulas, her mouth a blood-red drooping orchid. I, ingenuous to the end, didn't catch on at all. Every seam seemed ready to burst, the few buttoned buttons of her baby-doll blouse aching with the strain, her black mini a skin graft on racehorse thighs. She had come from Oxford and wanted to find out about this young American who had the hubris to propose to teach the English their own poetry. Her plan was to bury me.

Only later when we had drenched the sheets and closed the blinds to the sun did I know the future is contained in the present as sure as in amber.

Piety

Now I have been fucked nearly to death. There are large tracts of skinless meat on my knees, elbows, and the tops of my feet; I have purple-black bite rings on my shoulders, around my neck, and down my arms; I've thrown a muscle in my lower back; my neck and shoulders are stiff as hell; and every time I touch her or even think about her I get so erect I think my penis is going to split like a polebean along its seam.

It's never been like this and it does little good to use the word *happiness* to try to describe it. I feel more like a laboratory rat pressing the pleasure bar, ignoring food, ignoring water, ignoring society. . . . We dream only of enclosure, to be phoneless and walled up like an Amontillado, paired but anchoritic in endless white-knuckle worship.

The Sex Scene

I wake her with dirty fingers. Fresh stained with Vespa grease, I slowly run thumb and index along her sleeping brow, following the arcing line with moth-wing–tender kisses. The parabola widens down past her clavicle, running my tongue along its slow ridge till my fingertips catch the edge of the duvet. In a steady tug I pull it off her body and there she lies golden and tousled in the late morning sun. The touch recommences below her left breast, tracing kisses down to the gentle swell where snow-white down first turns dark. She trembles, but does not wake. I unbutton my jeans and gently part her knees with the back of my hands. As she begins to stir, I lean my naked torso long out across her body, place my lips to hers, and slide myself into the warm and familiar aperture. Now she is awake and aware and kissing me back between a smile and arching her back and raising her knees. I tuck my hands under her ass, stand up slowly, and pull her to the edge of the bed. She arches a bit to the left, guiding my movement with her left hand on my stomach, feeling each groove and ushering forth the long steady thrusts. My zipper is digging into her thigh and she'll have bruises from my belt buckle and button marks on her shanks, but she keeps biting her other thumb and circling faster and faster movements on my stomach. I lift her gently, pushing her legs back with my shoulders, and her left hand moves from my stomach to reach between her legs. She grinds, loses the composure of her expression, stroking herself with fore and middle fingers paired. Her breath comes heavy, and in an instant she is glazed with sweat. The pace quickens to the breaking point, my strokes are tight pulses, her ringlets replaced by a side-to-side mania, and then she gasps, pitches hard against me, does a long, last grind, opens her eyes, and unfurls a slow smile. She looks deep into my eyes and I just laugh, release her legs, and kiss her full and wet on the lips. We know we've only just begun.

I try not to pull out after the first orgasm, just pause, drink a bit of water, bite her on the curve of her neck, and then recommence in delicate, attenuated circles. Her come glues me to her walls; I can barely pull backward. It feels like fucking a stalled cement truck. Then I slip my shoulder round and roll her on top of me. She takes my hands and puts them high on her hips, then starts working in tight circles, leaning back little by little to take in ever more of me. She bites her lower lip, her hard, high breasts are shining with sweat, her mouth opens, eyes close, and she smiles the smile of a fallen, defiant angel. Lisa, my sweet Lisa. Of my sugarplums, my deep drives, my hemoglobin.

Toccata

"Lift it for me. Show it to me. Lift it for me slow. Speak to me with it baby, lift it, tell me you love me, you know I love it. Show it to me, oh yes, show it to me honey, do that thing you do. I gotta have you baby, gotta touch you, let me rub my face all over it. Take the pillow, yeah, use the pillow honey, you'll be more comfortable, I gotta rub my face all over it, gotta touch you. Fuck I love you baby. Shit I'm trembling all over. I'm losing it baby, I'm gonna split or fall apart or something. No don't do this to me baby, don't, don't. Oh don't fucking do this to me baby. No you can't possibly move it that way, you can't baby, no please don't. Oh just let me just let me touch, oh shit, oh shit. Oh yeah, oh yes, yes baby yes, oh you can't be doing that you can't. Oh jesus, holy fuck, oh baby please. Yeah shake it, oh yes move it, oh yes, oh I can't take it baby, I just can't. No you've gotta be kidding, you have got to fucking be kidding, oh let me, let me let me let me. Move it baby, show me how you can move it. Holy fucking shit, oh I like that baby, fuck that's good, that is so fucking good. Oh yeah honey, go baby, fucking christ, I'm gonna fucking lose it, I'm gonna fucking explode, I'm just gonna fucking die. A little fucking more baby, oh yeah, a little, just a little more, oh shit, oh shit, oh my fucking god, oh . . ."

Fugue

Butterfly your arms to their furthest extension, arch your scapulae pinioned beneath your lover's weight, then rotate your palms and bury nail and knuckle through the sheets and deep into the foam; then pull, pull, squeeze, stretch, buckle; then, when you're about to snap, when you hear yourself scream and feel the sweat run in rivulets down your face, you will begin to have an idea of what I'm talking about.

She tells me that when I die she'll have me cremated, put my dust in a douche and run me through one last time.

I, however, remain a bit stymied. The closest phrase I've found is "I love the shit out of you." These seven words, as I halt the millionth time from repeating them, emerge again as the final frontier, the last outpost of language on the range. In my dreams I see the hordes of bison, the unmassacred millions of bison, the massive, sanguine, mindless triple-hearted bison ever charging the further field and each thundering footfall the mute's testimony of my singular truth.

Beneath a footprint, below a gopher hole, under an oil well, deeper, deeper than the blackest sea abyss where the transparent fish traded eyes for malice and kill not for sustenance but to syncopate the monotony, that is where my echo sounds.

I have died but that doesn't keep me from dying again and again. A whisper—death. Two minutes late—death. A hemline—death. Like a field of sorghum, the folly of identity has been surrendered to the lilt, whistle, and push of an eternal wind.

She seems to feel likewise.

KEVIN KILLIAN
Spurt

The blood jet is poetry/
There is no stopping it.
—Sylvia Plath, "Kindness"

My little car vibrated under me, as though its engine were announcing exciting plans to fall apart, but I didn't pay much attention. Tears were drying on my face. I was preoccupied, you might say; I simply hadn't the time for car trouble. For a week the temperature had stayed high above ninety degrees, and the radio announcers kept saying it was going to rain. Even at night the heat was thick and hot, like a soup, but I kept driving, for when you're drunk, no challenge is quite beyond you. Traffic was light on the Long Island Expressway. Full moon, and moonlight revealing huge purple clouds scudding east, always before me, moving faster than I could. Squinting, I tried to read the hands of the dashboard clock. It was either 4 A.M. or 4 P.M. I was driving east, into the moonlight, away from the belt of lights that surround New York, and I was so drunk I could hardly keep my eyes open. My lids felt heavy, as though while I was crying some evil genie had implanted them with iron filings. My face felt like one of those cast-iron spigots that pour water into old-time zinc-lined, claw-footed bathtubs.

"I'm spent," I mumbled—that seemed dramatic. For luck I grabbed the bottle of Glenlivet that stood propped between my thighs, its long glass neck tapping the vibrating steering wheel. Single malt whisky that had lain undisturbed in some Scottish cavern for more years than I'd been alive and now, *glug glug glug*—created just for me, on my dumb day of grief. On Monday morning I'd start cracking the books and really put my nose to the grindstone and work on the dissertation. You must keep going, I said to myself, like a coach giving a pep talk to a reluctant player. All the same, tonight, I would try to imagine that I wasn't returning to school; that I was done with writing and thinking; that I'd never met Tim Baillie.

Something magical about really flogging your car, and the clear stretch of highway ahead; and feeling the motor and its complex accoutrements shudder under your heavy foot. And dipping an elbow out into the hot summer night and watching towns go by like reflections in shop windows—whole towns and neighborhoods, gone, gone, gone. You lose touch with the world—a car is an island all its own, another world; a world from which, perhaps, you might never return.

The radio, staticky and shrill, burst out with bass-heavy Motown: "I've known of your, your secluded ni-ights, I've even seen her, maybe once or twice . . ." A low-slung, dark car passed me on the right, gleaming like a streak of phosphorescence under a Jamaican sea. Sucker must be doing a hundred easy. Lotus. Then the driver seemed to slack in speed and I was passing him. I saw his face—couldn't help it, he was staring right at me.

Cute guy, in a sleeveless T-shirt, tanned, beach-boy look, shock of curly blond hair on top of his head, big pink rubbery lips and dark eyes staring at me. Like he'd seen a ghost.

One hand rested on top of the wheel, lazily, as though he could drive without looking ahead. I sped up, and he sped up too. Cruise control. I caught him looking at me, again and again, and he flicked on the driver's seat light, a plastic dome that filled his car—for a brief moment—with a thin plastic light, like cheap statuary of the church. I guess he knew how hot he was. His lips parted. I could see him trying to speak, or signal. Eighty miles an hour and his mouth was saying, "Wanna fuck?" I nodded, he nodded, I got hard, I shifted the bottle, the Supremes kept singing—"Think it o—o-ver . . . think it o-o-ver." Fat chance, Diana! Our cars kept passing each other, and his image faded in and out of the open passenger seat window. "Let's," I heard him call, and my car leapt ahead a length or two. Then he was beside me again. A sheen of sweat made his upper body look wet, as though someone had pulled him out of the shower and thrown him into a moving car and said, "Drive!" He was my dumb guide race-car stud boy, come to lift the cover off this hot sultry night and show me love's underside. Or something.

I swung in behind the tail of the Lotus and we slowed down to a sedate 65 mph into the right-hand lane, and a few interchanges later fishtailed out onto an exit, by a gas station and a diner. Under the purple neon lights of the diner we parked side by side. The Lotus was a gorgeous lime green, a color that the purple neon and the purple clouds overhead kept remarking on, whispering among themselves. Buzzing about. *Bzzzzzzz.* "Where we going?" I asked—don't even know if I asked in words. When I jumped out of the car, the air smelled of burning rubber, and he was pulling off leather driving gloves. He was six feet tall, disheveled, with long ropy arms, supple with muscles and fading tattoos. Steam covered the parking lot to a level of about four feet high, up to our chests. The net result was I couldn't see if he was hard, but knew he was. A thick white steam like dry ice, or the hot air that pushes up Marilyn's skirt in *The Seven Year Itch*.

"I'm Scott," said my new boyfriend. "You know where the Meadowbrook is?" "The motel?" Calculations spun in my head like the apples and oranges in a slot machine. He shrugged and the muscles in his shoulders rippled. He said to follow him. But first he kissed me, his big lips pressed flat against mine. When he broke away my mouth was aflame. "How old are you?" Scott said, like a challenge. I couldn't think if he wanted me older or younger, so I told the truth. "Twenty-five." One time in life when truth seemed to do the trick. "Grand," he said, sliding into the Lotus butt-first. "It's room 813," he said. "We've got it all night." Foolish me! I thought "we" meant me and him; boy, did I ever get that one wrong! I got back into the Maverick and took another slug of Glenlivet, checked my wallet, then followed Scott down an access road past strip malls and gas stations and into the huge, eerie, almost empty motel lot. They should have called it "Salem's Lot." . . .

Any of you ever been to the Meadowbrook Motel? I don't even know if it's still standing. In 1978 it was a sex motel, catering to the needs of suburban adulterers who could steal an hour from the PTA and the IRS and rent by the hour—what my cop pals called a hot-sheet pad. The Meadowbrook reared up its proud head like some Vegas monstrosity, its huge lobby studded with Italian crystal and a marble fountain. On either side of this lobby two endless wings extended, big rooms joined by a kind of faux-balcony with wrought-iron railings. Privacy and discretion a must.

I couldn't see the Lotus, but I saw room 813. The door was ajar, and bright light edged the crack of the doorway.

"Hello?" I mumbled, tapping, and slowly the door swung open. I stepped into a dazzle of whiteness and was grabbed from behind by a big burly guy: a thrill shot through my lungs like pure oxygen. "Hi," said a voice, teasingly. Big arms like bolsters against my chest. "What's *your* name?" His voice was dark and low, like some underground stream choked with weeds. When he ordered me to shut my eyes his words came out in a gargle. He twisted my wrists behind my back and held them there with one tight fist. I suppose I helped a little. "Where's Scott?" I said.

"Shot," said my captor.

"What?"

"I call him Shot," he replied, pinching my nipples through my white Brooks Brothers shirt. "I guess his name is Scott, but I call him Shot."

I relaxed a little and surveyed the room. "Why?" The salient feature of the Meadowbrook rooms was, and maybe still is, the walls—every available wall surface covered with mirrors, like the end of *Lady from Shanghai*. Mirrored ceiling, too, hung with the primitive track lighting of the seventies. Again and again my reflection gleamed back at me, and I could see the face of my captor. He shut the door with his bare foot, *slam*. Even the back of the door was a mirror. I guess there was a thermostat on one wall, but other than that there was only me, him, a TV, and a bed. Endlessly. And silent air-conditioning—its thin metallic smell seemed to bounce back and forth between us. The TV was showing some closed-channel sex film starring Marilyn Chambers. Marilyn was laughing her fool head off while jerking off one white guy and one black guy. The sound was turned down, so I couldn't catch the dialogue.

"Because he's, like, well . . . he's shot," said the man behind me. "Didn't you see his eyes?" I'm thinking, God, I'm
supposed to have sex with *this* guy? He was about fifty-five
and must have weighed three hundred pounds, wrapped in
an oversized white terry-cloth bathrobe, its sash underfoot
on the red rug. "What is he, your scout?" "Ha ha ha," he
laughed, as though I were joking. His unruly beard and
jolly grin would mark him today as a daddy type, a big
bear, but back then we didn't have that type: to me he was
just fat. But I was drunk enough to not really care. Weakly
I held up the bottle of Glenlivet, waved it around. "Want a
drink?"

"Shot's into bondage," said Bear Guy, making a face.
"But not me—I'm only into eating beautiful ass. How
about you?"

"Whatever," I said. The ruined king-size bed looked
good to me. On TV Marilyn's face beamed, dripping with
cum on her temples, eyes, lips. Okay, the linen wasn't exactly pristine—a thin strip of blood streaked the top sheet.
"First I just want a drink."

Suddenly solicitous, Bear Guy led me to the bed and
vanished into the bathroom. "Don't run off now!" I sat on
one edge of the bed, removing my shoes and socks. Soon
he reappeared with a glass of ice. *Glug glug glug.* He said
his name was Schuyler, but all his "friends" called him Sky.
"You've been crying," he said. I wondered if he was some
kind of counselor in regular life. His big kind brown eyes.
"Yes," I said, as I helped him insert his big hand through
the zipper of my pants. "I've just been to a wake."

Sky squeezed my balls in that tender way some big guys
have. "Ah, one of those long drunken Irish wakes. You
look Irish."

"Yes," I said. I could see my face in the mirror, and beyond that I could see my own back. Everywhere I looked I saw me, sipping this motel glass full of that wonderful Scotch. Sophisticated. My dick was hard. I saw it. I saw it in the mirrors. It was everywhere, sluicing up and down through his hand. "This'll make you feel better," said Sky. He grabbed some change from the nightstand and put a couple of quarters into the frame of the water bed. Instantly the bed started sliding and shaking up and down, to and fro, like an ocean liner on stormy seas. "Whoa," I said. "Relax," said Sky. Obediently, I shut my eyes and rolled onto my stomach. I didn't want to see his belly, tons of flab folding over and reconstituting themselves as he bent to work. I lay slumped amid the big coverlets and stained sheets, hid my hot face in a pink satin pillow, ruffled with black lace. "Good night," I said sadly. I didn't want to puke. Sky tugged my pants down to my ankles, then peeled off my tight white underwear, oohing and aahing like a connoisseur, touching and nibbling. The bed kept shaking as he parted the cheeks and licked the crack. At his muffled request—"Mmmftlmm?"—I raised my hips. I imagined my legs sprawled, my bony ankles dull under the weight of his knees, his bearded face buried inside my butt, a buffet. Comfortable. His tongue darted in and out, in time with the whirring vibrations of the water bed, licking the walls of my asshole. Nothing could have surprised me at that point, so when I became aware there was another boy in the bed near me, already passed out, snoring, I wasn't shocked, only pleased. I held on to his waist, pressing my cock along his long thigh. Hispanic guy with nubbly little pubic hair surrounding this enormous flaccid organ. His body was warm, he was naked, *zzzzzz*. An hour later, when I came to, he was gone. I've always wondered who he was and what became of him. The bed was still. Sky's quarters had run out.

And Sky must have run out too. Inside my ass I felt a little stretched, but not much. My mouth was parched. Five-thirty A.M. Scott was sitting on the other end of the bed by the mirrored nightstand, fully dressed, making a phone call. "You're up," he said to me, scratching the bridge of his nose. "Grand."

There was still about an inch of my drink left—*thank God*. Scott had two grams of cocaine that he said were worth a hundred dollars. "On me." This was his hint for me to fish them out of his clothes. They were in the right-hand pocket of his blue jeans. I slithered to his end of the bed while he talked on the phone, I think to his girlfriend or wife. I patted him down to find them, to find the tiny lump the vials made in those slick blue pants. The inside of his pocket felt warm, greasy, like sticking a hand into a Joseph Beuys sculpture of fat. I looked over his shoulder and saw our two faces. I could barely make mine out; it looked like the mirror was melting it, like rain on spring snow. But his face glistened, tan and sweaty, brilliantly smiling. His eyes were blue, like mine, but darker, almost black. I pulled the stash out of his pocket and dropped the vials, lightly, on the big sloppy bed. He hung up and then we scarfed the coke. What the hell. After we kissed some more he jumped to his feet to remove the belt from the loops of his jeans. "You work in a garage or something?" I think I said. "Your clothes are dirty, man." Even his boxer shorts had grease stains, as though he worked on motors in his underwear, then wiped his hands on them.

Ever been really drunk, in a room full of mirrors?

Liquor, brown and warm, slops down the side of your mouth. You can't swallow fast enough. Your kisses get sloppy; your vision too. All of a sudden there's a little click in your head, and the first person turns into the second person. That's you—Kevin. Have another drink. Don't mind if I do. You stroke the warm cock in your hand, you can't decide if it's yours or another's. Click. The second person slips into the third. Kevin rose suddenly, the chenille bedspread sticking to his butt, and made his way unsteadily toward the far end of the room, where a picture in a neo-Rosenquist style hung on the wall of mirrors. He thought it was marvelous.

Fine scars striped Scott's chest and back—thin shiny veins, like long gleaming tapeworms—and across both cheeks of his butt a thicker scar, of rough skin, as though he had backed into a hot pipe. Inside his head Kevin was, like, ????, but he kept grinning as though it was nothing out of the ordinary to see a guy whose outsides looked like insides. "So, you're into bondage?" Now it was Scott's turn to make a face. "Who told you that—Sky?" "Oh, no," Kevin said sarcastically, "Lana Turner told me."

He wore Kevin's hands around his waist like a belt, but Kevin took them off and lit a Parliament, backward, nonchalantly lighting its "recessed filter" so that acrid smoke filled the air of the mirrored room. Scott walked nude to the bathroom and flipped on the light, and, blinking, he tipped a plastic glass sideways in its holder, one limp arm pointing at it, his fingers working, weakly, as though he wanted to grab it. "I'll take a drink too, you got any to spare." Like any other alcoholic, Kevin measured what was left in the bottle and tried to figure out if, indeed, there

was any to "spare." Scott was naked in the threshold of
the bathroom, and Kevin kept ogling him blearily. His
body had the extraordinary angles of the junkie, the
bumps and bones, the big thick red cock like a wind-up
handle for the toy it set to motion. "Turn around," Kevin
said. Scott complied. Kevin peered at his ass. It was big
and full, a whole novel's worth. I could eat breakfast off
that butt, thought Kevin, scar and all. He saw Scott's
elbow working, moving like a piston from behind. Like,
he's jerking off, kind of. When he turned again he had a
hard-on bigger than a mackerel, and Kevin had seen a lot
of fish. "Want another drink?" Scott said, pointing to the
bottle that stood on the bedside. The alcohol sweat from
Kevin's body gave him a chill on this hot, humid night, just
before dawn, and he shivered as though—*as though,* he
thought, *a goose was walking over my grave.*
    Brrrrr.
    "Let's take a shower," Scott said. "I'm filthy." He told
Kevin he liked being tied up to the shower pole. Is it called
a "pole"? Whatever it is that holds up a shower curtain—
whatever it is that he was now tapping like a woodpecker,
in a rare burst of excitement. "Nah," Scott said flatly. "It's
called the rod!"—a word he seemed to find excitement in,
as did Kevin: a phallic word, concealed yet radiant, like
Poe's purloined letter, among the bathroom's pedestrian
fittings. Then Scott wanted Kevin to take the knife he held
out and slice him with it. "After that it can be *your* party."
Trouble was there wasn't any rope in their mirrored motel
room. On all four walls, on the ceiling, their faces, multi-
plied to infinity, represented an infinity of puzzlement,
thousands of eyes darting around drunkenly to look for
rope. Finally Scott gave up, shrugged. "No rope—let's improv." Improv? Very Second City, that boy! Very Lee Stras-

berg! For a few minutes Scott pretended he was tied, but that got tired. He stood facing away from Kevin, wrists crossed above his head, clinging to the rod as though lashed on. He kept looking back over his shoulder, trying to panic. Trying to feel trapped.

"Hey," whined Scott. "I really could, you know, use some rope. And I'd like to do this before Sky comes back, if you don't mind."

There was a second click in Kevin's head—a click of clarity. He saw clearly, vividly, where he could find some rope—in the trunk of his Maverick. Viewed the mental image in 3-D. It was like getting sober. The third person vanished. The second person lasted only long enough for you to whip one of the motel towels around your waist and prop open the door with your pants. Then you were out in the parking lot, and pop! I opened the trunk, staring down at the rope Tim Baillie had hung himself with.

A tiny wind whistled under the thin cloth of the towel, tickling my balls. I bent over and took the extra rope. The leftover rope. Tim Baillie was dead now; I had just come back from his wake. He was my advisor in grad school, and I had slept with him to pass my orals. Do they still call them "orals"? I guess I used him, without many qualms: just did it, set him in my sights and knocked him down like a bowling pin with charm, Irish whisky, and my big basket in the front row of Victorian Studies. "Kevin," he said, "you could have been a real scholar if you had anything in your mind." And now Tim Baillie—"*Dr.* Baillie, if you please!"—was dead.

Coiled loosely on the floor of the trunk, among pieces

of an oily jack, the rope looked harmless enough. But just looking at it made me jittery, as though it concealed cobras. I remember fantasizing about an inquest where I would have to get up on the stand and some Perry Mason type would be snidely asking me, "Didn't you know he would use that rope to hang himself?" "No! No! I've gone through this a thousand times! Dr. Baillie said he wanted to pack a trunk!" "A trunk to death?" "No, no, an ordinary trunk!" "Mr. Killian, may I remind you that you swore to tell the whole truth and nothing but the truth?" What could I say? I knew I didn't love him, but wasn't giving him all that head enough for Tim Baillie? He had been closeted for forty years or more; I thought I was bringing a little sunshine into his elderly life. I remembered lying in his bed in his awful condo in Rocky Point with all his books on Alfred, Lord Tennyson stacked sideways on the bookcase, as though he didn't care enough about them to stand them up straight. I remembered listening with him to Willie Nelson's doleful *Stardust* album again and again— his favorite album, whereas mine was either *Radio Ethiopia* or *Sexual Healing*. Maybe I should have loved him. But nobody respected him, why should I have? He was just this flabby fool with spots on his face that might have been freckles. He left a note, they told me: "I can't stand this heat." I didn't know, when he asked me to get him some rope at Smithtown Hardware, what he'd use it for. I remember his pursed lips when I showed him all the rope I'd bought, saying to me, "I only need about twelve feet, it's just for a trunk, I'm not Christo wrapping the Eiffel Tower." He cut off what he needed with a pair of cooking shears. Least he paid me for the whole hundred feet. Always this sarcasm, always the mockery, the checkbook, the despair. I thought *I* drank a lot till I met him—his eyes were the color of grappa, all the way through, no white, just this sick, luscious, purple tinge color. *Gulp.*

When I heard about Tim Baillie's suicide, I was sitting at a table in a bar in Port Jefferson, reading a book and nursing a bottle of beer and a glass of rum and Tab. The bottle kept leaving wet rings in the pages of the book. You know how Seurat worked? Placing millions of tiny dots of color into pointillistic masterpieces? I began to think, well, maybe you could do this with the wet rings of a beer bottle, and later Chuck Close took my insight and became way famous doing so. Oh Tim! If I made you feel second best, Tim, I am sorry I was blind. Maybe I didn't hold you, all those lonely, lonely times. Little things I should have said and done, I just never took the time, et cetera!

Room 813, Scott was lying on the bed whacking off, keeping his dick hard and his heels cool. "Grand," he said when I showed him the rope and mimicked lassoing him. Expertly he tied himself up, lashing his wrists to the shower rod and needing my help only for the last knots. The rod was L-shaped, to match the contours of the bathtub below; its two ends screwed into two different mirrored walls, and a sassy full-length shower curtain of hot pink vinyl hung from it dramatically, the drag queen of all shower curtains. I stood behind Scott, kissing and biting his neck and shoulders, my hard-on poking between his thighs, his big butt. I gripped the knife in one hand, my knuckles white around its heft. He was on tiptoes, arms braced tautly against the frail metal rod. I flipped a hand between the part in the pink vinyl curtain and turned on the shower; a rush of cool water beat on the other side of us. "You know what you're doing?" he said sharply. "I'm not a piece of meat, I just want to let some blood out. You don't hack me like you're at some butcher's shop." I saw him full length in the mirror facing us, on the other side of the tub. The hair under his armpits was blonde, darker than the thatch on his head. His nipples were brownish red, spaced far apart on his magnificent chest. "Right under my ribs," he said. "Let's start there." I could see how hard he was. His erection lifted his balls right along with it—everything pointed to the knife. I just wanted to fuck him, but thought, Well, later, later it'll be *my* party.

I took a deep breath and lifted the knife to his skin. First I heard a kind of screech, like two cats fighting. Then another screech, more protracted, from above my head. The shower rod screws sprang half out of their sockets in a noise of splitting glass and metal. My instinct was to jump back, anywhere, but there was nowhere to jump to. The knife fell from my fist. I tightened my hold round Scott's middle, his skin a blur. Another screw flew out of its seating and the shower walls collapsed. "Uh-oh," whispered Scott, and we began to drop, he right on top of me, he getting the worst of it for sure. Splinters of glass shot through the air, then whole panes peeled from the steamy bathroom walls, sticky with glue and loud with crackling and smashing. The room was imploding. With a sudden crack, the rod bent again, into three broken parts, and all the curtain rings fell to one end like poker chips clicking on a croupier's table. Scott's body, still knotted to the mangled metal rod, fell to the bathroom floor with a heavy thud, though I tried to cushion his fall. Hot pink vinyl fluttered and descended over our heads. Slumped to the floor, Scott's torso sprayed blood, pink mist erupting up the side of the bathtub, mist that grew red at its edges. His hands were still tethered, with the hemp now wet, swollen. I sat on the floor, afraid to move, for the glass was everywhere—on the rug, on the pink tiles, strewn across the tan of his naked body like sand. And also I was afraid of sitting on the knife I had let go.

Mirrors, with bright colors zigzagging across them; his dick seemed a thousand feet long, like a string of sausages in a Chuck Jones cartoon. I kept seeing him bleeding out the corner of my eye, the way you might think you're seeing something when you're really paranoid. Peripheral vision.

"Guy, you all right?" I said.

His eyelids pulled up to reveal blue irises swimming in twin seas of pink. His lashes were incredibly long, and from overhead the gaudy light of the motel's fluorescent tubes threw long shadows onto his picked-over cheekbones. One large shard of mirror stood, like Stonehenge, embedded directly into his stomach, about an inch above and to the left of his navel. Another shard toppled over on his right thigh, propelling a piece of pink flesh that looked like dog food across the rim of the bathtub. The blood was everywhere. I was covered with blood: spots, streaks, puddles. But somehow I hadn't been hurt. I ran back into the bedroom to grab a drink and to fetch a pillow to stanch Scott's blood; I had the word *tourniquet* in my head.

"I'm all right," he gasped. "Wow, I just wanted a little cut, dude, but you brought in the whole artillery, didn't you?"

"FX," I said.

"Now help me," he said. "Help me come now."

I sat back on my haunches and used one hand to stroke my cock. With the other I held his dick, which hardened and throbbed to a vivid red brightness—its natural pink intensified by desire. I studied it before I began to pump: it looked angry, swollen, as though stung by bees. Blood and pre-cum, greasy in my loose fist. The aroma of blood: stale, tangy, older than either of us. Scott stirred, smiling, moved his head across the wet shiny tile. Gently I placed the pink satin pillow between his head and the floor; its black lace ruffle grew instantly darker with blood and water. This is like some Mario Bava film! I thought, scared to death, but horny, too. Scott's dark blue eyes fixed on some point on the mirrored wall, from which another face gazed back at him, mine or his. His tongue protruded from his mouth, like a dog in summer lapping up water. "Cool," he said.

His tan flesh, which should have been lightly dusted in sand; his beach-boy look, spoiled or accentuated in scars; and everything pricked with glass, like a St. Sebastian I felt so sorry for, yet couldn't help. All I could do was jerk him off. That's all he wanted from me. His tongue touched the tip of my dick as I labored over him. Lick. Rustle. Spurt.

Again. Spurt. Presently I straightened up, creaking from my knees, and tossed a towel into the bathtub so that I could stand in it without cutting my feet on the broken slices of mirror. Then I stepped over his body and into the shower, let cool water rinse the blood from my arms, hair, crotch, legs. Through a streaming veil I watched Scott sink into sleep, as blood continued to pool up in all the concave sites of his fading body. Was he sleeping? Unconscious? His blonde hair matted red, brown, black; his smile gave no clue, his big lips slack, happy, purple and gray as the petals of a sterling-silver rose. I nudged him with the Glenlivet. He didn't seem to want a drink, again I'm like—*?????* Then I dressed, found my keys, left the motel. I guess.

MARIAN PHILLIPS

Three Obscene Telephone Calls

The phone rang the other day. I picked it up and said "Hello" in my cool, distant telephone voice.

"Hello," said a sultry female voice in my ear. "What are you wearing?"

"I am wearing," I said, "a purple and green polka-dotted clown suit, with a big yellow ruff collar and huge white pompom buttons down the front."

"Oh, that's so sexy," my caller whispered.

"—And also," I continued, "black men's socks with black knee-garters to hold them up. On my feet I am wearing huge rubber flip-flops. The socks," I added, by way of explanation, "have been slit so that the thong of the flip-flops will fit between my big toe and my second toe." There was a low moan as I paused for effect.

"Do you know what I'm wearing on my head?" I asked.

"A rainbow-colored wig?" said the husky, familiar voice.

"No." I could hear her breathing, as I paused again to let the anticipation build.

"An arrow through the head," I said.

"Oh, Jesus, I'm so turned on," my caller gasped hoarsely.

"What are you wearing?" I asked.

"Nothing but a cock ring," she purred.

"And is it the cock ring that inflates into a seahorse inner tube, or is it the one that has coat hangers projecting out from it like the spokes of a wheel, that you can attach spare change and dollar bills onto?" I said relentlessly.

"The one with the coat hangers."

"All right," I continued evenly. "Here's my fantasy.

"You're standing on a street corner aggressively panhandling the passersby. As you follow someone down the street, screaming obscenities, I run out from an alley and knock you down, leaving you to flail helplessly in the gutter, while I steal all the spare change and dollar bills from your cock ring, and run away laughing."

"Of *course* you're laughing, for God's sake," she snapped, "you're a *clown*. Clowns *always* laugh."

Click.

I had started out the evening alphabetizing my fiction, but had gotten sidetracked into re-reading the good parts of *Pride and Prejudice* instead, when the phone rang.

"Hello?"

A pleasant, unfamiliar male voice said, "Hello, who's this?"

"I," I said, "am the King of the Cats. Who are you?"

"Uh, my name's Bob," he said, sounding a little nonplussed. Picking up confidence from my silence, however, he continued: "and I just wanted to tell you that I have a huge, nine-inch-long cock that I'd like to—"

"Don't you want to know what I'm wearing?" I said in an offended tone.

"Uh . . . what are you wearing?"

"I am wearing a suit made entirely out of aluminum foil that covers me from head to foot, leaving only eye holes and a mouth hole. I wear this suit to deflect radio transmissions from the National Security Agency, which is beaming commands to me through the steel plate in my head. In addition, I have roped my cat to my head, with its feet tied together so that it forms a turban and can't scratch; its intermittent yowling also helps block the transmissions.

"I have a friend here," I continued: "Would you like to know what she's wearing?"

"Um, well, I—"

"My friend," I plowed on, "is dressed up like a martini. She is wearing close-fitting white clothes, and around her neck is a clear plastic cone shaped like the bowl of a martini glass. Her head is bald—she shaves it—and she has painted it up like an olive, green with a red spot on the top. Instead of that arrow-through-the-head prop, she has a sword through the head."

There was a distraught silence at the other end of the line.

"Now here's my fantasy," I said. "I—"

Click.

The telephone rang.

The last time anyone at the telephone company asked me, I told them to change my listing from S. Wright to Susan Wright. Previous to this change, I had gotten about one wrong number a week. After the change, the wrong numbers mostly went away and were replaced by obscene callers who addressed me familiarly by my first name, and heavy breathers.

The telephone rang again and I picked it up.

"Hello?"

"Well, Susan, you cunt, so you're at home for a change."

An obscene caller with a wrong number—truly the best of both worlds. Also, obviously, a man with a grievance. Although I'd never heard the voice before in my life, for a fleeting moment I considered apologizing anyway. Fortunately, he wasn't expecting a reply, and he pressed on:

"You fucking whore, why aren't you out sniffing the streets for men to fuck, getting down on your knees to suck their cocks, isn't that what you like, you bitch? You couldn't be bothered to fuck me when we were together. I don't know why I call you a whore, I've met plenty of whores who are better than you."

I was getting so caught up in this random call that I almost asked indignantly where he'd been meeting all these whores, but he raced on.

"Well, you'd better watch out, because some night you're going to be crawling around offering your twat to be fucked and I'm going to come up behind you in a dark alley and rape you with the barrel of my gun. What do you think of that, scumbag?"

"I think it sounds hot," I said. "However, I should warn you that I carry a gun in the left inside pocket of my leather jacket, so you'll want to make sure to pinion my hands and disarm me first. I suggest some kind of restraining device."

There was a long silence.

"What kind of gun?"

"A Ruger compact semiautomatic seven-shot .45 with a 3¾-inch barrel," I replied.

There was another long silence.

"You're not going to get much range with a gun like that," he said finally.

"How much range do I need? If you're close enough to

grab me, I'll be close enough to hit you. Anyway, what do you care? You're going to pin me and take it away before I get a chance to shoot, aren't you?"

Silence again.

He started to laugh.

Click.

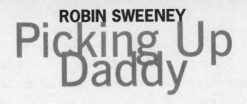

ROBIN SWEENEY
Picking Up Daddy

You will know me, boy, by the way I cut through the crowd, like an animal tracking its prey, until I find you and make you mine."

That's what Griffin's latest e-mail said before she got on the plane in Philadelphia and came to claim me, a continent away, in San Francisco.

I stood waiting outside the gates of United Airlines. The collar she had sent me was in my right rear pocket, my boots polished, my jockstrap holding my packing dick in place just like Daddy told me. My on-line daddy was coming to make me her boy, and I was going to pass out from anticipation.

Griffin had found me my first night on-line, and she spoiled me for all other cybersex and on-line cruising. Hell, she spoiled me for most in-person sex and cruising too.

It was a complete accident that she was able to find me. My first night wandering around the possibilities of America Online, barely computer literate, I found the gay message area. There I found the leatherwomen board, and I posted an ad:

Jaded boy looking for other boys to play with, although her heart would still belong to Daddy if she'd show up already. Not into fakes or pretending. Looking for a real connection. I'm a sick fuck into most kinks who likes to pitch as well as catch and who is looking. . . .

Turns out that "sick fuck" was a little too much for the family standards of America Online. (The pitching and catching part was apparently okay, though.) The on-line monitors who pull "objectionable" ads deleted my post, and I was certain no one would see it.

Griffin had seen it, though. In that window of opportunity between posting and pulling, Griffin read my ad and decided to respond.

"Fairly presumptuous, aren't you, boy?" her first subject line to me read.

Holy shit, I thought. *It worked.*

"You sound like the sort of lost boy who starts acting loud and tough to try and scare away the noises in the dark. You've probably started topping the girls in town, maybe even being someone's daddy, in an attempt to get your needs met. After all, if you can't get what you want, you might as well make someone else's fantasy come true, right? That's not working, or you wouldn't be putting personals on-line.

"I am willing to allow you to write me if you lose the poor attitude and present yourself properly. If you are not capable of this or are not interested, you need not respond. Otherwise, you have twenty-four hours, boy. Yours truly—Griffin."

I was a newbie on-line, but I had been around the block as far as women go. I wanted a daddy badly, but I hadn't found one. I dated a lot and had flings that I really enjoyed, but I always ended up topping my girlfriends. Griffin had pegged me right. I had been doing S/M for a while and had gotten a fair bit of experience. The type I like—women who look like sixteen-year-old boys—tend to be novices. I liked playing with them just fine, but having to explain to somebody how to tie my wrists to the bed just didn't inspire me to bottom.

Also, like most people I met, I was afraid of getting what I wanted. I didn't like to give it up to just anybody who asked. Daddies were supposed to know how to take a boy down. Most of the ones I had met weren't up to the follow-through I craved. I didn't want to be just submissive, I wanted to be told how to behave.

That's exactly what Griffin did. I checked her profile:

Griffin. Also known as Sir.
Female, single.
Macintosh PowerBook 145.
Occupation: student, cook, and daddy top.
Likes leather, dykes who are boys, taming the untamable.
Quote: "Come closer. I won't bite . . . until you ask me nicely."

I wrote back. I had no idea how she wanted me to present myself, much less how to do it in writing. If we were at a party or a bar, I'd bring her a drink, be respectful, and call her Sir. How was I supposed to do that on-line?

"Good evening, Sir. I appreciate your letter to me and hope that you find my response timely. I am interested in learning more of what interests you in a boy. True, I haven't found many people I want to submit to, but I try to remain open to the possibilities.

"Sir, I apologize if my ad was too brazen. I never expected an answer, much less from someone who was going to give me an opportunity to present myself properly. Please, Sir, would you tell me exactly how you would have me present myself? Respectfully yours—Jay."

Twelve hours later my computer "said" to me, in a way that was grammatically incorrect but delightfully enthusiastic, "You've got mail."

"On your knees, boy," it started, "is how I would expect you to present yourself to me. On your knees, head up, and eyes forward until I told you different. Arms behind your back, left hand holding right wrist. Legs spread—and don't let your ass touch the heels of your boots. Look me in the eye, boy. You're not a dog, and you're not a slave.

"You're a boy, and I expect you to do us both proud.

"Now, tell me more about yourself, boy. What should I know? How would I tell who you are in a crowd if we were to meet at a bar?"

That was the start of almost endless letters back and forth. We didn't do what I later found out was typical in cyberspace. I didn't lie to Griffin, and she didn't tell me anything less than the truth. I explained my life in San Francisco, working at a retail store on Castro Street, living with a bunch of roommates, and playing with lots of women.

And looking for Daddy.

"My friends call me Jay, and my mother still calls me Janice. I prefer Jay, although I'm sure that's not a surprise. I'm not as tall as I act, Sir, which means I end up looking up at people more than I'm comfortable with. Five-two should be taller than it actually is, Sir. I'm a big boy, not fat, really, just solid. (I like to think that makes me more fun to hurt, but I'm not sure if that's out of line.) I'm pale, with light brown hair that I keep in a flattop. I wear jeans and T-shirts to work and dress shirts and ties to play parties. (It's that F. Scott Fitzgerald fetish, Sir.) I just turned twenty-six and have lived in San Francisco for three years.

"My eyes are blue when I'm calm and go green when I'm horny or sick and turn gray after I've been beaten. And please, Sir, will you tell me about yourself?"

"A younger daddy," her next note said, "is what you're going to get with me. Are you a sick enough fuck to still treat me with the respect due Daddy? I turn twenty-one next month.

"I'm a student here in Philadelphia, although my family lives in New Hampshire. I miss that part of the country, but I don't miss my father and his homophobic bullshit. I came out my senior year of high school—which reminds me, boy: Tell me your coming-out story.

"I go to college at the University of Pennsylvania, which is exactly as uptight as it sounds. Full of frats and the boys who fill them, who aren't half as interesting as the boys I meet on-line. I'm out of place here and wouldn't have survived if it weren't for the people I meet on-line and the women in Dangerous Women, the S/M support group here.

"I work, study, read, write, terrify my dorm mates, and cruise perverts, both live and on-line. I'm five-ten, dark-haired, dark-eyed, part Irish, part German, part Cherokee. I lift weights, cook professionally, and can't wait to be done with school.

"Now tell me what hankies you'd be wearing when you'd cruise me at the bar and how you would get my attention."

I did just that, spinning a fantasy about picking her up at the Eagle during a beer bust in front of all the fags who don't understand why two women would be there and going out into the alley and fucking like wild things, me on my hands and knees, getting plowed by her from behind. She wrote back, adding flourishes like handcuffing me over a motorcycle and inviting other people to join her in fucking me.

I loved it.

With words she painted a picture that I longed for. I tried to offer her as much from my writing as possible. We exchanged fantasies and conversations about our real lives. We gossiped about people we knew on-line and even managed to have arguments.

We wrote back and forth and sent pictures. At one point we exchanged phone numbers and started talking on the phone as well. We kept fairly different schedules, though, and I've never been that comfortable with phone sex. The phone didn't match the intimacy of our writing somehow. Early on I knew that I wanted to meet her and be her boy FTF—face-to-face, in computerese. Griffin cinched my interest and made me want to really be her boy about two months after she first answered my ad.

One day there was a package on the kitchen table for me when I got home. I didn't recognize the address at first glance. Who did I know in Philadelphia? Then I realized. The package was from Griffin.

I was so excited, I could barely open the box. There was a note on top of the tissue paper that filled the small box.

"Boy," it said on the outside, and I unfolded it.

"I found this collar on one of my travels along I-95. In one of those little towns in New York in a mom-and-pop store. I bought it that day and have kept it oiled and ready for the person I wanted to wear it. I didn't know who that would be or when I would find them, but I knew I would someday have a boy who would deserve this.

"You must oil it once a week and wear it whenever you write to me or whenever you read your mail from me. You are also to wear my collar to the next leather event you attend where you are not otherwise engaged, and when you are asked whose collar you are wearing, tell them it's your daddy. Much love—Daddy."

The collar was a plain black band of leather with a shiny chrome buckle. I held the collar up to my nose, and I smelled the oil she had rubbed into it and swore I could smell her too, even though she was thousands of miles away. I had never met her, but she had reached out, found me, and claimed me as her boy. I had never worn a collar before, though I had wanted to, and had told Griffin that when I was someone's boy, I wanted to wear a collar to mark me as belonging to Daddy.

I wore it that night when I wrote to her on my knees in front of my computer.

"Daddy," I wrote, "thank you for the collar. i am wearing it now as i write to you. i can't begin to tell you how thrilled i am by having a collar from you, how much it makes me feel cared for and like i am your boy. i can't wait until i can actually see you, feel your touch, and be in your service. i treasure the token of your esteem that you have sent me. thank you, Sir. Your boy—jay."

We continued writing for several weeks, the collar never far from me. Griffin made me tell her all my fears and fantasies and would leave messages in e-mail telling me to put clothespins on my chest or ordering me to beat off while I read. I crafted long and complicated stories for her involving more and more of my desires to please her and serve her as my daddy. I practiced polishing boots so that I would be competent to take care of hers. I started wearing my keys on the right and telling people, "No, thank you, I'm taken."

Except snuggling up with a computer isn't easy, and even the most delightful messages don't fill emotional needs after a while. Griffin realized this, of course. She was my daddy, and she was perceptive.

"Boy, I know that it's hard being so far away, and I would understand if you need to find a flesh-and-blood top to serve. However, you should not make plans with anyone for the week of March 2nd through 10th. Be at the airport to pick me up. Attached is my itinerary."

So here I stood, at the airport as instructed. Daddy's flight was announced, and passengers started filling up the gate area. I didn't see her in the first crush of people and worried fleetingly that she wasn't on the flight.

Then, just like that, there she was. The grin on her face I recognized from photos, but now she was real and in front of me. Her black leather jacket hugged her broad shoulders over a black turtleneck tucked into blue jeans. Her crotch bulged in a way that let me know she was wearing a dick, and her boots glittered with their shine.

"Hello, boy," she said as she dropped her carry-on bag and wrapped her arms around me.

Finally I was touching Daddy. Even better, Daddy was holding me. I put my head on her chest and tried to breathe calmly. She smelled like sweat and leather and some sort of spicy scent, and it was intoxicating.

I felt her pull the collar out of my back pocket, and she put it around my neck. I watched her face as she buckled the collar on me. She looked at me and growled.

"Mine."

"Yes, Sir. Please."

She kissed me then, first soft and friendly and exploring. Then she grabbed me hard and pulled me against her, one hand reaching for the collar around my neck. Her mouth took over mine, the kiss becoming ferocious, and I melted into her arms. All my fantasies, all my desires, and all that e-mail were fulfilled with that one kiss.

She pushed me away and turned on her heel. She didn't look back to make sure I followed; she just assumed that I would. That was a safe assumption too as I grabbed her bag and scurried to keep up with her long strides.

She headed into the women's room and moved to the far stall, one of the larger handicapped-accessible ones. She held the stall door open for me, and I blushed as I hurried past the lone woman at the sinks.

Daddy sat on the toilet, legs spread, playing with her bulge.

"Down, boy," she said, and I dropped to my knees. I couldn't believe she was doing this in the San Francisco airport, but I didn't want to stop.

"Take care of my boots, boy."

For a second I thought she wanted me to polish them, and I panicked. My boot-polish kit was at home. Then I remembered one of her earlier e-mails to me about a boy needing to love Daddy's boots with every part, including a boy's mouth. I leaned over and put my lips on Daddy's boots.

She groaned and shifted her weight and put her other foot on my back, pressing me onto the tile of the floor. I spread out full-length and tried to put my entire being into licking the boots of the woman I had just met and knew so well. I licked and kissed and moaned under her boot and thrust against the floor, rocking my hips. My packing dick pressed up against my cunt and drove me crazy, and I heard Daddy unbutton her jeans above me.

"Up, boy, and suck me off."

I scrambled to follow her instructions. Her dick hung out of her pants, and I dived for it. For so long I had beaten off at night fantasizing about a daddy to service and, please, a big daddy dick to fill my mouth. After Griffin started writing me, I created endless dreams about her, how she would take me and make me her boy, make me suck her big cock.

And there I was, forcing as much of Daddy's dick down my throat as I could. Daddy grabbed my head and groaned. I closed my eyes, rocking back and forth over her crotch. I opened up my throat and swallowed her as well as I could. Daddy was real, and her dick was too, at least as far as we cared.

Griffin pulled me off her dick, grabbed me by the collar, and pulled me closer. She started kissing me hard, harder than she had at the gate where I had waited for her. She undid my belt buckle and unbuttoned my jeans. I held on to her shoulders as she groped my packing dick, the pressure against my cunt almost overwhelming, my psychic attachment to my dick making me throb.

Daddy pushed her hand past my dick, past my dripping cunt, and, kicking my legs apart, started playing with my butt. It felt so good, I moaned in her mouth. She fingered me gently, and I could tell she had smoothed her manicure down to almost nothing for this. She pumped her fingers into my cunt once, twice, then pressed the moisture into my ass. My butt opened around her finger, and I let her inside me.

"Oh, please, Daddy," I whispered. "Please fuck me, Daddy. Please?"

Griffin nodded and kissed me again.

"Yeah, boy. Daddy's going to fuck you. Take my dick in your ass and make me happy, boy. Yeah, I'm going to fuck you." While Daddy said this, she pushed my jeans all the way down past my knees and turned me around. She pushed me over so that my nose almost touched the floor and I could see the pumps of the woman two stalls over. "Beat off, boy, and come for Daddy while I fuck you."

I felt lube trickle over my ass, and Griffin's fingers started spreading me open. I had practiced with butt plugs so that I could take Daddy's dick, like she had ordered me to in e-mail, but I was nervous. Griffin's dick wasn't the biggest strap-on I'd ever seen, but it was pretty hefty. I felt her press her dick against my ass. I started touching my clit under my packing dick, breathing deep and trying to take her cock in my ass. Daddy pulled my hips closer to her, rocking me back toward her, and her dick started going inside me.

Then, so slowly that I could barely tell she moved, her dick slid into my ass. Daddy pulled me back, and I moved against her, and her cock filled my ass completely. Just as slowly she pulled back out until her dick almost left my ass, and I heard myself whimper.

"Yeah, boy," she murmured above me. "Daddy's here. Fucking you. Making you mine. My boy."

She plunged back into me and started to move in a rhythm so sweet, I had to bite my wrist to not cry out. She grunted and moved inside me, and I rocked back in response. I beat off as Daddy hit her stride, pushing me on and off her dick. Soon, almost too soon, I came, with Daddy fucking my ass.

I lay there panting as Daddy pulled out. I felt her clean me off. I couldn't move; everything felt too good. Daddy buttoned her jeans and slapped my ass once to get my attention. I got up onto my knees and turned around.

"That's my good boy," she said. She wrapped her arms around me and hugged me close, like Daddy should.

"Let's get out of here," Griffin said. "Take me home with you, boy. I need to have you fuck me now, and if we wait much longer, it'll be here in the airport bathroom. And I don't come as quietly as you do."

I left the stall in front of Griffin. I walked proudly in front of my daddy and smiled at the woman doing her makeup at the sink as she looked quizzically at the two rumpled and grinning leather dykes leaving a single airport bathroom stall.

BEN NEIHART

The Number One Song in the Country

I **was twenty-eight,** tall, bony, a bit stooped when I walked. Maybe it was a little bit late in the season for another sexy, rage-filled singer-songwriter chick, and maybe I wasn't that angry or horny, but I got a contract anyway, with Warren Brothers, after a photo of me getting my pussy shaved by Mr. Michael Stripe appeared in *Playboy*. The photo accompanied his interview, in which he said he wanted to fuck me. A bitch profiled me in *Salon*. I fucked ICA agent Benet Little, from the L.A. office, and got a bit part as a witch on *Days of Our Lives*. The suits at Warren Brothers tried to fix me up with Ballart and Warden and Kidface and the Rust Bros, but I was like, "We can talk about producers, no problem, when it's time for me to go into the studio, but I'll write my own songs, okay?" I said, "I'm moving home to Lancaster, Pennsylvania, as a matter of fact, until I finish them. There's a music scene, Ed Kowalski from *Alive* is in town, and he's definitely fuckable," and so on.

I rented the top floor of a rowhouse in the city. I wasn't used to being alone, so I wrote fourteen songs in a month. The suits loved them, called them tight and hook-filled, and they went on about the sampling we could use in the song they thought would be the second single, but for the first single they wanted a song with hard-core lyrics. Couldn't I talk about my pussy or maybe pee in a guy's lap? I got on the phone with my agent, but she was no help, so uncreative. I got Michael Stripe on the line and asked him what I should do. "I need urine for the single, and it can't just be a fucking blowjob where he dribbles some piss into my mouth," I said. "I need raunch. I mean, it can't be an accident. I think if I'm going to do this I need to pee on a guy so I know what it's um like."

"Let me ask Ed Kowalski," Michael started. "He might know a guy."

"Call me back."

An hour later, Michael called. "Ed set it up with a guy who needs the money. If that's okay, meet the guy tonight at a park, I think the address is . . ."

"I know the place you're talking about," I interrupted, and hung up.

I went near dark. I watched ducks slide across a mucky pond. A few cars were following the park roads, headlights off and tires rolling across the loose gravel. The sound made me smile. I wasn't sleepy, and the air had achieved its cobalt heaviness. The ducks were really just a splash I couldn't see.

I wasn't there long before a boy rounded the near shore and came up to me, dropped to his knees. "I could smell you from way fucking far away," he said, "so I followed my nose. I'm glad that I did."

"I'm the singer," I said. "I hate asking you this. I mean, if you don't want some chick pissing in your lap . . ."

He licked the palm of his hand. "I want you to piss in my lap more than anything." He had shaggy brown hair parted in the middle, thick eyebrows, a fat, round nose. He wore a tight tan T-shirt and jeans. Good shoulders, flat belly, strong arms.

"Can I tell you how genuine you sound?" I said. "You're good."

"I'm in a band, too. Ed's gonna maybe produce our record."

"Oh, I'll totally mention you in my publicity for my disc."

"I have a great body. I work out all the time. You wanna like touch it?"

I reached out and gave his arm a squeeze: soft, soft skin over hard, round muscles. He flexed for me, and I was impressed. "Look, I need to be up front with you," I said. "I'll pay you a hundred an hour, but you have to be creative. I'm looking for sensations I can use in my single, and I've been fucked before and I know what it feels like. There's the pee and all, but I mean, I might have to prod you and lick you, like that. Let me taste your hair? I mean, I'm sort of famous, so I'm used to being objectified, but for now you're a nobody and so maybe you don't like it."

"I want to fuck you. You don't even have to pay."

"No, I wanna pay. I can expense it. And then I won't feel bad about the pee. Now, I really do wanna taste your hair."

He laughed, but when he understood that I was serious he bent his neck and presented me with the top of his head. I took a lock, a big mouthful, and held it there. My mouth was slippery, pumping out saliva as I moved across the top of his head, wetting him, and then, before I knew what was happening, the boy slid his hand along my inner thigh and pushed a thumb up my panties.

"You like shave your pussy?" he asked. "I thought that was a thing just for the magazine."

"I like the way it feels," I said. "By the way, you taste so, um, briny. Let me taste under your arm?"

He held out his arm as if I were going to give him a shot. I rolled the short sleeve of his T-shirt up over the hard round cap of his shoulder and dipped my nose and mouth into the nest of hair. He brought his upper arm down tight against my cheek and along the side of my head, clamping my face in his pit, and I took deep, deep breaths, almost laughing, licking and wetting the hair. With my other hand, I played with his nipples. Slowly, he loosened his hold on me, and slowly I pulled my face away from him and told him we should go to my place.

He followed me up the stairs—three flights. My apartment was the only one on top. As we trudged the final couple of stairs, he pushed his face up my skirt and traced his nose down the crack of my ass and licked my crotch. I stood there, feeling the wet of his tongue, and then I started to squat, and I could feel my ass sort of open as I let him support some of my weight. The boy had a bull neck and those shoulders, so I wasn't worried. He wrapped his arms around my lap from behind, with his face still buried in my ass, and tipped me forward so that I was on my hands and knees. My door key fell out of the slit pocket of my skirt. As I reached for it, he put his thumb and forefinger in my pussy and took my ass in the rest of that hand, flipped me over, supported my back with the other arm, and picked me up, carried me to the door.

"I have to pee," I said.

He smiled. I liked the way he looked, holding me.

Shoulders straining, neck veins and muscles standing out. "Piss on me."

"Yeah," I nodded. "You're good."

As soon as we were inside, with the door still hanging open, I started to pee, through my underwear, down his fingers, down the front of his T-shirt and the lap of his jeans.

"The record company wants me to call the song 'Territory,' but I don't like that. It's too cerebral. I don't want real punk, you know, either. Like not 'Golden Showers' or 'My Yellow Stream.' Am I too heavy? You can put me down, although I have to admit I really like a guy who's clearly physically stronger than me. You wear a T-shirt well."

"How about 'Jasmine Wine'?" he asked.

I gulped. "That's so damn Steelie Nicks; I love it."

He sat on the toilet while I hung my pissy clothes inside the stall shower. I got a fresh washcloth and rinsed off and stood in the shower and douched with something fruity and put in my sponge. "I'm going to start fucking myself," I said, two fingers still up my pussy.

"I don't know why you cleaned up," the boy said. He pulled off his T-shirt, unbuckled his jeans, and just sat there, legs wide, wide open, and I pulled the denim off, down his hairy, thick legs. I was in a sort of kneeling position in front of him, and he lifted his feet, rested them on my knees so that the pouch of his white briefs was right there in my face. "You might as well fucking taste this now, if, I mean if you like stick as much as you like hair."

I peeled the waistband down and cupped his dick out of the fabric and he leaned forward and sort of rested his balls on my chin.

"I have to pee now," he said. "You want it?"

I started to hear a melody. It was simple, strong, it was a great fucking tune, but it was just outside of me. I nodded, and he put the head of the dick in my mouth.

I spit it out.

"Keep your dick pressed against my neck," I said. "I don't want any on my face. Stream it down the front of my body."

It was warm, and there was a lot of it, some pooling in my belly button, my lap. As soon as he was done, I took his balls in my mouth for a quick kiss and then I told him to start beating off, we could get off together. I heard the melody again. God it was sweet. A song was coming together. The words warm like blood kept going through my head. Warm like blood, saffron, and then, with twin rhythm guitars, the chorus: *I can smell you from far far away, far far away, ooh I can smell you from far far away, far far away . . .*

The boy sat back down on the toilet and I lay at his feet on the bathroom floor, rubbing my swollen labia with my knuckles.

The head of his dick looked like a fat extra thumb in his fist—and as he stroked it, spitting down there, wiping his mouth with the back of his other hand, I looked at his nipples beneath the hair of his chest and they were the same color as his lips and I liked that and I told him and he said, "I want to come over and fuck you."

I didn't say anything at first, but then the chorus of my song came to me, and the melody, and I sang it to him:

I can smell you from far far away . . .

He got down on the bathroom floor beside me, supporting himself on one thick elbow, and pulled me onto his lap; I watched the dick go inside me, shaved pussy lips swallowing him, and I started to come right away. We tangled our fingers up together as he bucked against me. I heard my words, I heard my melody, my fucking song, my first single. He was singing it back to me, and it occurred to me, in a flush of generosity, that the song would work as a duet.

The rest, of course, is fizzy bitter pop music history: the infamous "yellow wine" video, *Nightline,* the fights over the boy with Iona Apple and Murielle Shocked, my bomb second single, the one I sang alone, my triumphant power-ballad comeback with the remixed version of "Crest-fallen," the flings with Tawnie and Nick Clexum, and the very public debacle of Thick Boy, as he was calling himself now, dissing me at the Grammys and walking out of the Maverick party with that bitch Jule.

I ran after him, out into the crowded plaza swarming with fans and media.

"Hey," I called out to him. "Are you sure you want it to end this way?"

He stopped in his tracks. Jule took him by the elbow, but he shook her off and took a couple of steps in my direction. "The way we started," he said, shaking his head, "I mean that was beautiful and real, but now you're all about glamour and gowns and shit. What do we have left?"

"We've got jasmine wine, baby, *jasmine wine.* We shared that. You've got to admit we shared that."

"Yeah," he said, touching the crotch of his Versace leathers. "But Jule knows that vintage, too." He winked at me, those cruel, cruel eyes. "We're going home now to uncork."

JOHN MASON SKIPP

All This and Heaven, Too

Omigod, omigod, omigod, JANEY? Are you awake? Are you busy? Do you have a minute? Yeah, I know it's late. I'm really sorry. But this is too wild. I've just gotta tell ya.

So . . . are the kids in bed? Are you alone? Are you sitting down? Do you have a drink and a vibrator handy? Good. Yeah, it's that *kind* of story. Ready?

You will not believe what just happened to me.

Well . . . okay. You know I'm out in Vegas, right? Exactly. The adult video trade show. It's like a *Star Trek* convention with boners: lots of bald sweaty men who've memorized every frame of every movie I was ever in, and they all wanna talk about it in great gushing detail while I sign their eight by tens. No, no, they're VERY sweet, and very respectful—well, at least they all TRY to keep from staring at my tits.

But you remember when I had that column in *High Society*? Right. I showed you some of those letters, especially the ones I got from prison. They all started out very respectfully: "Dear Ms. Brandy Anne Lace, you are the most beautiful and intelligent woman in adult films, and it is my dream that one day when I'm paroled, you and I could have a nice dinner together, just to talk." Right? And so the first three pages or so are about that—the sparkle of my eyes by candlelight, my warm understanding smile, the delicate curve of my breasts.

But if you flip ahead to page twelve, the writing's all in humungous caps, and it's like, "AND THEN I'M FUCKING YOU IN THE ASSHOLE, AND YOU ARE SCREAMING 'OH GOD, *MASTER ME*, PIGPEN! YES! YES! OH, YOU'RE THE BIGGEST AND THE BEST!!!' "

Ay-yi-yi. *Exactly!* Well, everybody needs a dream, ya know? But after ten hours of this in a live-action setting— I mean, the guys in prison probably have better sex lives than most of *these* boys—all I really wanted was to be alone. So I checked back into my room at the Hacienda, which is the best those cheap bastards at VCI would spring for.

But lemme tell you: I will never complain about those accommodations again. . . .

Okay! Okay! I *am* getting to the good part! Just gimme a minute!

Jeez!

So anyway, I'm fucking exhausted, so I throw off my clothes and jump in the shower; and it's right about this time that I get the unmistakable feeling that *I am being watched,* okay? Yeah. You know when it's happening. You can feel it on your skin.

So I start looking around for secret cameras, but the air by now is so thick with steam that I can barely see. So I figure, whatever. *I'm taking a shower.* Let 'em go blind trying to jack off to this . . . yeah, right! Just like the good Lord intended! Hee hee!

But after the shower, the feeling persists, and I start to get annoyed. So I slap on a towel, right? And I start searching around. But there's nothing. No hidden panels, no holes in the walls, and no windows. Just this feeling that won't go away.

So now I figure that I'm just being paranoid, chalk it up to the residual psychic buzz of being ogled for hours on end. I go back to the bed and slap on the TV, just to try and distract myself.

And what do you think was on pay-per-view? You're never gonna believe it: *Hot Bitches on Ice!* Exactly! The one where I fucked the ice sculpture! You *know* I've been dying to see that scene ever since I shot it, but I never got the chance.

So now I'm totally jazzed, so I decide to make it an event. I pop open a bottle of wine and get the candles out of my bag, light some incense, load a bowl, turn down the lights, stack the sex toys on the bed, and settle in for some fun.

The first scene I catch is a three-way between Joey, Ron, and this dizzy new bitch they call Lily White; and I'm like, oh, God, this is too funny. No, not just because it's Ron. Because the whole time I'm watching them, I can't stop thinking about this scene I heard about that recently went down, where Lily got tag teamed by Debbie and Jeanie, and they just went fucking nuts. They had this chick so fired up that she didn't know *what* was going down; and just as she was about to get off, Debbie took a piss right into her cunt, and Jeanie *lapped it up!*

NO, I'm not kidding! I'm totally serious! See, that's the thing about a lot of these new girls. They always have to prove how bad they are. Me, I'm still a sucker for a little romance, but—yeah. Exactly. Like swigging piss is the new frontier. *You go, girls.* That's all I've got to say.

So, anyway, in the midst of my hilarity, there's also this great sense of relief, because I know that my scene is coming up soon. And the anticipation is getting me more than a little horny, which is cool. So I pile up the pillows and settle back . . . sure, I can hold. Hurry back, okay?

Dum-dee-dum . . .

Okay. So that's your new boy on the side? I wanna hear all about it. But let me finish this first.

Yes, it's gonna get good! I mean, if I tell you that this was the *weirdest sex I've ever had in my life,* will you chill out a fucking second? Thank you very much.

So Lily finally fakes her orgasm, while the boys grunt and groan, and I am mercifully spared the cum shot via the miracle of soft-core editing . . . yeah, it pisses me off that they can't show cock, but the whole thing is so retarded anyway that I can't say I miss . . . right. You got it. The obligatory cream facial.

Anyway, the next thing I know, there I am on the screen, and I know that this is it. So I make sure the batteries are still in working order, put a dent in the wine, set some fire to the bowl, and bring a couple fingers down to warm my pussy up for action.

Mmmmmm. Just like that, exactly. Yeah.

When I close my eyes, I can see you doing it.

Now picture *this,* sweetie: On the screen, I walk into this room, and there's this glorious ice sculpture perched on this pedestal. The guy who did it is this amazing artist—he does these huge catered gigs at, like, the Beverly Hilton; we're talking *incredible* detail—and he had totally outdone himself with this thing, which is like a classic Greek statue: no head, arms, or legs. Just this incredibly cut torso—sorry, no pun intended—and this magnificent ten-inch glistening prick.

Well, I move in on this sculpture, embrace it from be-hind; and because it's already starting to melt a little, it slicks my blouse to my boobs, and I can see my nipples get hard through the translucent nippled chest of this amazing ice-stud. I remember how turned on I was by this scene, and I can see it in my eyes as I start to grind against it; and in the real world, all this is making me *totally* fucking hot.

So I'm starting to get into some serious clit action, and I think about grabbing Gigantor—you know, the Hitachi—but I decide to hold off for a while. It was one of those moments where I remember what guys must go through all the time, watching this shit . . . *you* know. Trying to hang in there for the cum shot, time everything just right?

Exactly. Like you're doing right now. So I slow down a little, while, on the TV, I'm ice-water licking my way around front. And just as I drop to my knees on the screen, I hear this INCREDIBLE MOAN; and it is, like, coming from *inches above my head.*

Well, YEAH, it freaked me out! The sound was so close that I could feel the breath behind it; and that breath was so fucking cold that it cut through the serious air conditioning I already had blasting in the room. It jerked me out of my heat so fast I almost forgot what my right hand was doing.

Then I looked up.

And you will not believe what I saw.

No, it wasn't Casper. But you're awfully goddamn close. And I know that you're not gonna believe me when I say this, but work with me, okay? 'Cuz it's the honest fucking truth.

There was this cock, and it was glowing blue, like a special effect in a half-assed monster move . . . no. It was just hovering in midair. Very erect. Definitely circumcised. Big veins hangin' out . . . no, not severed. Just your basic cock veins. No bloody stump. And no balls.

Just cock. And lots of it.

Attached to nothing at all.

Well, I stared at this thing for a couple of seconds. I blinked, just to see if it wouldn't go away. It didn't. Then I looked at the screen, to see if maybe the ice dick had burned itself onto my retinas somehow. But no. The two dicks were immensely dissimilar.

How? Well, for one thing, the ghost dick was way shorter—maybe seven inches, max—and just a little bit thicker. But both of them were, after all, glowing blue; and that was the only real basis for comparison I needed.

Then the ghost dick moaned again.

And this time, I saw its little mouth open. Just like any other cock. Except that this one had lips. And when it opened its mouth, I saw *little tiny teeth* against the teensiest little red tongue. . . .

No, I am not making this up.

So what do you *think* I did? I started LAUGHING MY ASS OFF, of course! Which was totally the wrong thing to do, but I just couldn't help it. I mean, I'm sitting there thinking, man, this is *incredibly good pot!*

And the next thing I know, the poor little baby is starting to wilt.

So suddenly I'm going "OH, NO!" and without even thinking, I reach up and grab it . . . you know, the way you'd grab *any* hard-on that starts to go away when you're not done playing with it yet . . . and suddenly, there's this wild kind of *electrical surge* running through me. I swear to God, it shuddered all the way down to my soul.

That's when I knew, without a doubt, that this was actually happening to me.

Next thing I know, I'm on my knees in front of this thing, just kind of stroking it reassuringly and going,

"Shhhh, it's okay," like I'm talking to some kind of frightened animal—yeah, *exactly;* like I'm talking to a man—and this little mouth is just taking these *deep, shuddering breaths* . . .

Well, this was the amazing thing. Right at that moment, on the TV screen, I start to go down on that glorious dripping hunk of ice. And Wesley's got it lit so well that it looks like it's glowing from within.

So the second I saw my lips sliding over the head, it's like, all hesitation was gone.

It wasn't just a matter of weird synchronicity, or life mirroring art, although I was tripping on all that. It was more a sense that this was so perfect—so undeniably not just right up my alley but unmistakably *meant to be*—that all I could do was go, "THANK YEW, JEESUS!"

So I leaned forward, opening my mouth, and went to lick the head of this dick, when this *little tongue comes out to meet me.* So there I am, French-kissing this penis that is floating in midair. And, yeah, I gotta say that I've never kissed a cock that could kiss me back before. It was SO MUCH FUN, I could not fuckin' stand it!

The next thing I know, he's at the back of my throat, and I am *goin' to town* on this boy: slurpin' and slidin' and tickling and nibbling and biting and slippin' and slidin' some more, letting my tongue trace the length of him down to that mouth and then back up the shaft to the root. And just when it occurs to me that he *has* no root, I feel balls on my chin, and there's an ass within my grasp.

I open my eyes and see shimmering thighs . . . yeah, and I'm a poet but I just don't know it . . . and the first twinkle of a ghostly belly button, like a half-moon on its back in an otherwise empty sky. There's no rib cage and no knees, but the middle is coming together just fine, and this ethereal penis is making wild animal noises straight down my esophagus.

Now you *know* how much I love to suck cock; and you know I've never seen another cock like this one. But at this point, all I can think about is, I want this thing to fuck me bad. So I roll it around in my mouth for a minute, just to let it know I really care. Then I pull it out. Look it straight in the eye.

And it screams at me, "DON'T STOP!"

I lick it. Twice. It goes, *"Ahhhh . . . ,"* and shudders.

"You're a ghost," I say.

"Don't stop," it begs.

"Don't worry," I say. "You couldn't stop me if you tried. I'd say I'll fuck you to death, but it's already too late. You are a ghost, right?"

The cock nods its head, and I say, "Maybe I'll fuck you back to life. . . ."

Mmmmmm. Thank you, sweetie. I love it when you talk dirty, too. . . .

So anyway, I roll over onto my back, grab my ghost by the ass cheeks, and start to slide him cock-first down the length of my body. On top of everything else, he is *totally weightless;* though, as I mentioned before, the cock had a nice girth. So it is enjoying the hell out of its trip: licking my neck, nibbling my nipples, moaning with pleasure, and dreaming of hands. I take my time around the thighs, teasing myself as much as him.

Then I slide him along my crease, without letting him in. He's, like, desperately chewing on my outer lips. When he gets to my clit, he's beside himself; and pretty soon, so am I. I do this until I can't stand it any longer.

Then I start working him inside me. Hard.

And the feeling is so astonishing—this pulsing energy,

synced to the pounding thrusts—that I start losing it almost at once, going over from here to orgasmic there, parting the veil 'cuz I'm coming so hard that it *really is* more than a little like dying. And I hear myself crying out. And I hear myself crying out on the TV. And I look back in wide-eyed desperation at me fucking on the screen, humping on the ice-dick while I'm slamming, slamming, slamming this fucker into me . . .

. . . and I feel knees spreading my legs wide, and I look up to see the glowing torso above me, a blue neon paunch below a featureless head . . .

. . . and suddenly, I feel the hands flipping me over, flipping me over onto my hands and knees, the thrusts coming harder now, coming from him while my back arches, ass rises, grinding back to meet him . . .

. . . when suddenly he slides all the way out of me; and the next thing I know, he is up my ass, and the transition is so smooth and powerful that I SCREAM, practically jamming my whole fist up my cunt, instantly and massively coming again as he hammers and grinds and electrically blinds me with churning pure cosmic fuck energy.

And I hear this howling, from deep in my bowels. It's the sound of his cock, howling up at my diaphragm. And the sound fills me as I come again, like wave after wave, come again and again, until it feels as though I *am* the sound: his and my sound, filling the air . . .

. . . until I realize that the air *is* filled with his sound, a second mouth howling above my head. I twist around, craning my neck to see my strange lover, this dead man who is doing this insane shit to me . . .

. . . and you know who he looks like, this god among men? He looks like George on fucking *Seinfeld*! Like Jason

Alexander, only blue. Like if there were middle-aged Smurf accountants, he would be one.

Do you get what I'm saying?

I'm saying that he was *the spitting image of the hundred thousand guys I'd been signing autographs for all day!* In fact, I'm absolutely certain he *was* one of those guys, by the fact that his gaze kept going back and forth between me and the TV screen. He had no hair. He had a paunchy little body, pudgy sissy-boy arms, and little beady dark eyes.

He was also giving me the fuck of my life.

It was then that I noticed the blowhole.

At first I thought it was a shadow, at the top of his head. But then I saw it yawning open, like a third wild screaming mouth. His glow was nearly blinding now; and as he shifted to pelvic overdrive, the air began to crackle. I started to REALLY, really come.

And that's when he came, too.

The first thing that happened was, his heart blew up. Blew straight out of his body. Blew up the TV. The explosion synced up great with the sound of the blowhole.

The blowhole was erupting all over the place.

I mean, this guy came like a whipped-cream cannon, firing gallon streams of ecto-jizz right straight out the top of his head. It hit the ceiling and *pooled* there, spreading in flat-out defiance of gravity. I watched the air turn blue, as well, and felt myself starting to leave my body.

Then I heard the voices of angels.

And the *real* orgasm began.

Swear to God, I felt this warm, astonishing light flood over me, into me, deeper than I even knew I went. It was like a vibrator that *really loves you,* applied to every single cell in your body. I felt like I was floating in perfect bliss, like I was losing myself and not minding a bit.

I saw the angels, then. Pure light. They had my spookster Romeo, and they were airlifting him to glory. He had the sweetest smile on his face, and he said "Thanks," gave me a little wave just before he vanished.

Then an angel was there, beside me. I told him I wanted to go, too.

He smiled and shook his head and said, "No. Go back. And keep on fucking like that, okay?"

Which was really a great thing to hear, especially from an angel. I gave him a kiss on the cheek, and he put his hand on mine.

"So there's really an afterlife," I said. Which was kind of dumb, under the circumstances. So he said yes, and— gossip whore that I am—I asked him for just a little taste of the juiciest afterlife dish. You know, just a little something to share with my friends, give them hope for a brighter tomorrow.

"Welllll . . . ," the angel said, with no slight hesitation. "I guess the biggest buzz right now is: Every year, the ghost of Elvis has to go down on Michael Jackson, as part of an evil wedding anniversary ritual."

"Oh, you're kidding!" I said.

"No, I'm SERIOUS!" said the angel. "And the *weird* thing is, Michael Jackson's been without a dick for over seven years."

"No!"

"Yes! You know what he's got? A surgically constructed perfect replica of DIANA ROSS'S PUSSY!!!"

YES!!! Isn't that just the cat's pajamas?

I was so happy, I almost cried.

So anyway, that was all I needed to know. There is a

God, and It really *does* care! I said I could go back to earth again. The angel gave me a great big hug and didn't even cop a feel. Then he said, "Remember what I told you."

And the next thing I knew, I was back in the room.

So how do I feel? Real goddamn good about myself! I guess it's pretty gratifying to know that you *really can* make a dead man come, not to mention fucking him so good he really *has* died and gone to Heaven!

And, ya know, it's really making me think twice about my fans. I mean, if a quarter of them were *half* that much fun, I might never walk again!

So does this mean that I'm going to start fucking nothing but nebbishy guys from now on . . . ? Right! *Exactly!* ONLY AFTER THEY'RE DEAD!!!

DONALD RAWLEY
Mother of Pearl

Los Angeles is bursting with bad men named Hector, Felice, and Paco, with eyes like a glass of Kahlua and sharp teeth. They have tattoos of mermaids and crossed knives above the word "MIEDO," and their arms are muscular and scarred.

They are men at fifteen, corrupt at eighteen, sometimes dead at twenty. They have moist lips and a way of walking that clears sidewalks. They are perfumed with Jockey Club and Aramis, and they hold the scent of limping women on their fists.

And they'll hustle you out of everything you've got. Because Los Angeles is a town built by hustlers, for hustlers, and left in wills to hustlers, bad men with loins so stiff they have to dance and fight to keep them down. When they finish with you, whatever room you might be left in reeks of them, whatever room you're crawling out of with wobbly legs from too much sex and a dry throat that won't disappear.

They like fast cars, late nights, guns, and knives. Girls named Suzy who swallow, with fishnet stockings and a real American accent. Sometimes they'll want a man who's got money, who's debauched enough to do as they say. And sometimes they want a kiss that lingers.

I cannot give any of these things. I am forty-five, a pretty young man who faded in middle age. Now I am poor, shy, and lonely, living in a small single apartment with a view of an alley. The doctor tells me there is a shadow on my lung. How I've wanted a strong man to wrap his arms around my skinny shoulders until I can't breathe. How I've wanted his come to shimmer on my chest, every slow thrust an innuendo and a trance. How I've wanted him to promise me his soul.

But I have nothing to trade. Watching the bad men strut like parrots with their wings clipped, I know nothing comes for free. Something is taken. As I see their heads crooked for sex, I say never for me. No, not ever for me.

I am taken to a welterweight fight in East Los Angeles, past an overgrown park and a graveyard where hibiscus is growing out of graves. It is in an ancient two-story warehouse. Felice Garcia versus Angel Jesus del Toro. Past Cuban cigar smoke and grime, past men with gardenia oil in their hair and dirty white polyester suits, I see Felice Garcia on his stool, his mouthguard in place. He's staring right at me. His eyes are a sable brown, and I cannot catch my breath. He is too beautiful, too young, too pure for me.

His arms are very muscular and there is a small tuft of black hair on his chest. He smiles at me, in the second row, scratches his nipple and wipes the sweat on his purple satin shorts. He shifts his legs as he thinks I might be able to see up his shorts. I cannot, but I pretend I can.

My friend Henry hands me a paper cup with bourbon in it. I hand it back.

"I don't drink," I say quietly, not taking my eyes off Felice.

"What DO you do?" Henry asks with a leer. "You into Mexican food? You into big hot burritos?"

I turn and look at Henry. He is seventy-five and obese, with pink skin and a penchant for ex-cons. One shot at him and missed, another stole all his furniture. Someday, I know, he will be murdered. He's dancing toward it with glee, and he frightens me.

I am ashamed to be here. I am too effeminate for this crowd and I have to guard my gestures, make sure I don't cross my legs the wrong way. Straight men generally sit at games with their legs spread and shoulders slightly hunched, as if they're sitting on the toilet. This is the posture I assume.

Angel, with a pug's face, a crewcut and bullet hole eyes, walks proudly into the ring, holding up his arms. The crowd applauds. Over an echoing loudspeaker an announcer, speaking in a velvety, rapid Spanish, introduces the fighters and the bell rings.

"If you want to see real blood," Henry says to me, "in two hours there's a cockfight. Two mean fucking roosters. You've never seen anything like it."

"Why do you think I want to see that?" I ask, annoyed. Henry shrugs.

"Because you like danger," he shouts over the roar of the audience.

"No, I don't," I say to myself, watching Angel Jesus del Toro hit Felice so hard blood trickles out of his mouth and slides over his nipples, some of it getting caught in his chest hair.

Felice must be about nineteen, I reason. I like how his thick hair shakes as he does the boxer's hop. And how his muscles are tense and lean.

The crowd begins screaming invectives at Felice in English, then in Spanish. Two middle-aged women behind me are in a rage over Felice. They sound like bluejays fighting, cawing in a Castilian lisp.

"No. I'm sorry, but I don't like this at all," I say as loudly as possible to Henry, who glares at me and turns his attention back to the fight. I know this is the end of our friendship, which was a minor one at best. I get up to leave, but at this moment Angel punches Felice with such ferocity the oil from his hair flies on my face. I am suddenly flushed, my eyes bright.

It is the most singularly exciting sensation I have felt in ten years. I run my hands along my face, and watch Felice, who, as he crumples to the floor, smiles at me and closes his eyes.

"You took quite a punch," I murmur soothingly as Felice comes to on a rickety cot. It is close to midnight. I have waited in this dim room for four hours. Felice had been thrown in here after the fight, then just a few minutes ago, an ancient Mexican with no teeth and an Elvis Presley toupee threw water on Felice and broke an amyl nitrite ampule under his nose.

The boxing hall is empty, as is the old warehouse. Elvis Presley nods to me as if to say, "I'm leaving now, *maricón*. You take care of the bastard. You lock up."

Felice has been stripped out of his purple boxer shorts. He is wearing a red jockstrap. I'm amused. I wonder if he keeps leopard skin bikini briefs at home.

"You. Come out of the shadows. I can't see you." His voice is deeper than I imagined.

I am not sure if I should walk into the light of the bare bulb in this makeshift locker room. He will see that my hair is falling out, that I am thin, white skinned. A stutterer, a whisperer. Ready to be picked over. Like a corpse in the desert.

I walk into the light. Felice's pubic hair is flaying out of his jock strap. He wiggles his feet and smiles.

"What lonely eyes you got, baby." He wipes some dried blood away from his ear with a curious expression, then wipes it on his cot.

"Where did you learn English?" I ask.

"El Paso, Texas. I saw your lonely eyes. You're bad for Felice."

"I should go. I was worried," I say quietly.

"But they're pretty eyes, baby." Felice tries to yawn, but it hurts. "Oh shit, that dog fucker hurt me. Son of a bitch has no dick, thinks he's a big man like me."

Felice looks at me with a satisfied smile.

"You want Felice, don't you baby? Felice is expensive." He gets up stiffly, in a sore heave.

He stands in front of me. He is exactly my height, but he seems so much taller.

"What time is it?" he asks, touching my cheekbone. His hand is thick, almost rubbery. I look at my watch.

"Ten minutes to midnight."

"Jesus, you stay here all that time for me? You must *really* want Felice."

I realize now I have gone too far. I should sink back into the shadows, find the door leading out with the back of my hand. I should find my friends, others with shadows on their lungs and broken hearts. I should try driving at night, to no place at all, with my doors locked and my windows rolled up.

• • •

"What's your name?" Felice asks, running a finger along my chin.

"My name is Claude."

"You French?" Felice asks, cocking his head.

"No."

Felice shakes his grogginess off and gestures toward a filthy sink.

"Take that towel, wet it. You rub the blood off me. Okay? You're my new friend, right?"

"Right," I say.

As I rub his shoulders and chest the lightbulb flickers above us.

"You take me out for tequila tonight, okay? And hamburgers. Loser don't pay, loser never pays. I saw you got a watch. I lost my watch."

"It's a cheap watch," I murmur. Felice grabs my arm and looks at it, then takes it off my arm and puts it on his.

"It tells time. You got some money for Felice?" His voice is reptilian.

I stop rubbing his chest and look into his eyes. His eyebrows are spiky and black. One eye is beginning to swell up.

"No, Felice, you probably have more money than me."

"You old whore! *Viejo puto!*" He coughs, spits some saliva and blood into a tin can. "Okay, I pay for tequila and hamburgers, but you do as I say. Later, you make Felice come. Okay?"

I nod my head slowly. I don't know what to say, and I start rubbing his chest again. I imagine Angel is with his manager and his girlfriend, plump, with teased red hair. Angel Jesus del Toro won't remember Felice Garcia tomorrow morning.

•   •   •

"Where are you from?" I ask. My questions sound high pitched, like a nervous woman. One loser confiding in another.

Felice doesn't mind the question. He smiles at me, then closes his eyes and licks his upper lip.

"I was born in a corral in Tecate and walked to Acapulco when I was ten. Open those doors." I walk over to a set of heavy, industrial cast-iron double doors and open them. They swing out to a second-floor fire escape.

Below us several Cadillacs and El Caminos are parked near a liquor store called "El Bambino." I can hear salsa playing from not one boombox, but two or three. Same song and station. I can see a crescent moon, peach colored in the dank Los Angeles night, and a sky punctured by stars.

"What are you looking at? Get back here, lonely eyes."

I turn and walk back to Felice, who looks at me coolly. I begin rubbing him. He wants to talk.

"There was old men and young boys like me, little baby horses. I was the most popular. I stay at the El Presidente, at Las Brisas with the guys. There were coins to dive for. There were old gringos with white shoes and flowers on their shirts, big wallets. There was a boat, I know, ready to take me away."

"To Hollywood?" I ask archly.

"Yeh, baby, Hollywood. But first El Paso, Dallas, then Ensenada. Yeh, Felice *es muy popular*. Going to be a movie star." He laughs.

I suddenly imagine Felice in a tourist villa at the top of Las Brisas, twelve or thirteen years old, hair just beginning to grow under his arms, holding a candy cane from Christmas. He's sucking it carefully in the Mexican sun until it's a sharpened spike, then puts it in his jeans for later.

I see him dive naked into a tiny round pool as baby cockatiels test their wings and banana leaves quiver.

"You gonna finish me?" Felice asks, grabbing the towel away from me. "You dreaming, huh, lonely eyes?"

I step away from Felice and stare at him in silence. I am too frightened to say anything foolish.

Felice is built like an attack dog. When he moves he crunches his shoulders like a wrestler, little man with big balls. I bet he comes all day and dances all night, snapping his fingers at waiters and pimps. And I cannot stay away.

Looking at Felice and seeing bruises suddenly appearing on his hips and shoulders and arms, I want to kiss him. I realize I am the imprint on a shroud, my face's oil and sewn lips only leave a hard metal mark for Felice to decipher.

Felice balances himself as he stands up and stretches, then pulls his jockstrap down, kicking it off with one foot. Lazily he knocks the lightbulb and it swings on its cord.

"You like Felice? You like big Felice?"

I nod my head. He walks over to his cotton pants and takes a penknife out of his pocket. I lower my head. So this is the trade. A watch for a knife. A blowjob for a stab wound. I become frightened.

"Don't back away. Touch it. Touch my knife."

Felice ambles up to me. I can feel his penis against my leg. His knife has a mother-of-pearl handle and it is warm in his hand, in front of my face, doubled up like a fetus, its handle glowing dully. I can smell Felice, and it is overpowering, like sewage and rose water and heavy fog.

A mambo is drifting up from the street. Felice clicks the blade out and rubs the handle slowly on his chest to make it shine, then tests with his thumb the serrated edge of the blade. Then lightly rolls it on my neck, my chest. He cuts two buttons off my shirt and whispers in my ear.

"I cleaned abalone in Ensenada with this knife, faster than anybody. You gut it, one cut and it flips on this big wood table. Then it doubles up, no noise. Just like a heart. Just like loving me, lonely eyes. No noise. Like a fish out of water that dies, when rainbow comes up on its scales. I washed a thousand shells in river water, sugar, and sun. The mother of pearl rises, shining like your eyes, old man."

I realize there are tears in my eyes. If this is my last embrace, then I will fall into it. Felice raises and cuts off a lock of his hair. He throws his knife at a cork bulletin board, empty of bulletins, where it sticks. I feel like I'm going to pass out. Felice takes my waist with a swollen hand; with his other hand he throws his hair on my face and shoulders like confetti, laughing.

"Now you belong to Felice. You never leave."

The mambo from the street has gotten louder, rapider. It's Tito Puente and Celia Cruz. It's playing from open windows in crowded apartments where the smell of *mole* sauce drifts past the palm trees and stars that dot my peripheries like talismans. Felice's cock is pressing against me like a mariachi's golden guitar, pulsing like a high tide. Like a winded sunset in the desert. Like a heart.

"You like to dance? Felice will teach you how to dance, *el baile,* baby." I see how welts are rising on his head and neck. Such black curly hair he's grown to make him a man.

A vein leads from his loins to his hard belly. Next to it there is a li'l devil tattoo with a baby's ass and a tail, pitchfork, and smirk.

Felice undresses me and it dawns on me that I am naked too, old, unkempt. I cannot decipher what will happen, but I tenderly put my hands around Felice. I am careful not to touch his bruises, but he still winces in pain.

"You wrinkled old man," Felice says, breathing heavily. We are pressed together, moving our hips slowly, and I know Felice does not see my sad little chest, my scrawny legs. I put my hands further down, around his buttocks, and look up into his eyes.

It is midnight and I am not poor and sick and old anymore. I am moaning. Felice is listening, his teeth clicking like a rattlesnake, and his hair is still on my skin.

"See, lonely eyes, when you dance, *en el baile,* you got to hold the girl close. Like this."

MARY ANNE MOHANRAJ
Fleeing Gods

Helena struggled out of sleep, blinking her eyes hazily against the darkened room. It had been a most vivid dream. Since she'd left her spineless husband and the regular supply of dull sex, she'd often had erotic dreams. Somehow none had been quite this . . . explicit. A tongue had licked her instep, her toes. Teeth had nibbled on her calves. She had almost been able to feel the muscled body, the sensuous hands caressing her thighs, her hips. She could almost hear his heavy panting and smell his strong breath.

Actually, she could still smell that strong breath, that unmistakable mixture of strong spirits and poor oral hygiene. There was a strong scent of aroused male in the room. Helena suddenly sat up and switched on her halogen lamp, ready to grab it and crack it on the skull of any would-be rapist.

As the light flooded the room, an immense man reared up on the bed and away from her, raising a hairy arm to block his eyes from the light.

"Shut that off, wench! You'll ruin the mood!"

Wench? What kind of man calls a woman wench? Helena relaxed a little, still retaining her firm grip on the lamp, and peered at the impressive stranger in her bedroom.

"What are you doing here?" she asked him, quite calmly, she thought.

"Seducing you!" he thundered. "What does it look like I'm doing?" He lowered his arm a bit, piercing blue eyes blinking in the light like those of a dazed deer. Helena stared intently at him, hungrily drinking in the obvious strength in those arms, that chest. The man was positively bristling with hair, and muscles bulged under the thick brown coat. Something else bulged too, an enormous penis that stood out proudly from his naked body. Helena had been married for seven years, and bar-hopping for three, but she had never seen anything to match this before. She licked her lips.

He blinked at her, looking a little confused. Then he seemed to gather himself together. He started shouting again.

"Fear not, fair maiden. I am the greatest of lovers, renowned in seven kingdoms and across seventy seas. No harm will come to thee!"

Helena winced at the volume. "Could you lower your voice a little?" she asked, as she started to shift her body, preparatory to sitting up. The man immediately flung himself down on her, pinning her to the bed. Helena just lay there, enjoying the weight of his body on hers, the teasing scritch of curly chest hair against her nipples.

"My apologies, maiden, but I cannot have you turning into a fawn or a swan, or trying to run away," he said, in a voice slightly softer than before.

A fawn? A swan? A strange suspicion started dancing through Helena's head. "Just what did you say your name was?" she asked him.

The man's chest swelled proudly, incidentally crushing her breasts beneath it. "I am Zeus, ruler of Olympus, seducer of maidens, wielder of the thunderbolt . . . and you shall not escape me!"

"Why would I want to?" Helena practically cooed, as she laced her arms around his thick neck. That would explain how he got into her locked bedroom, the odd dream she'd been having . . . it would explain a lot of things. She began rubbing her naked body against his, maneuvering so that he could slide that gorgeous tool into the place where it belonged.

"What?" he said. His voice suddenly seemed much less like massive thundering and more like a pitiful squeak. He held his body very stiff as he stared down at her. While stiff was good in some ways, his stillness was somewhat of a problem now, as she couldn't get to quite the position she needed. "Are you not afraid of me? Will you not shift your form into a thousand others so as to escape? Will you not turn into a tree, a pebble, a breath of breeze?"

"Honey, I can't shift my form into even one other," Helena replied. She raked her nails along his back and writhed her body underneath his, hoping to stimulate a response. His response wasn't quite what she expected.

"But it is simple. Even the shepherd maids of Greece knew how. Let me show you," he said. And with that, she felt an odd sort of twist in her brain, strange enough to make her pause a second in her feverish groping. Suddenly she knew how to change forms, how to become a thousand creatures of wind and flesh and earth. Zeus smiled in triumph above her. "Now, will you run?" he asked.

"Mmm . . . I don't think so," Helena said. With that, she used her newfound knowledge to stretch her body, adding several inches to her height, and not so incidentally enabling her to finally slip that stiff penis inside her dripping cunt. Helena gasped then, and bit down on his rock-hard shoulder. She started to slide back and forth, almost gnawing on his skin as she did so.

"But they always run," Zeus said. He sounded dismayed. "I cannot believe women have changed so in the mere millennia that Hera and I spent traveling . . . surely you are unnatural, a freak?"

Helena kept moving as she replied, "Well, my appetite's maybe a bit bigger than most women's, but I think I'm pretty typical nowadays." Suddenly, that feeling of delicious fullness started to disappear. Helena looked up in sudden suspicion. "Hey, if you're a god, surely you can keep it up?"

Zeus started to pull himself away. "You are a hellish imitation of a true woman. I will go and find a more feminine being in whom to spend my heavenly seed. You cannot expect me to perform with a creature as unwomanly as yourself. It would be . . . unnatural!"

Helena suddenly clung even harder, wrapping her long (extremely long) legs around his muscular form. "Not so fast, boy. You look to be the best lay I've had in a long time." Helena's mind continued the sentence: *with potentially infinite endurance.* "You're not getting away until I get what you promised earlier. And not until I get it several times."

Zeus moaned in dismay and suddenly changed himself into a porcupine. But Helena changed her skin into an odd fur and stuck to him like Velcro. He wailed in horror and changed himself into a lightning bolt. But she changed into a storm and blew out all the windows as she surrounded him. Zeus moaned as he turned into a waterfall, pouring out of her forty-seventh-floor windows. But she turned into a river right below him and engulfed his sweet essence. It was then that he really started to run.

Helena chased him down the highway, causing the early morning traffic jams to become early morning wrecking sites, as the heavenly dawn filled the sky. Irate businessmen in suits leaning out their car windows could hear a male voice, whimpering on the wind as the pair disappeared over the horizon. It was clearly calling, "Hera? Saaaaaaaave meeeeeeeee . . . !" The ones who listened carefully even heard a soft chuckle of what might have been goddess laughter as they hurriedly pulled their heads back inside and quickly rolled up the windows.

TSAURAH LITZKY

The Balm That Heals

Windy, too cold for a November day, and I am on my way to the subway home with my chin tucked into the neck of my jean jacket. I am looking down for some epiphany in the street like a message scratched into the concrete—*you are not alone*—but all I see are feet preceding me, feet on either side. It is rush hour and as I turn the corner of Sixth Avenue I bump into a knot of people that stops me short, forcing me to look up and around. A tall, morose-looking woman in a green down coat is standing behind a card table set up in front of the Dalton's bookstore, the table is loaded with pamphlets, and next to it is this larger-than-life stand-up figure of a naked *Playboy*-type babe with huge round breasts like honeydew melons; that honey would do me fine, I think. The nipples are covered with masking tape and across the genitals a sign is taped that says, "This exploits women." I make my way through the little crowd in front of the table and go down the steps into the subway, but now I have the vision of those wonderful breasts in my head. Standing up squashed in the subway car between two women both reading Sidney Sheldon's *Nothing Lasts Forever* I think about how I wanted to tear the masking tape off the nipples of those breasts and suck them, but of course I knew she was only a cardboard figure. I wish Michael and I were still together because if we were I would put tape over his nipples and then lead him to the bed, lie him down, tuck his cock between his legs to make a pretend vulva, and tie his legs up at the ankles with the black leather belt he uses to hold up his jeans, then I'd get my makeup case and make him up to be the belle of the ball—Chinese-red lipstick, black eyeliner, blue eye shadow to match his sky blue eyes, lots of blusher—then I would make love to him, I'd rip the tape off his nipples, and suck them till he screams. This pleasing fantasy gets me through the subway ride home to Brooklyn, my cunt gets wet, and I almost come right there holding onto the pole between the reading women, I wonder if they can smell me.

Once inside my apartment I kick off my shoes, throw my jacket on the floor, get the bottle of scotch out of the cabinet, and pour myself a big slug. I need some magic, maybe a genie to appear in my life, a genie who can dance the tango, but the genie that pops out of the glass looks just like Michael, it's been six months since he split and I am nowhere near over him, I am afraid I will never meet anyone else who knows all my codes. The scotch has stoked the constant itch between my legs and I think about getting my new pink vibrator or maybe I should do yoga, but another scotch is in order before I decide, and as I am pouring it the phone rings. It is Jane West inviting me to a party Saturday night because it is her 40th birthday. She says she is feeling kind of down, 40 years old and still going through life alone, I try to reassure her that someone will soon turn up, but I am talking through my hat and she knows it. I get off the phone and get the vibrator from its honored place beneath my pillow, I must have washed the sheets 50 times since Michael left, but his smell is still on them, if only he would stop haunting me, if only I could heal myself, free myself from his memory, I switch my vibrator on, but three orgasms later I can still feel Michael's hands on me.

As the week progresses I write three poems about lost love, my funk lifts somewhat, and I find myself looking forward to the party, it's been so long since I've had a chance to strut my stuff. On Saturday night I make up carefully, put a false beauty mark under my eye, make my brows dark and thick like Frida Kahlo's. I choose a long, tight, red velvet thrift-store dress that shows off my big firm ass. I stop at the liquor store and buy the starving artists' requisite bottle of acceptable cheap red wine, I used to make chili, potato salad, bake cakes for parties, but I cannot remember when I last had the time. I wonder if the approaching millennium will be ruled by convenience, compromise, complicity, or will it be pure anarchy, I would prefer anarchy because it would be easier to sneak away into my own countries of lunatic illusion, but who knows.

The downstairs door is ajar, and as I walk the four flights up to Jane's, the sounds of laughter and talk and the Counting Crows singing "Mr. Jones" reach out to me, my excitement mounts, and I climb faster. Jane's big one-room studio is crowded, full of smoke, someone is blowing weed, and a half-dozen people are dancing. My eye is caught by a short, wiry guy in a tuxedo and a '50s vintage gray fedora, he sees me too but I am too shy to smile. Genia waves hello and there is Hal and there is Sasha who tried to soul-kiss me one time at the bar. Jane paints cats and her big cat paintings cover the wall, I look around for her and finally see her talking with two very young men holding skateboards, they look maybe 15, when I go over Jane introduces them as Joe and Joel, Joe is very cute and I tell him I wish I were 20 years younger and he blushes. Jane looks a bit piqued and I wonder if maybe I have stolen her thunder and she had some plans for this Joe. I want to make her smile, so I tell her she looks beautiful in her black cat suit—it is the truth. She takes my wine, thanks me, goes to hang up my coat. I move to the food table, take up a chip, aim it for the babaganoush, but my hand halts in midair when suddenly out of the side of my eye I see Michael seated on a couch in the corner of the room with a woman who has such large tits she reminds me of the cardboard figure. I am a 32A. They are looking into each other's eyes and he has his hand on her knee. The bile rises up in me and I get so filled with jealousy and rage that I cannot see. When my eyes clear I find I am grasping the big bowl of salsa, have lifted it several inches off the table, and I probably would have hurled it right at them if I hadn't been saved by three women I did not know who came up to me just then to tell me how much they liked my erotic stories and inadvertently pinned me against the table. They talked at me for a while and when they moved away Michael and his companion were no longer sitting on the couch. I looked around the room and was relieved not to see them. Someone jostled against my arm and I turn to find a tall, blonde man looking down at me, his hair is way down his back and he has a handsome, equine face, a full mouth, those big lips could gobble me up, I think, and maybe he is reading my mind because he says, "I know it's not cool to say this, but nothing excites me as much as a sexy woman in a red dress." I tell him, "Thank you, I don't care about being cool, I like hot best," and then he asks me why I am not drinking wine and gets me some and an hour later finds us sitting on the same sofa on which Michael and his companion had been sitting, but this man whose name is Steven now has his hand on my knee and he is gazing into my eyes and telling me about his leather sculptures, as he is talking he gently takes my hand and holds it palm up to the front of his silk trousers, I can feel how strongly he is attracted to me and I am impressed, then we kiss and I know right away I want to give him what I've got. As we are kissing I see over his shoulder that Michael is standing in the middle of the room looking at us. *Stick it in your ear,* I think as Steven and I break our kiss, he tells me he wants to show me his work, and when I say when he says right now and I say why not and we rise as one from the couch and move through the room to find our coats. We look for Jane to say goodbye but find her engrossed, kissing Joe in the kitchen, and we do not disturb them. Walking the few blocks to Steven's loft we are quiet, what is there to say; do you read poetry, isn't it a lovely night, I want you inside me, please don't hurt me—it's best to keep silent. We take the freight elevator up to his floor, in the hall outside his door he fumbles with the key, I wonder if he is as nervous as I am. Once inside the door, to reassure him of my interest, I grab him, put my arms around him, stroke his tight, hard, small ass, if he is surprised he does not show it, nor does he appear startled when I step back and undo the buttons of his fly, and when I put my hand inside there is no restraining underwear and he is already there to greet me. I cup his swollen cock in my hand and gently squeeze and release it, squeeze and release it until he throws back his head and moans, then he seizes me by the wrist, extracts my hand, pulls me to him, and kisses me until my panties are wet and my thighs tremble, then he buttons his pants back up and switches on the light. We are in a huge white room, one whole side is windows, there is an efficiency kitchen along one wall, a loft bed, several workbenches piled with tools, about thirty high platforms stand spread out in the center of the room, each draped in white muslin. Steven walks around pulling the muslin sheets off, on each platform rests a black leather mask or belt, a vest, codpiece, crown, corset, or gauntlet. The leather is exquisitely stitched together and studded, they could have been insect parts, but they look more like armor for a futuristic horde of sex warriors. *I love it,* I say, and he says *good,* as I move across the room to stand beside him I have the sense that my life has changed and I am entering a brave new world. He leads me to one of the pedestals, on it is a black leather corset with many tiny, silver hooks in front, a thick, leather strap is buckled from front to back to pass between the legs. Steven lifts it off the pedestal, holds it out to me, *I'd like you to wear this,* he says. I take it from him, go into the bathroom, strip and put the corset on, it pushes my tits high up and they poke out in front of me like an offering, the edge of the leather strap feels cool and sharp, it chafes between my legs yet I do not mind. I pile my clothes on a hamper, leave on my black suede high heels, when I step back into the room he is naked except for a black leather mask with crescent-shaped holes for his eyes that covers the top half of his face. He is fully erect and his pride bobs and sways in front of him as he bends over a table made from a bedspring and milk crates covered with glass. I join him there and see a spoonful of fine white powder on the glass table top, I watch as he shapes the powder into four neat rows with a butter knife. We use a straw to each do up a row, then he takes a little of the blow and dabs it on one of my nipples, he sucks and nibbles there until I am chirping like a bird, I grab his rigid cock, it is as hard as wood, and I pull on it again, this time not so gently, he swells so much I cannot contain him in my hand, then I go for his big nuts and milk them until his head rolls back on his neck and he sighs with pure pleasure *OOOOh,* but when I start to trace my fingers up his back he stops me, lifts me, and lays me out flat on the table, he positions me, arms up and out to the side, legs spread wide, I am happy to be his big butterfly. He unbuckles the leather strap between my legs and bends his head and licks me back to front, back to front, he tongues my clit until I want to die with him, then he stands, tapping his cock up and down on my ready mouth, I want to run my tongue round and round the tip, I want to hold him in my mouth and suck him down into my esophagus, into my heart, into my belly, but he does not let me; instead he steps back. "What a pretty picture," he says, then he takes that big cock in his hand and holds it just above my hungry love hole and a clear liquid begins to flow out in a steady jet onto me, at first I think I have never seen such clear sperm, then I realize it is pee bathing me, it is more than a little warm but not too hot, just right, it feels so good, maybe, I think, this is the way amniotic fluid feels, maybe at last I have found the balm that heals.

MICHAEL BRONSKI

Doctor Fell

OCTOBER 5, 1995

Made notes on "Flesh and the Word" essay. Nothing feels right. I have no idea of what tone to strike—lurid, medical, religious, psychological, confessional? The whole thing makes me uneasy. It should be simple: for six years in several relationships part of my sex play with my partners was that we cut each other with razors, scalpels, X-Acto blades. Sometimes we did temporary piercing with needles—usually to draw blood. No big deal. Assume an honest tone and simply describe the experiences. Mention the potent sexual stimulation. Leave out the drugs (you wouldn't want to give cutting and blood sports a bad name).

OCTOBER 17, 1995

Essay going nowhere. Realize the problem is that it is supposed to be sexy. The actual experiences were sexy, but how do you convince readers who may well be appalled by the very idea? On the other hand, everyone likes gory movies, slasher films where sex and anxiety are bound together and released in the oozing and splattering of red fluid. The problem with writing about cutting and blood is that nothing much happens: cut and bleed. No thrashing legs, pulsating cocks. It is not the stuff of pornography but of dreams and unreason; the fairy tale, fearful myth; the elliptical spaces left unarticulated.

> *I do not like thee, Doctor Fell,*
> *The reason why I cannot tell;*
> *But this I know and know full well,*
> *I do not like thee, Doctor Fell.*

I've always loved this nursery rhyme. It resonates with dread, which is so often sexual. Odd that the man—Jim—who introduced me to cutting, whose scars I still carry and who died more than a decade ago (with the scars he carried from me), was a doctor and a Vietnam vet. Sometimes on acid he would remember the horrors of battlefield surgery and cry and praise me for having protested the war. And then we would cut each other. I would try not to cry because this was *his* time, his way of finally gaining control. He was not simply transferring the bloodied flesh of men from the battlefield into his living room, but shedding the shame and humiliation that were the constant companions to his sexuality when he was in Vietnam: he was making his desire real, palpable. The intensity was suffocating; heart-binding. "Do you trust me?" he would ask. "Do you trust me?"

The question felt superfluous. Trust, like love, is diminished when articulated. Fear, like love, can vanish when examined. The cutting and the gradual flow of blood—first a trickle, then a tributary; never more than that—was a physical and emotional release. And it was so sexy, so *driven:* I have a hard-on writing this. The fifteen years between then and now slip away, I can feel my heart beat, place my hand on the breastbone: a tattoo, a pulse: blood, blood, blood. I still love thee, Dr. Fell, the reason why I cannot tell, or even remember clearly, but I remember those long nights with hot black tea laced with bourbon, lemon, and MDA, and the almost unimaginable intimacy of scalpel to skin, of steady hand to willing flesh.

Essay (part one)

The living room in Jim's South End apartment is dark, candlelit. A hard music beat on low volume comes from the radio. It is 3 A.M. We came home from the Ramrod twenty minutes ago, high on energy, cruising, MDA, a little acid, and each other. We've been going out for four months. Walta, my lover of six years, is at home; Jim is my other life, my nondomestic dark side, where the wild things are. At home I feel loved and secure, bookish, smart, even respected. Here I feel beautiful, desired, wanted, needed. I am no longer the friendless high school kid jerking off thinking about juvenile delinquents and hoods, James Dean and the wild ones with their antisocial attitudes and slicked-back hair. In Jim's eyes I become someone who lives in the world, lives in my body. With Jim I move through the bar like I should be there, like *we* should be there. Ripped dirty jeans, T-shirts, leather jackets: these were the uniforms of the rebels of my youth. I have become my childhood dreams. I have become the men I feared.

We are alone. The room is hot, the heat turned up against the winter outside. On the far wall, above a low, long chest, is a mirror—seven feet by seven feet—that dominates and enlarges the room. We move the candles in front of it and the cavelike room becomes magical. We make tea and carefully doctor it with sweet bourbon and sugar to mask the bitterness of more MDA.

We talk and laugh about someone at the bar, my arm around Jim, his hand under my shirt. We kiss and allow ourselves the pleasures of small movements, affectionate gestures. I feel myself both leaving my body and entering it. Like a transformed beast in a fairy tale, I can feel my flesh changing around me—it is a body I like, that I want to touch, that feels right. Jim's hand is on my nipples; my hand is in his pants, kneading his cock through the jock-strap, feeling the foreskin shift and move with my fingers.

We kiss again and Jim gets up to piss. I begin to re-arrange the room, moving candles away from the mirror, adjusting the music to increase the volume and lower the bass, and take the scalpels from where they reside, hidden deep in the drawers of the antique captain's desk. The in-struments are meant for healing. In my heightened con-sciousness I think about the "art of healing"—a derisive term Jim uses to blaspheme and dismiss his experience in Vietnam.

Jim comes from the bathroom as I turn on the crane's-neck lamp and focus its 150-watt bulb on the mirror. The effect is mesmerizing; the intense illumination seems to ra-diate heat as well as light. The reflected room has become a stage on which we are to perform as actors playing our-selves, fantasy projections who are both us and not us. Jim has taken off his shirt and jeans. He wears only boots, socks, and his jockstrap; his six-foot-five-inch body—long sinewy arms, flattish ass, slight potbelly, shaved head—moves in and out of the mirrored light.

I remove my shirt, pants, boots and cast them into the

corner. Jim opens a sterile package. The plastic crinkles; my body responds. I stretch my arms. I've done this before. You have to get the blood moving through the skin, bring it to the surface. I run my hands over my pectorals, down my thighs, play with my nipples, watch my body in the mirror. I am beautiful, I think. Who is this person? Not me, surely not me. Not as I know myself in the real world, the world of books and politics.

I stand in front of the mirror and inhabit the warmth from within and without. I run my fingers through my long hair and throw my head back—half Garbo in *Camille,* half Brando in *Streetcar*—and feel Jim's hand roam my chest as he chooses where to cut. I reposition my head and, staring at the body in the mirror—my body— watch as Jim makes feathery cuts around my nipples. I flex my pectorals. Pink lines form on my upper chest—Tina Turner chants "What's Love Got to Do With It?" in my subconscious, or on the radio, I'm not sure which—the pink turns rose, then vermilion, then crimson as it gathers and trickles, eddies and flows. I flex and breathe deep, stretch my arms above my head, savoring the pull of muscle and the tightness of skin. But most of all I watch. Watch as the blood—my blood—begins to run down my chest, glistening and gesticulating with a life of its own. This is who I am, I think. This is my body. Jim whispers in my ear, "Look at it look at it I love you look at it." I am in my body and beyond it, I have made it do what I want it to. I am transfigured, scarred, and left wanting more. More cuts, more pleasure, more warmth, more refuge from the hard life of the real world, from my past, from the person I was as a child, an adolescent, yesterday. I am the man in the mirror, the man standing next to me, holding me and cutting me, the man in my body and the man outside of it watching it live and bleed, move and breathe. I am . . .

PART 2

JOURNAL

NOVEMBER 3, 1995

Essay is too difficult to write. I'll be misunderstood, misinterpreted. I would think that I'm beyond worrying about most of that—after years of cultivating a reputation as a sexual renegade. But what here is making me uncomfortable? My depictions of my cutting experiences are detailed and verifiable (I just looked at the fading scars on my chest and legs, running my fingers over them in memory and dispassionate awe), but the essay feels false to me. Is it overromanticized? All those candles and references to fairy tales? Is it too consciously spiritual, with its insistence on high-Catholic kitsch? Or is it that it is simply too, well, literary?

NOVEMBER 7, 1995

Journal entry of four days ago is complete shit. I know perfectly well what is missing from the essay: honesty and truth. Not that the cutting didn't happen, and (at its best) was romantic, affirming, potent. What am I leaving out? That as much as I loved Jim, I thought he was fucked up about sex? That his S/M practices—including cutting—were mostly vain attempts to break through the crushing repression of his southern boyhood and his horrible feelings about himself? That in our first year together he would have to leave the room after coming so that he could be alone and cry? Or that Jim died of AIDS in 1986? Acting out doesn't always bring you through to the other side. And what does this mean in an essay that is promoting sexual experimentation in the name of freedom and health?

What else am I leaving out? That while I was seeing Jim I was involved in a deeply committed relationship with Walta Borawski, a relationship that lasted twenty years until Walta's death in 1994. Walta and Jim and I spent a lot of time negotiating how to be nonmonogamous. Sometimes it worked; sometimes it didn't. But what does it mean that while I rhapsodize now about my cutting experiences with Jim, I *never* talked about them with Walta? That I would wear sweatpants and T-shirts to bed for weeks at a time to hid the fresh scars, as if Walta couldn't figure it out anyway. What does it mean that I trusted Jim—my boyfriend, my fantasy—enough to cut my flesh with scalpels, and yet I couldn't trust Walta—the man who gave my life meaning—enough even to speak to him about this? Was I lying to Walta?

The idea of what is truthful and what is not is arbitrary; an approximation. We write to give the appearance of truth, and hope readers believe us. But even careless readers must realize that these "journal" entries are fake, a literary device used to move my story along. All, of course, in the pursuit of "truth" and "honesty."

Moments after Walta died—at 9:05 P.M. on February 9, 1994, at home in the bed I'd inherited from Jim, in which he had died eight years earlier—I sat next to him and talked to him for the last time. My first thought was to apologize for all the times I might have hurt him by my relationship with Jim. Why is *this* harder to confess than precise details of erotic extravagance?

Should I also mention that, while taking care of Walta during his illness, I accidentally gave myself several sticks with potentially contaminated needles? That if I am HIV-positive—I've never been tested—it was because transmission occurred (accidentally, incidentally) while nursing to his death the man I loved? That the blood running down my chest—Jim's blood—conflates in my mind with the blood of my dying lover? That the romance of the scalpel slicing through my skin is nothing compared with the sharp, frightening reality of the needle's jab in the thumb, the fear that pierces the heart and disorders the mind?

Essay (part two)

The living room is glowing now. Not only with the candles and the reflected lamplight but with the heat of our sexual energy. I stand in front of the mirror and watch myself. A simple flex will increase the trickle of blood down my chest; arching my torso to one side will change the course of the fluid, now carmine in color as it oxidizes and finds its way in the world, outside of the body. Jim lies on the couch watching me, enjoying my self-involved pantomime. I pull on my cock. It is soft, but full of feeling. I can feel the sexual excitement in my belly and down my thighs; I feel dazed by my own lack of inhibitions and overwhelmed by desire.

My self-entertainment lulls and I go to the kitchen and begin to make us more tea. Waiting for the kettle to boil, I look at my chest and marvel at the patterns, now crusting. Jim is in the bedroom looking for the restraints (tossed beneath the bed after he took them off last night's trick) and appears in the kitchen wanting my help fastening the buckles. We adjust the black leather cuffs, finish making the tea—sugar, lemon, bourbon—and sit on the floor, our backs resting on the couch. We hardly speak. We are lost in our own worlds as well as our shared one, and words seem superfluous. The tea is hot and sustaining; its heady fragrance intoxicates. Jim says it smells like hibiscus; a memory of his youth. We kiss and I run my hands over his chest, pulling the skin taut and relaxing it like a moiré silk or the most subtle of velvets.

Tea finished, we stand in front of the mirror. I flex and watch the now-dry blood crinkle and flake. Jim holds up his arms, and I stand on a chair to slip a long rawhide cord through the D-bolts of the restraints and around the not so subtly placed hook in the ceiling. I pull the rawhide taut; he raises his arms, relaxes. The cord holds tight and I deftly knot. Climbing off the chair, I readjust the light— Jim is taller than I am—to highlight his form in the glass. He plays with the tension—up on his toes, down again, shrugging shoulders, and then forcing them down—until he is comfortable. I stand to his side and run my hands over his skin, play with his nipples. Jim's eyes are closed. What is he thinking? About me? About last night's trick? About being a teenager and the smell of hibiscus and the terror of sex with other boys? About Vietnam? He sways and I hold him still with my hand and then carefully open the hermetically sealed package and remove the blade.

"Open your eyes," I whisper. He does. "Where?" I whisper. "Here?" I touch the skin above his nipple. "Here?" I run my hand along his breastbone. "Here?" I touch the flesh on the uppermost part of his abdomen. "Yes." "Where?" "There." I press on the soft center, pinch the skin, knead it, redden it, make it ready for the cut. "Watch," I say. "I love you." I steady my hand and slide the blade, ever so gently, across the expanse of white epidermis. A three-inch arc appears. We both look in the mirror amazed, confounded by the beauty of it. From pink, to rose, to vermilion, to crimson (who knew there were so many shades of red?), it rises to the surface magically and begins to weep. Slow at first. Jim tenses his body, holds it, relaxes. Tenses and relaxes. The blood rises and then begins to run: rivulets almost afraid to give in to the gravity that pulls them down. "Do you like it?" I ask. "Do you want more?" The question is needless. "Here." "Here?" "Here." I create a feather pattern over his nipples, alternating light with deeper strokes. Jim likes to see a lot of blood. It is not a matter of cutting deep, just of time and tension, patience and gravity. I cut lower on his belly and we watch. Wait and watch. "Shave me," he asks quietly. There is a hospital safety razor on the chest. I reach for it and remove the stubble of his pubic hair—we did this two weeks ago—with short, quick strokes. Around the soft cock, the inner thighs, the top of the scrotum; carefully, carefully. He is clean, more naked than ever. And suddenly he tenses his whole body: once, twice, again and again and again. This is what he wanted. What he has waited for. The blood runs more freely, past his nipples, his rib cage, each one showing as his body stretches, over his belly and down onto his cock and balls. It runs down the foreskin, slowly. He watches in silence, rapt with the extraordinary grace of it. This is what he wanted. This is what he always wants. Suspended, displayed—like some martyr in a Renaissance painting—unable to help himself, and watching as rivulets of blood dam at the tip of his gathered foreskin and then fall, drop by drop, to the floor. You can almost hear the droplets, tiny amounts of precious, jewel-like fluid, fall and shatter as they hit the floor. I look in the mirror. It is like a dream. But whose? And then I see that Jim is crying.

PART 3

JOURNAL

DECEMBER 2, 1995

Have just reread what I have written after putting it away for a few weeks. Does it work? Is it sexy? Or sexy enough? Is it "truthful"? Is it truthful enough?

Jim and I had an intense sexual relationship for almost five years. The dynamic between us was that I took care of Jim—sexually, emotionally, psychologically. The last time we had sex, I had him tied to a chair and beat his chest and arms with a switch, and then cut him with a scalpel. There was much blood. We were angry at each other, yet he still trusted me to enact our old rituals. After we broke up, my fury at him was nearly out of control. How could a man who trusted me to cut him not trust the depth of my love for him? We broke up and continued speaking, if only to argue. Walta was both upset and relieved. Jim left me for another man—Patrick—who loved him without any demands. Maybe in the mirror, Jim's dream was to find the perfect lover, the man he did not have to be tied up to love, the man who would not remind him of his guilt about Vietnam. Where had we gone wrong? Can you trust with your body and not trust with your heart? Walta felt more betrayed by my grief at losing Jim than he did by my sexual relationship with him. It was easy to hide scars in bed with T-shirts and sweatpants; it was nearly impossible to hide my desolation when Jim told me, "I just want to be friends."

DECEMBER 12, 1995

Can I write about "honesty" and "truth" without writing about Vince? I started seeing Vince after Jim and I broke up. I never mentioned it to Walta. Or rather, Walta and I never talked about it. Vince was a distraction from my loss of Jim. Our sex was energized and extravagant. He let me beat him, tie him up, cut him. His capacity for this abuse and pain was endless. He fell in love with me—a fact he never felt permission to state—and I used him to get over Jim. My grief and anger fueled the affair. Was I hitting Jim when I hit Vince?

Once, in the middle of a long, somewhat drunken night, I said that I loved him. The words hung in the air. He had never said these words, but it was true for him. I did say them, but it wasn't true for me. The next week he asked tactfully if I had uttered those words. He remembered I had, but thought he might have made it up. I said I didn't know. We continued the intense sex for another year and a half. Did I love him? I don't know. Was I using him? Probably. Was he using me? For what? Attention, sex, love? I gave him some of that. When I cut him it wasn't like cutting Jim—it was exciting but perfunctory, surgical. It was about Jim. It was about me wanting control again. "Trust," "love," "honesty." Is it enough to say that those words have no real meaning detached from actions and intentions? Is it enough to say "I'm sorry" now?

My last date with Vince was June 13, 1986. The day Jim was diagnosed with PCP. I was at the hospital and stayed there for the night. His body was so depleted that he needed red blood cells immediately; he had ignored the fact that he was sick for at least six months—was this the doctor-in-denial or the saint-in-the-making? I watched the blood—thick and heavy concentrated plasma—drip from the plastic bag into the clear tubing, through the large-gauged needle into Jim's vein. I never slept with

Vince again, or tied him up, or beat him, or cut him. Jim needed me. I won. I was back in his life.

DECEMBER 28, 1995

I sit here running my fingers over the scars on my chest and legs. They are fading now, most of them gone. Here or there is a line, a bump, a bit of raised skin, perhaps whiter than the surrounding flesh. I touch my flesh and pull at it. I look at the bed next to me—its brass in need of polishing—and think of Jim and then Walta dying in it. I look at my life and think, "It's not too bad. I'm here. I am writing this." My fingers roam my chest, pinch my nipples, I think about Jim's white, fish-belly flesh; Walta's hairy, darker skin; Vince's pliant scarred arms. I think of Walta and Jim and love and trust and where we fail and where we succeed, but sometimes, in the end, fail. Flesh is what brings us together, what joins us, and what keeps us apart.

I always thought Hamlet's line was "Oh, that this too, too solid flesh would melt." But someone just told me it is "sullied," not "solid," and that made sense. Flesh isn't solid, it isn't marble, but tender. Like "truth" and "honesty" and even "love," it can be inexplicably ruptured, torn apart. It is ripe for decay on its inevitable journey to become lifeless, what we—as a last resort—call "dead." Like "honesty," "truth," and "love," it is negotiable: we can make it do what we want (sometimes); we can do to it what we want (often); we can misuse and abuse it; but we cannot deny that it is there, that it is us.

I think about cutting Jim, about being cut. I feel my scars and think about cutting again. But with whom? Jim is dead. I never even talked about this with Walta. Vince is sick; we haven't spoken for a decade. Feeling my skin, I decide—one last time—to cut myself. Will it be sexual? My cock feels nothing. Would it be an experiment in remembrance? I can remember. I have remembered. Is it an easy way to end this essay? A cheap, exploitative shot? What do I feel writing this? What does my skin feel aging as it is on its journey to death?

Essay (part three)

I've turned up the heat in the house. It is cold outside. I've made a strong cup of tea with bourbon and sugar and lemon and have warmed myself within and without. I find the needles I saved from when Walta was sick and look at them in their sterile paper and plastic wrappers. I forget which is thinner—20G1, or 25G5/8? These are things I used to know. How odd to hold these slim packages in my hand. Three years ago I would deftly open them, remove the needle, and irrigate Walta's Hickman catheter or flush his feeding tube with saline and heparin. Fifteen years ago I would open these packages and carefully push the needle through Jim's and Vince's flesh. Which has more meaning for me now in memory? I nursed Walta and at times even made him better; he needed me and I was there. I gave Jim and Vince pleasure, at times even ecstatic joy. Did they need me? Could someone else have done this for them? And me? I learned, I received pleasure, I grappled with the mysteries of flesh, my own and others', I entered worlds I never dreamed existed—of sex, of fantasy, of fear, of AIDS, of death—and I became who I am today. Oh, that this too, too sullied flesh would melt.

I am lying on the brass bed next to my desk. I rub my chest, my nipples, warm them with my palms. I unwrap the needle and breathe deep. I've done this before. I can do this now. I hold the tip of the needle—the thinner of the two—to the almost pink-beige areola of my nipple. I breathe, I look at my chest and remember the whiteness of skin, the tension of muscle, the love of other men, their bodies and their trust. I trusted them, and why not now? Why not myself? I hesitate and then I push without thinking, without feeling, without memory. The needle slides, clean, and then sticks. I see the skin on the other side of the nipple poking pointed; the needle has not broken through. I breathe and push again. There is little pain, a poke and that is it. The tip of the needle is exposed and its shaft emerges clean and bright. My breath comes back and I stare at the gleaming needle. What does it mean? Have I re-created a moment from my past? Did I think this would bring back Jim or Walta? Bring back some sense of their presence, of their desire? Or is it to bring back my own desire for them? Will it ignite my passion, which feels long asleep, quietly resting in my flesh, my heart, my cock, my past? The needle feels hot; the skin surrounding it feels warm. I rotate the tiny steel rod and feel nothing: a slight pull, a tiny tug deep inside my flesh.

I reach next to me and open the single-edged razor from its package—not sterile, but clean, shiny—and hold it up. Can I do this? Without pausing or hesitating I reach down with my left hand and stroke the skin around the pierced nipple. I can feel the tension from the needle below. I stroke and warm the flesh and again without pausing I look down, and with the blade in my right hand sketch— delicately—an arc across the skin. There is no pain; there is no feeling at all. I breathe and wait. Nothing. I breathe more. My hand trembles: tension, anxiety, fear? I remember Jim in the mirror, Vince on the floor, Walta in bed sick and frail, hardly able to talk or help himself. Do I cut again? I'm too tense. There is no blood because I can't relax: tense, relax, tense, relax. There is no gravity; I am lying down. Tense, relax, tense, relax. I am holding my breath as I remember Jim in his hospital bed, his face gaunt; Walta at home holding my hand so hard it hurt. Tense, relax, love, trust, truth, pressure, tense, relax, trust, truth. All of the men I have loved, really loved, in my life are dead. I am here. I think about Vietnam and Jim and dead boys covered in blood. I think about the needle in my thumb, my panic. There is no blood. Tense, relax. Tense, relax. I stand up. Breathe. Tense, relax. I look in the mirror on the wall across from the bed. The room is dark. I see Jim's picture on the wall above my desk. Walta watches from across the room. I feel hot and look again in the mirror. The arc is pink, almost rose. I breathe, tense, relax. Suddenly the rose turns deeper—a lovely color—and almost imperceptibly the new color emerges from the top of the arc and slowly travels to its end: as if by will alone a single drop of crimson, scarlet, carmine blood forms and runs down my chest. It stops and I stare at it in the mirror. I don't feel like a saint, I don't feel beautiful, I don't feel sexy. I just feel alive.

EDO VAN BELKOM
The Terminatrix

Sex is power.

I know this because sex is what killed me.

And no, I didn't die in bed in the middle of an orgasm or anything like that. I died in a car accident—and a messy one at that. But the way I died isn't what matters here because the truth of it is that I was dead long before my car slammed into the front of that truck. In fact, I was dead the moment the bitch stepped into my life.

Correction!

I was dead the moment the bitch stepped into my *husband's* life and began her slow, methodical plan to get rid of me, nudging me out of the way a little bit each day until it was time for that one final push and I was gone for good.

Then she took my place as his wife.

Mrs. Bitch.

Married to Mr. Bastard.

She knew that sex was power, and she used that knowledge like a weapon to rub me out.

But after I came back and learned about the power of sex, I used it against her . . . to get *even*.

I'll tell you all about it, but first things first.

My name is, *was,* Margie Donnard. I worked in the classified department of the local daily newspaper, and I'd been married to the Bastard for over six years. I guess I would have called our sex life "okay." I mean, I enjoyed it all right, and we seemed to do it often enough, or at least I thought we did.

Apparently not, since the Bastard felt he had to go looking elsewhere to find whatever it was that I wasn't giving him. And it must've been something great, too, because it was enough to make him kill in order to get it more often.

You see, sex is what killed me, but he's the one who did it.

And while I can't prove it was him, what else would you think if one Sunday afternoon the Bastard is tinkering under the hood of your car and the next day the brakes give out on a stretch of road the local teenagers call "Dead Duck Run"? And how often do two-year-old Chevrolets completely lose their brakes anyway? And I mean *completely,* like in those old movies. You know the ones with the car barreling down one of those steep, swerving mountain roads, with the guy stomping on the brake pedal and nothing happening, so he tries working the steering wheel to keep the car on the road. In the movies the guy always jumps to safety or gets stopped by some strategically placed tree. Me, I went under the front end of a Mack truck.

I was dead almost instantly, my head punching through the windshield and halfway into his radiator like it was shot out of a cannon.

Of course, the driver of the truck didn't get a scratch on him. Isn't that always the way?

Watching the firemen and ambulance attendants cutting me out of the car and then trying to revive me was sort of interesting. The paramedic who finally gave up on me seemed sorrier to see me go than the Bastard did.

You see, by the time I got used to this afterlife I got stuck in and managed to make my way home, a couple of days had passed. I entered the house and found the Bastard giving it to the Bitch right in our bedroom. And to make matters worse, she was wearing the black silk teddy and stockings the Bastard had bought me for our third wedding anniversary.

I never did like wearing that stuff, but she looked like she was born into it like some magazine centerfold who sat around the house all day wearing lingerie, keeping her legs spread just in case some pool man stopped by to fuck her brains out.

My first thought was to beat the crap out of the Bastard. So that's what I tried to do, but every time I brought my fists down on top of him they just slipped through his body like he wasn't even there.

That's when I realized that while I could move around and act like I was a part of the real world, I couldn't do a thing to it. Not touch it, not move it, not affect it in any way.

Death was getting more depressing all the time.

And the more I wanted to get even with the Bastard, the less I was able to do it.

So, with nothing else to do, I found a comfortable spot in the corner and watched them go at it.

And that was when I got my first lesson about how sex is power. You see, she was lying stomach-down at one end of the bed, her face bobbing up and down between his legs like she was licking the dripping ice cream off some superdeluxe sugar cone.

The Bastard was loving it too, his head arched back, moaning "Ohhh" and "Yeah" like he was in some other world. Well, he'd never acted that way with me, so I moved around the bed to get a closer look at just what she was doing.

At first she ran her tongue up and down the length of his cock, licking his balls and then working her way back up to his big purple head. When she got there she brushed her lips over the tip and then sucked his entire cock deep into her mouth like she was trying to see just how much of it she could inhale.

Let me tell you, it was a lot.

I'd tried doing that a couple of times, but it always made me gag, which got me out of the "mood" faster than a knock at the door.

But she just kept sucking him deep down her throat, farther and farther, until the Bastard didn't have any more to give her. And then he started moaning again, louder this time, as he moved his body in these slow gyrations, as if he were trying to fuck her mouth like it was a pussy. She actually let him do it for a few seconds, but then she pulled her mouth away from his cock, leaving it glistening wet in the dim light coming from one of the nightstands.

I was amazed.

His cock was long and fat with thick veins running up and down the length of it.

He'd never been that big or hard with me.

Never!

The Bastard looked disappointed that the Bitch had stopped sucking him off, but she either didn't notice, or didn't care. She just laid down on the bed next to him, spread her legs and said, "Your turn now."

Turn for what? I wondered, but not for long.

As obedient as a schoolboy, the Bastard moved to the end of the bed and made himself comfortable between her legs and began licking her cunt.

I couldn't believe it.

He was licking her from top to bottom, bottom to top, sucking on her swollen clit with his mouth, and fucking her sopping-wet hole with his tongue.

He'd never done any of those things for me.

Never!

Of course, I'd asked him to do it plenty of times, but he'd always complained that it was dirty down there. Dirty and disgusting.

Well, if *she* was dirty down there, he'd made sure he licked her clean a long time ago.

Like I said before, it was then that I first came to realize that sex is power. The Bitch gave him sex like he'd never had before and then used the power it had over him to make him do whatever she wanted.

Like licking her cunt.

Like killing his wife.

If he didn't do either, she'd cut him off.

So he did them both.

And she rewarded him.

"Oh, that's it, stud," she cried.

Stud!

She began to buck and grind her sex against his lips, massaging her breasts and squeezing her nipples all the while like she could barely control herself.

"Oh, yeah, babe, that's it!"

It looked and sounded as if she were going to have one hell of an orgasm. And although I couldn't take my eyes off the two of them, it was hurting me to watch.

To think, I was murdered . . .

For a good fuck.

"I'm coming. . . . I'm coming. . . ."

I sat motionless, watching as she wrapped her stockinged

legs around his head and pressed her vulva hard against his sucking mouth.

And then she came.

And a part of me died all over again.

It ached something awful, but it gave me an idea.

That night after they went to sleep, I tried something. I moved over next to the bed and touched the Bitch. Nothing fancy, just a simple, gentle touch. This time my hand still passed through her body, but there was definitely some feeling there . . . as if my hand were touching water or something a little more solid, sort of like gelatin.

The sensation was so strange and unexpected that I pulled my hand back and examined it to see if it had been damaged. It was fine, even felt sort of pleasant as a cool tingling sensation danced the length of my fingers.

When I looked over at the Bitch, it was obvious that she'd felt something too because she was rubbing the spot on her thigh where I'd touched her. And it didn't look as if I'd hurt her since she was rubbing her leg slowly, almost like a caress. Maybe it had felt as good for her as it had for me.

I wondered why I was able to touch her now when I couldn't connect with the Bastard before and figured that the fact that they were sleeping must have made a difference. Maybe while they slept their minds and bodies were closer to wherever I was and the gap between our two worlds was smaller.

Seemed plausible enough, but I really didn't care.

All I knew was that I could touch them while they slept and that my touch felt good. It was all I needed to know.

I moved back over to the bed and reached down to

touch the bitch again. This time, instead of her leg, I touched her breast. It felt even more fluid than her leg.

As I moved my hand around in slow, languorous circles, the Bitch stirred. Her movement startled me and again I moved back. She continued to tremble slightly as she experienced the pleasant tingle of my touch, and her nipple hardened and distended into a stiff nub of dark brown flesh. She brought a lazy hand across her chest and fingered the nipple as a slight smile appeared on her still-sleeping face.

Encouraged by her response, I moved closer and touched her breast again. As I did so, her hand fell away as if inviting me to do more. I moved my hand through her nipple and watched her body shiver with delight. . . .

And then I stopped.

She let out a low, hungry sort of moan, begging me—or whoever she thought was pleasuring her in her dreams—to continue, but I wouldn't.

How could I control her if I gave in to all her desires?

How good does candy taste if you can have it whenever you want?

I left her there wanting like a bitch in heat and moved to another part of the house where I could rest. . . .

And plan my revenge.

The next night after they'd gone to sleep, I paid another visit to the Bitch. Like the previous night, she'd slept in the nude and, since the night air was a little hot and humid, she was lying on top of the covers, giving me easy access to every part of her body.

I watched her sleep for a while, gathering up the

courage to do it. Of course, I was hesitant because touching a woman that way wasn't like me. But the more I thought about it, the more I realized that *I* wasn't like *me*. I wasn't Margie Donnard anymore—I was a ghost now, or a special kind of ghost called a wraith, since my only reason for existing seemed to be to exact revenge for my murder. Knowing that made it easier for me to touch her in that way. After all, revenge has always been a prime motivator in history and fiction. Why not in the afterlife too?

So, with the Bastard snoring away, I crept onto the bed and placed my hands through the fleshy part of her inner thighs. Already, her unconscious mind was responding to my touch, spreading her legs wider for me as tingles of pleasure moved up her thighs toward her vagina.

After one last moment of hesitation—*This is it!*—I leaned forward and touched my tongue to the soft outer lips of her pussy. She gasped in her sleep at my touch, adjusted her legs one last time, then began to move her cunt slowly against my tongue.

I have to admit that doing it with a woman wasn't as bad as I'd thought it would be, and after a few minutes I was actually beginning to enjoy the feel of her hungry lips and swollen clit pressing against my mouth.

She seemed to be enjoying herself too, since she reached down between her legs and began to move her hands over her slit, rubbing it softly and stretching the lips gently apart as if inviting me to venture inside.

I took her up on the invitation and slipped my tongue into her warm, wet cunt, filling her up with a kind of pleasure she'd never experienced before. Not only was my tongue inside her pussy, but it was also *inside* her, meshing with her body and providing direct stimulation to the thousands of nerve endings in that most delicate and sensitive part of her.

She let out a loud, breathy moan that almost woke the Bastard up. "Huh?" he mumbled, before quickly falling back to sleep, oblivious to the smoldering sex going on just inches away.

I continued to slide my tongue in and out for a long, long time, and felt my own nipples beginning to harden, my pussy getting warm. It almost made me wish I'd tried this when I was living. If I had, maybe I would have left the Bastard before he'd had a chance to kill me.

She continued to hold her pussy lips apart for me with the index and middle finger of her right hand while her left hand slid back up her body and began to caress her breasts. Even though she was lying on her back, you could tell her breasts were large and full, which was probably the thing that first caught the Bastard's attention. She squeezed them gently, fingered a stiff brown nipple, then tweaked it between her thumb and index finger.

Another moan escaped her lips.

That's when I knew it was time.

I concentrated on licking her clit gently with the tip of my tongue the way I'd always wanted the Bastard to do it to me.

She moaned again, long and loud this time, and thrust her pussy hard against my mouth.

Then she arched her back as her body spasmed.

The tiny tingles of pleasure that had racked her body like individual drops of water had become swollen to the bursting point, spilling pure ecstasy into her system like a highly narcotic drug.

She'd be wanting more.

And I looked forward to giving it to her.

Only now, she'd have to come to me to get it.

I visited her again the next night, and the next and the next and the next. I wasn't sure my nightly visitations were having the desired effect until the Bastard came out of the shower one night with a raging hard-on jutting out from between his legs and a coy little smile on his face.

"For the past two days, I've been thinking about what you could do with this," he said, stroking his cock like he was polishing some custom-made cue.

"Sorry," she said, looking over at him but failing to notice his big, thick cock. "I'm beat, and I've got to get up early in the morning. Maybe on the weekend."

That's when I knew she was ready for the next step, which was to move our nightly encounters out of the bedroom.

After she fell into a deep sleep, I passed a hand over her breasts, fingering her nipples before bending over and taking them between my lips.

As always, she responded eagerly to my touch.

I continued to move my hands over her large, soft breasts as I brushed my lips past her ear and whispered, "Follow me."

Whether she actually heard the words through her ear, or her mind had picked up the command through some sort of ESP link-up, I don't know. All I know is that she did as she was told and got up from the bed and followed me, out of the bedroom and into the adjoining bathroom.

The doctors and lawyers would later agree that she suffered from sleepwalking, the act or state of walking, eating, or performing other motor acts while asleep, of which one is unaware upon awakening.

Somnambulism.

That's the fancy word for it, but the truth was she wasn't even really sleepwalking.

She was just horny.

She wanted . . . no, *needed,* the sex only I could give her, and she was willing to follow me just about anywhere to get it.

Like I said before, sex is power, and that power was going to kill her in the end. The funny thing about it was, I wasn't sure who was enjoying herself more. The Bitch, or me.

After following me into the bathroom, she lay down on the cold, hard ceramic floor tiles, her eyes still closed and her mind locked in some scorchingly erotic dream.

In her mind . . . I was some well-endowed football player with a foot of long cock that would remain hard for as long as she wanted . . . I was a millionaire lawyer who called her into his office to take some dictation and then ravished her repeatedly on top of his solid oak desk . . . I was a fluid and handsome dancer who swept her off her feet, seduced her with his eyes, and then made slow, gentle love to her long into the night . . . and I was her love goddess, who visited her each night and brought her to climax after shuddering climax, leaving her fully satisfied but always wanting more.

I rewarded her for following me into the bathroom by sucking on her nipples a bit more, stimulating them simultaneously from both the outside *and* inside. Then I moved my hand along her firm belly, past the dark patch of neatly trimmed pubic hair, and down over her slit. As always, she responded to my touch by spreading her legs as wide as they would go, opening up the way for me to come inside.

I slid two fingers into her, massaging her inner lips before slipping them in deeper.

The Bitch gasped.

Encouraged by the sound, or perhaps wanting to get more out of all this than simply revenge, I moved around so that I was kneeling over her head. Spreading my legs slightly, I lowered my pussy onto her lips and gasped as her tongue dutifully snaked out from between them to lick at my sex.

It felt good, too good. Instead of simply enjoying it, I grew angry at the Bastard for refusing to do it to me when I asked him. And maybe, just maybe, I was a little angry with myself for not leaving the Bastard to find somebody who would. But despite my anger, I continued to hold my pussy over her lips, feeling an orgasm—or whatever its afterlife equivalent is—gaining strength from her touch.

Knowing my own climax was imminent, I slid more of my fingers inside her, then my entire hand, touching her insides like no man—or woman for that matter—ever could.

She began breathing harder, so I decided it was time to let her orgasm. I curled my fingers back, found her clitoris, and applied slight pressure on the nerves leading away from it and directly to the brain.

The pleasure had to be intense because the Bitch arched her back and let out a tiny chirp of ecstasy as she came in a long, drawn-out series of orgasms.

Seeing her in the throes of ecstasy sent me over the edge as well; a series of bright sparks shot up from the junction between my legs and caused my form to tremble with pleasure.

When it was over, we were both exhausted.

Pleasantly so.

I left her there to sleep, getting her used to the feel of the hard floor beneath her.

She woke up well rested, although a little confused as to her surroundings.

"What the hell are you doing on the floor?" asked the Bastard when he got up to take a pee in the middle of the night.

"I don't know," said the Bitch, a little groggy.

"Are you all right?"

"Yeah. I feel good."

Maybe, but not for long.

And so I continued working on her, turning her on, then asking her to follow me out of the bedroom to other parts of the house. So far she'd awakened bleary-eyed in the living room, on the dining-room table, in the basement, and upstairs in the attic. It was almost too easy. I'd come to her, touch her down there, and she'd start getting wet; she was like one of Pavlov's dogs after hearing the bell. Then, after she was good and hot, I'd suggest that she follow me, and she'd trail along behind me like . . . well, like a dog following its master.

The Bastard kept telling her to go see a doctor, but she just kept brushing him off. She wouldn't say it, but I knew she was afraid that if she saw a doctor, my nightly visits might stop. So, instead of seeing a doctor, she placated the Bastard by doing it with him on the weekend.

See, he didn't have any power over her—I did.

She went through the motions, but she looked kind of bored while he was doing it, like it was a here-you-go-now-leave-me-the-fuck-alone kind of fuck. If she was eager about anything, it was finishing up in a hurry so that she could get to sleep and be ready for me.

I didn't disappoint. In fact, I rewarded her devotion to me by bringing her outside so that we could do it under the stars.

We left the Bastard snoring away and went down the stairs into the kitchen. The door wasn't locked, so she slid it aside and stepped out into the backyard. It was a warm, cloudless night, and she followed me onto the cool, soft grass.

The air was filled with the sound of crickets, a few chirping night birds, and the constant *hush* made by the cars on the highway on the other side of the forest behind the house.

I set her down on the grass on all fours, rubbing her slit with my fingers so that she'd curve her back and hold her pussy high in the air like she wanted it doggie style.

I moved back a moment, looked at her, and almost laughed.

She even looked like a Bitch.

A Bitch in heat.

I knelt down behind her and placed my hand between her legs. I began by inserting a finger into her pussy and watched as she ground her cunt against it. I inserted two, then three fingers, and she began to move back and forth harder and harder, as if she were dreaming about being fucked by some giant cock.

So be it, I thought, and slowly began to push my entire hand deep inside her. She continued to grind and buck against me, wanting more and more of what I had to offer.

So I gave it to her. All of it.

I pulled my hand from her, then reinserted a finger in her cunt and another in her anus. Then I moved beneath her so that I could suck on one of her large, hanging breasts. Finally, I slipped two fingers into her mouth.

It was a little awkward for me, but I knew it was worth it. In her dreams she was being serviced by four men, each of them insatiable, each of them pleasuring her like no man had ever done before.

Especially the Bastard.

It took less than a minute for her to come, and when she did it was an explosive climax that almost awakened her, not to mention the neighbors.

I moved out from beneath her and watched her collapse onto the grass, utterly exhausted, a contented smile on her face.

I smiled then too.

My plan was almost complete.

Sex is power, and through sex I had gained total control of her nocturnal mind and body. She would follow me anywhere now, perhaps even to the ends of the earth if I wanted.

Fortunately, we wouldn't be going that far.

The way I figured, about a mile or so would do it.

When the Bastard woke up that morning, he frantically ran through the house looking for the Bitch. When he saw the open kitchen door, he ran outside and found her lying naked on the grass.

"Wake up," he said.

"Huh?" she mumbled, still deeply asleep.

"You're outside in the backyard."

"I am?" Her eyes fluttered open.

"Yes, now come inside before you catch cold." He helped her off the grass and led her back inside. "What were you doing out there?"

She just smiled.

And for the next few weeks, the Bastard made sure to lock the door before he went to bed each night. So, I had to bide my time, leading her around the house again and leaving her in all sorts of places, just to keep her in practice.

Then one night, early in August, the Bastard worked late and she went to bed alone.

My first thought was to enjoy her for myself and put off my plan for another night, but seeing her lying on *my* bed, in *my* house, and remembering that it was *my* life she'd stolen, I quickly put aside any ideas I had about self-indulgence and clouded my mind with thoughts of revenge.

So I went to her, brushed my long hair over her legs, belly, breasts, and pubic hair and whispered in her ear, "Follow me!"

She rose up from the bed almost instantly.

"Yes," I said, rubbing my fingers against a nipple. "Come with me!"

She walked out of the bedroom, down the stairs, and through the kitchen. The door was unlocked. She slid it aside and stepped out into the backyard.

I slid a finger inside her already-moistened pussy. "Come with me!" I whispered.

She walked into the center of the backyard and began to get down on the grass. "No," I said, gently touching her clitoris. "This way!"

She stood up again and began walking.

The forest behind the house was thickly treed and dark, but it didn't matter. I guided her along the path, careful not to let her step on any rocks or broken sticks, lest a sudden jolt of pain should awaken her.

As we neared the highway, the roar of the traffic grew

louder so that now the sounds of individual cars and trucks became recognizable as they passed.

She began to tire, to slow.

I quickly laid her down on the path and began licking her body from head to toe, starting with her neck, then moving down to her breasts and finally ending up between her legs.

She responded with newfound energy and enthusiasm and began moving her body against my probing tongue. That's when I stopped, leaving her wanting more.

"Come with me!" I whispered again. "Lover."

I wasn't sure what the new word would mean within her mind, but it seemed to spur her on, since she rose up off the ground refreshed and eager to follow me further down the path.

We were there minutes later.

The interstate was always busy, but at night the traffic became somewhat erratic with cars and trucks passing in groups with long stretches of nothing in between. Soon, a few cars approached from the right in single file, heading west.

I waited for them to pass, then led the Bitch onto the eastbound lane.

There I laid her down on the warm asphalt and began manipulating her with my tongue. As always, she responded, spreading her legs and moving her hands over her body to heighten the stimulation I was providing.

I looked to the left and saw a pair of pinprick points off in the distance. They were growing larger.

I continued to lap at her pussy, bringing her closer and closer to orgasm.

I checked the highway again and saw that the lights had now grown into small circles.

They'd be upon us in seconds.

I turned my attention back to the Bitch and brought her to the very edge of orgasm.

One last check.

The lights were almost there.

I pressed my lips and tongue directly onto her clit, sending arcs of pleasure shooting through her body, causing it to shudder and spasm.

She was coming.

But unfortunately for her, so was an eighteen-wheeler.

I looked up . . . and quickly got out of the way.

The driver must have seen the Bitch at the last second because he slammed on the brakes of his long, black semi less than twenty feet from her quivering body.

But it was too late.

Way too late.

The truck skidded across the highway, the sound of its screeching tires jarring the Bitch awake.

The look on her face was priceless.

Pure, absolute terror.

It was there for a split second, then was obliterated by the hulking mass of the truck as it ran her over, the lead wheels on the right side of the rig bumping roughly over her body before the trailing wheels ran smooth.

As I watched that truck come to a stop, I couldn't help thinking about how sex is power because, to be honest, I'd never felt more powerful than I did at that moment.

But instead of hanging around and congratulating myself on a job well done, I turned and headed back toward the house.

You see, now it was the Bastard's turn.

EDWARD FALCO
Tell Me What It Is

Ten steps back behind a pair of blue tents pitched side-by-side under thick trees on Cape Flattery, the ground ended abruptly at a thirty-foot vertical fall to the Pacific Ocean. A campfire in front of the tents had burned down to red embers. Alongside the fire, two card tables pushed together made one longer table topped with a battery-operated fluorescent lamp and a bright yellow plastic game board and crisp black tiles. Enclosed in the circle of light emanating from the lamp, two couples seated in folding chairs around the card tables were deep into a session of Acquire, a board game involving the placement of randomly selected tiles on a numbered grid. The tiles formed companies in which the players bought stock and either gained or lost money as their companies merged and grew or were taken over and disappeared. It was Barrett's turn to move and he had been staring intently at the board for several minutes. In the intense quiet of his concentration, the others listened to water lapping at boulders and rushing through sea caves that lined the shore below them.

Finally Barbara said, "For God's sake, Barrett, will you just merge Worldwide and end my misery?" She didn't have any stock in Worldwide and was almost out of money. If Worldwide were merged she'd be out of the game.

Barrett said, "What makes you think I have the merging tile?"

"Oh, please!" Barbara shouted.

Adam said, "Here they go." Adam and Adele were the second couple. Adam and Adele. Barrett and Barbara. They lived in adjacent apartments in Manhattan, and they referred to themselves as the alphabet couples, because of the unfortunate alliteration of their names—or sometimes they called themselves the A's and the B's, as in "Barrett, see what the A's are doing tonight," or "Adam, see if the B's want to come over for a drink." Adam owned The Body Works, a physical fitness center, and Barrett acted in *Days of Our Lives*, an unending daytime soap opera. They were on vacation now, camping a few days on Cape Flattery, which was part of the Makah reservation.

"Do you think I'm an idiot? Do you think we're all stupid?" Barbara put her elbows up on the table and leaned toward Barrett. She was a woman in her early fifties who looked twenty years younger, easily. Some of her youthful appearance came from the fortune she spent on skin-care products and minor cosmetic surgery, and some of it was genetic. In any case, she looked good. Her naturally sandy blonde hair was dyed a brighter blonde, and it contrasted strikingly with her pale green eyes. She wore jeans and a sheer green blouse that showed off the shapeliness of her breasts. All of her beauty, natural and purchased, was at that moment however swallowed up by the anger that surfaced in her face. She shouted: "You've been buying stock in Worldwide for the last three rounds! You don't think we know you have the merger? You either think we're all idiots, or else you're an idiot for buying the stock!"

Adele laughed and said, "You guys. . . ."

Barrett placed the merging tile on the board. "Okay,"

he said. "Worldwide comes down." He smiled broadly at Barbara, his white teeth catching the lamplight. "Bye-bye, Barbara," he said, and he laughed out loud.

"You love it," Barbara pushed her chair back from the table. "Anything that screws me, you love."

Adam said, "Talking about screwing you, Barbara . . ."

Adele reached across the table and slapped him playfully on the head.

"Yes?" Barbara said, perking up. She leaned seductively toward Adam.

Barrett said, "Let's do the merger first. Then you can talk about screwing my wife."

"Okay," Adam said. He pulled the bank toward him and began counting out money.

Barbara said, "I'm hot." For weeks now the Olympic Peninsula had been hot and dry—weather conditions almost unheard of in the region. She stretched, extending her arms over her head and pointing her fingertips to the sky. Her blouse rode up on her stomach. "I'm going to go take this thing off," she said, referring to the blouse, and she walked away from the table. As she bent to enter her domed tent, she pulled the blouse off, revealing a bare back and a quick flash of her breasts swaying in the pale outer reach of the lamplight.

Barrett said: "Too bad, Adam. You missed it."

From inside the tent, Barbara answered: "Go to hell, Barrett."

"What?" Adam looked up from a stack of hundreds. "What did I miss?"

"What did she do?" Adele said to Barrett.

Adele and Adam were a much younger couple than Barrett and Barbara, younger by more than twenty years.

Adam had met Adele at The Body Works, where she had started working out at age thirty-two, when her daughter turned thirteen, entered junior high school, and started living behind a locked bedroom door. Her fourteen-year-old son had been living behind locked doors since he had entered teenagedom some twelve months earlier. Adele couldn't blame either of them. She and her then-husband bickered constantly. Their principal forms of communication were the jibe and the insult. Adam, at thirty-four, was also married at the time, also with two teenagers. When he saw Adele, the first thing he noticed was her body—which was worth dying for, and which no one would ever believe had been through the wrenching changes of childbirth. Seeing her in a blue-and-red Spandex exercise outfit that clung to her like brightly colored skin, he offered immediately to be her personal fitness counselor. A year and two months later they were both divorced and remarried to each other.

Barrett said to Adele, matter-of-factly: "She pulled her blouse off before she got in the tent."

Adele turned to Adam. "And you missed it, honey," she said, her voice dripping mock sympathy.

"Damn . . ." Adam handed Barrett a pile of pink thousand-dollar bills and pale-yellow hundreds. "Why didn't you nudge me?"

Barrett sorted out the money and placed it in neat stacks next to his black tiles. "Haven't you seen her tits before?" he said.

"No!" Adam said, petulantly. "I haven't. And I don't think it's fair. After all, you've seen Adele's."

Barrett and Adele laughed. Barbara came out of the tent wearing a bikini top. "Shall I strip?" she asked Adam. "Shall we even it up?"

"Absolutely!" Adam said. He pounded his fist on the table, making the tiles on the game board bounce.

"Hey!" Barrett said. "You're messing up the game."

"I'm sorry," Adam said. He pouted, sticking out his bottom lip.

Barbara sat down at the table. "You first," she said to Adam.

"I can't," he said. "I have a very small penis."

Adele laughed out loud, and Adam and Barbara laughed in reaction to her. Barrett just shook his head.

"I've heard about that," Barbara said. "Adele's told me all about it."

Adam grinned wickedly.

Barbara said to Barrett, "You saw, didn't you? Are the rumors true?"

"Like a horse," Barrett said. Barbara was referring to that morning, when Barrett had found Adam and Adele bathing in a tidal pool under a stone arch. He had applauded their naked bodies. Adam had looked taken aback for a moment. He had looked toward Adele, as if he might want to cover her. Adele, however, had appeared unconcerned, and Adam had wound up clowning as usual, doing muscle-man poses before Barrett turned and walked on. Now Barrett slapped Adam on the back. "Like a damn stallion!" he added.

"Absolutely," Adam said. He touched one of his tiles and seemed to hesitate for an instant. Then he said: "Why don't we all go skinny-dipping?" He looked up at the sky, at a full moon that was about to disappear behind a long line of clouds.

"Fine with me," Adele said. "I love getting naked in the ocean."

"Are you two serious?" Barbara said.

"Sure," Adam said. "This is an Indian reservation, isn't it? Didn't the Indians used to bathe in the ocean?"

Barrett said, "I'm sure the Makah people bathed in the ocean—a hundred years ago, anyway."

"I'll do it," Barbara said. "Except the water's probably still cold—even with all this heat."

At fifty-six, Barrett was the oldest member of the group. He had been married three times before Barbara, and he had one child from each of those previous marriages. His youngest child, a daughter, was in her mid-twenties. He was still an attractive man, but his attractiveness didn't come from being in superb physical condition, as it did for Barbara, Adele, and Adam. Barrett's attractiveness was in his face, which was weathered and leathery, and in his eyes, which suggested an inner intensity. It was a look that many women over the years had found appealing. Women found his size appealing too. He was six-one, two hundred and twenty pounds. He looked up at the others and said, "You guys go. I'm too old and fat."

Barbara said, gesturing toward Adam: "You'd let your new bride go skinny-dipping with this sex fiend?" Barbara and Barrett had been married less than a year.

Adam said, "She's got a point, Barrett."

"You have to come," Adele said. "Otherwise you'll be the only one whose body's still a secret."

Barrett shook his head. He laughed as if he were nervous and a little shy. "I don't think so," he said. "You guys go. Really."

"Okay," Barbara said. She jumped up, rubbing her hands together with anticipation. "He's already seen you two naked," she added, with her back to the group as she ducked into her tent. She returned with two flashlights and tossed one to Adam. "Come on, Adele." She leaned down to Adele and whispered in her ear, loud enough for everyone to hear, "Not that I'm gay or anything, darling— but I'm dying to check out your body."

Adam laughed and Barrett said, "You believe the libido of this woman?"

"You lucky dog!" Adam grasped Barrett by the neck and gave him a shake.

"Come on, come on!" Barbara took Adam by the arm and led him to the path that went down to the shore. "It's getting late and we've got that dumb fishing trip in the morning."

Adele hesitated at the table, looking across the game board at Barrett, who was watching Barbara and Adam as they made their way along the path. When Barrett turned to meet her eyes, she said: "You sure you won't come?"

"Believe me," Barrett said. "I haven't got the body to show off."

Adele laughed, dismissing Barrett's modesty. She smiled warmly at him, touched his fingertips with hers, and then joined Barbara and Adam, calling for them to wait.

Barrett put the game board and pieces away as he listened to the others descending the path to the water. For a long time, he could hear their laughter and the shrill, playful screams of the women. When, finally, the sound of their voices disappeared under the constant low whistle of wind through trees and the white noise of small ocean waves breaking over boulders that rose up out of shallow water all along the shore, when the only sounds left were the elemental ones—the fire, which occasionally popped and hissed, water leaving and returning ceaselessly, wind moving along the earth—Barrett carried the Acquire game into his tent, put it away, and came back out with a flashlight and an expensive pair of high-powered binoculars attached to a black graphite tripod.

Carrying the tripod on his shoulder as if it were a rifle, holding the feet in his right hand while the binoculars bounced along up over his head, and carrying the flashlight in his left hand, its beam trained on the ground, he followed the same path the others had taken, only in the opposite direction, up to the cape, to the point where the land ended and he could look out over Neah Bay to Tatoosh Island and the Pacific Ocean. Earlier in the day, Adele had taken his and Barbara's picture there as they stood on either side of a makeshift, cardboard sign that read:

THIS IS CAPE FLATTERY,
THE NORTHWESTERN-MOST POINT
IN THE CONTINENTAL UNITED STATES.

Now, as he walked along in the dark, he was watching for the sign. When he reached it, he would be close to the lookout point, where he planned on setting up the binoculars and watching his wife and friends as they undressed and went swimming.

Barrett approached the cape amazed at himself. He was fifty-six years old and waves of sexual desire still pushed him along like so much driftwood. Desire swelled in him and still, now, at fifty-six, he couldn't find the will to resist it. That morning, for example, his coming upon Adam and Adele bathing had not been accidental. He had been lying awake in his sleeping bag, looking out at the green canopy of trees through the netting at the top of his tent, when he overheard Adele suggest to Adam that they bathe at the

shore. He had waited until he heard them leave the campsite before he got dressed quietly, careful not to wake Barbara, and he went down to the shore, hoping to come
upon them. When he first saw them, they had their backs
toward him. It was amusing to him that both Adam and
Adele, at thirty-five and thirty-three, thought of themselves
as old. To Barrett the two of them were luminous with
youth. Adam had the body you'd expect on a man who'd
made a career and built a successful business around physical fitness. And Adele . . . Adele's beauty extended from
the luster of her shoulder-length auburn hair, to the intelli-
gence in her eyes, and the creamy glow of her skin.

When he came upon them, they were standing knee-
deep in a tidal pool, Adam behind and to the right of
Adele, his right hand on her shoulder, his left hand turning
a thick bar of white soap in slow circles at the small of her
back. While Barrett watched them, partially hidden by a
pair of side-by-side boulders, Adam slid the bar of soap
down over Adele's buttocks and then under her and
through her legs. She laughed and turned around and they
embraced and kissed. Barrett moved back behind the boulders and waited. He looked around, nervous about getting
caught leering at his friends. Getting caught would be humiliating and he was genuinely afraid of it—and that mixture of real fear and sexual excitement, that was one of the
things that made him do it. It felt powerful, intense. He
waited a few minutes, and when he looked again, they
were kneeling in the water, splashing each other playfully.
Then he walked out from between the boulders and began
applauding—as if he had just accidentally come upon
them, as if their naked bodies were nothing more to him
than an amusement, something which of course in his ma-
turity and experience held no real power over him. Adam

seemed taken aback at first, but Adele met his eyes and smiled—and then Adam, jackass that he was, began posing.

When Barrett reached the head of the cape, the shelter of the trees ended abruptly. The moon was just emerging from a bank of clouds, and it was bright enough that Barrett felt confident turning off the flashlight and laying it on a boulder. He walked carefully, testing the firmness of the ground with each small step. When he was close to the place where the land dropped away, he crawled on his hands and knees to the edge, where he lay on his stomach and looked down to the beach. Forty or fifty feet below him, Barbara, Adam, and Adele had just reached the water line and were standing in the surf with their shoes off and their pants legs rolled up. Barrett set up the tripod behind some bushes and a small tree, and he focused the binoculars on Adele. He had paid thirteen hundred dollars for those binoculars, and every time he used them he saw why: through their powerful lenses, Adele appeared to be a few arm's lengths away from him. He felt as though he could touch her hair.

After several minutes of watching the threesome talking at the edge of the water, Barrett began to fear that they would chicken out and not go skinny-dipping at all. For a moment, he wished he were down there to urge them all out of their clothes and into the water. But, really, he didn't want to be down there with them. If he were down there, when they were all out of their clothes, he would have to pretend that it was no big deal. He wouldn't be able to leer and stare. He would have to pretend he didn't want to feel the weight of Adele's breasts in his hands, he didn't want to run his tongue over her nipples, he didn't want to reach down under her the way Adam had. The truth was that he wanted to look, and he wanted to look with concentrated attention—not a pretense of amusement. And, if the relationship wasn't sexually intimate, that required distance and anonymity. So he preferred being up on the bluff, behind a tree, with his binoculars.

At home, in Manhattan, on the set at work, he was surrounded by stunningly beautiful women—all out of his reach, by his own choice, because he was married again. The tension was incredible. He wanted those women intensely and he didn't want them intensely—both at the same time. He was fifty-six years old, with three grown children, a veteran of three failed marriages. He was lucky to have Barbara. He knew it. He knew it absolutely. And yet, whenever an attractive woman came near him, something happened in his blood, something over which he had no control. It was as if his blood heated up, the surface of his skin grew electric, his breathing changed. He didn't know if it was like that for all men, all the time—but he was determined, absolutely, this time, with Barbara, to stay in control. He had slept with so many women over the years. And he knew now, knew absolutely, in his heart, that what he really needed to be happy was one woman. He needed Barbara. In the years he was single before he met her, in those years when he moved constantly between one woman and the next, when his life felt like a habitual swirl of movement, he suffered from anxiety attacks, terrible attacks that on a couple of occasions included hallucinations. Since he married Barbara, he had been fine. He needed to stay with her, to stay with one woman, with Barbara. He needed to learn to stay still. He needed to learn to value what he had and to resist the desire to move from woman to woman to woman.

Barrett knew what he needed. . . . And yet, some nights, he still found himself out at Flashdancers on West 21st, where dozens of mostly undressed girls filled the room and the runways. All the women were beautiful and varied in form: with light skin and dark skin; with big breasts that floated over taut but ample skin, and small breasts tight to the rib cage; with small pink nipples on white, white skin, and large oval nipples, brown or nutmeg on darker skin; with asses that were round and asses that were long and flowed into youthful thighs: beauty everywhere on the pedestals of table tops, and what he desired was to look at it, what he desired was to see what was every day all around him hidden from his view.

In a sense, Barrett's voyeurism was a kind of compromise. He chose looking over acting. He was going to leer at Adele, but he wasn't going to make a pass at her. Adam was a jackass, but he was his friend. He liked betting football and basketball games with him, and playing poker with him on Friday nights, gambling being another source of intensity in Barrett's life. He didn't want to sleep with his friend's wife. Even though his relationship with Barbara had been strained for the last few months, he didn't want to mess up the marriage by sleeping with another woman. But of course he wanted Adele. He wanted to see her, to touch her. He wanted her. He didn't want her. It was maddening and confusing. It had always been maddening and confusing.

Down on the beach, Barbara slipped out of her bikini top, and Adam's loud whistle floated up to the cape. While Adam and Adele watched, Barbara stripped out of her jeans and then her panties, slowly, with an equal mix of seduction and play. Watching from the cape, Barrett felt the familiar tingle of sexual excitement—and it surprised him. He had seen Barbara naked on a daily basis for almost a year now, and he had thought that she no longer excited him—not even when she put on the flaming red teddies, or the exotic black garters, or the Frederick's-of-Hollywood panties with the crotch cut out. Now, here he was watching her secretly from a distance through binoculars and feeling that old, recognizable tingle in his groin. When Barbara was fully undressed, she trotted away into the water, where she watched Adam take off his clothes, her head bobbing on the surface, as if she were just slightly jumping up and down in the water. Adam got undressed quickly and yelped as he dove dramatically into the waves. Then Adele turned around and looked up at the cape, looked up directly at Barrett.

Barrett moved away from the tripod and took a step back behind a tree trunk. His heart raced wildly. He said to himself, "She can't possibly see me." Then he wondered if she had perhaps seen the glint of moonlight off the lenses of the binoculars. Or maybe he was wrong, maybe his body was somehow silhouetted by the moonlight and she knew he was up on the cape watching her. He slid down and sat on the ground behind the tree, and he was filled with wildly chaotic feelings of shame and guilt and anger and remorse. Why did he do things like this? He was a fifty-six-year-old man. He had a career. He had a family. Why was he hiding in the bushes like a pimply teenager peeking at girls? For God's sake, he repeated to himself, and he was filled with a ragged humiliation. Then he told himself he was overreacting. So what if they knew he was up here watching? Hadn't he been perfectly welcome to join them down on the beach? He'd make light of it if they knew. He'd turn it into a joke.

When he went back to the binoculars, he half expected to see Adele wave at him. Instead he found her reaching behind her back to unsnap her bra, still looking up at him, looking directly at him, as if she were engaged in a staring match and resolved not to be the first one to look away. She had already taken off her pants and blouse, and when the bra came off, she smiled, the same warm smile she had given him just before she left the campsite. Then she took off her panties and just stood there for a long moment, looking up at the cape, before she turned around and walked slowly into the water. Barrett watched them all the time they were in the water, and he watched them get out and get dressed, and then he hurried back to the campsite and put the binoculars and tripod away, and got undressed and into his sleeping bag.

By the time Barbara came into the tent, Barrett was almost asleep. He had listened to the exchange of goodnights through a sleepiness that was like being drugged. He heard the zipper to Adam and Adele's tent open and close, and then Barbara was climbing into their tent, almost stepping on him.

"Barbara?" he said, exaggerating the confusion in his voice, as if he were waking from a dream.

"Go back to sleep," Barbara said. She bent over him and touched his cheek gently with the back of her hand before pushing a strand of hair off his forehead.

"How was it?" he asked, turning onto his back and looking up at her.

"Fun," she said. "They have beautiful bodies . . ." She paused and bent to kiss him on the forehead. She whispered, "But I'm happy to be with an older man, someone with character and real strength."

Barrett laughed softly. "Are you putting me on?"

Barbara didn't answer. She kissed him again, gently, told him she loved him, and then pulled her sleeping bag close to his before she got in it and went to sleep.

Barrett was better able to relax once he was sure Barbara didn't know he had been watching them. For a long time he lay quietly thinking about the next morning's fishing trip, trying to remember what was exciting about holding a pole for hours while you waited for a fish to bite. Then he started thinking about himself, about who he was, about his relationships with others. Did Barbara really believe he had strength and character? He guessed she did. That was his image, the image he projected out into the world. He was an actor. He was a man of experience. He had suffered and he was world-weary. He was a man who lived with the knowledge of the nothing at the center of everything. That was the image he had been working on and refining from the time he was a boy. But who he was, who he was really, that was both his image and something more—and that something more. . . . He wasn't sure what it was. It was shaped by the people and places in his life, but it was something more. It was his angry father and the Brooklyn of his youth. It was the wives he had gone through one after the other and discarded or been discarded by because he was unhappy or unfulfilled or unsomething, or she was. It was his children, all grown now and into their own lifetimes of trouble. But it was also something more. It was his experience and his thought and something more.

But Barbara believed in the image within which everything came wrapped. As he lay in his sleeping bag, not seeing the dense bright stars in their patterns so infinitely complicated they were like a complex, visual music, he tried to think about that something more that he never had been able to apprehend as anything other than a feeling, an idea, that there was something under the images he invented and rendered for others—but he wound up feeling as though he were floating loose of the earth. He wound up feeling as though he were drifting. If no one knew you, who were you? And how could anyone know him if he wouldn't stay still long enough to be known? Outside his tent there was an amazing variety of noises as the nocturnal creatures of the local woods began their nightly foraging—but Barrett's thoughts made him deaf to their music long before sound truly disappeared in the genuine deafness of sleep.

At four-thirty in the morning the sky was an unbroken mass of dark clouds. Adele stood in a circle of lamplight staring out over a fleet of fishing boats to the black water of Neah Bay. Adam stood behind her, looking the other way, back to a small building, a glorified kiosk, set at the edge of a gravel parking lot. Through an uncurtained window, he could see Barrett and Barbara standing in front of a desk cluttered with papers, while behind the desk an elderly woman typed some figures into an adding machine with her right hand and opened a desk drawer with her left. Barrett handed her some money, and Barbara took the slip of paper that had issued forth from the adding machine and been ripped off precisely by the old woman. Adam said, "We shouldn't have let them pay for this. It's probably expensive as hell."

Adele grunted softly, a sound that meant nothing beyond acknowledging that Adam had spoken.

Adam went on: "Barrett makes me feel like a little kid sometimes, the way he's always picking up the tab. I think I may have a tendency to let him take too much control. Probably because he's so old."

"He's not that old," Adele said. She laughed quietly, as if to herself.

"Are you laughing at me?" Adam said.

Adele didn't answer. She was wearing white shorts and a bright yellow sleeveless blouse. A hooded, red vinyl rain slicker was folded over her right arm. She had taken the raincoat just in case—even though the weather report had called, once again, for clear skies and a temperature in the nineties.

Barbara nodded toward the raincoat as she approached Adele. She was carrying two Styrofoam cups of black coffee and she extended one to Adele. "You must be psychic, honey. The captain's mom says it might rain."

"Shit," Adam said. "Will we still go out?"

Barrett, who had been following behind Barbara, carrying two more coffees, handed Adam a cup. "We're just waiting for the couple that's going out with us. Captain says they're on the way."

"Is this latte?" Adam asked, looking down at his coffee. "I like a lot of foam."

"Right, latte," Barrett said. "And the captain's serving croissants and apple scones on the flying bridge at seven."

Adele stuck her hand out, palm up. "Is it starting to rain?"

Barrett looked up to the sky, as if he might be able to see the rain falling. "I don't feel anything."

Adam said, "I think it's just misting."

"There," Barbara said, and she gestured to the village's single blacktop road, where a station wagon had just come round a curve. As they all watched, it pulled into the gravel parking lot and a middle-aged couple emerged. The man was shaped like an egg, with a small chest and a huge stomach that sloped down to skinny legs. He was wearing a camouflage outfit. The woman was also heavy, but her bulk was solid and seemed evenly distributed from her shoulders to her feet. She gave the impression of a living rectangle.

"Good God," Adam said, as the couple approached them and the captain emerged from his office at the edge of the parking lot. "I hope this boat's solid."

"Stop it," Adele said, turning her back to the couple and giving Adam a look.

The man in the camouflage approached the group with his arm extended for a handshake. Barrett switched his coffee to his left hand and shook the man's hand. "Joe Waller," the man said to Barrett. He extended his hand to Barbara and he gestured to his wife. "This is my wife, Lady," he said. "Would you believe twenty-five years?" Lady nodded, confirming what he said. "Married twenty-five years yesterday, two kids through college and married, one in college, one in high school." He said this as he shook Adam's hand and moved on to Adele. "Can you believe it?" he said to Adele.

Lady said, "And we're only forty-three."

"No kidding," Adam said.

"Hey!" Joe exclaimed, turning around to face the captain as he approached them slowly, carrying a large white bucket in each hand. "We going to catch some salmon today, Captain Ron?"

The captain was a Makah. His skin was dark and lined with myriad creases and folds. His eyes were solemn and deep. "I hope so," he said, and then continued on toward the boats, the large white buckets dangling from his hands like balancing weights.

Adam said, "I guess we follow him."

"That's Captain Ron," Joe said, putting his hand on

Adam's back. "You ever been out with him before? Where you folks from, anyway? The wife and I are down from Alberta . . ."

Joe went on as the group followed the captain down the rickety boat ramps and over the narrow docks to *The Raven,* Captain Ron's fishing boat. Behind them, the village at Neah Bay was quiet and dark. The only lights came from the Thunderbird Motel, which overlooked the water and was bracketed by gravel parking lots, one of which housed the small rust-red building out of which Captain Ron ran his charter fishing boat business. When all six passengers were on board, the captain jumped off the boat, undid the mooring lines, and then hopped back on and climbed up to the bridge. He backed the boat out of its slip and onto the bay. From below deck a young woman came up dressed in boots, denims, a blue-and-gold Notre Dame sweatshirt, and a heavy yellow rain slicker. Her eyes were watery and her short, dark hair was pressed flat against one side of her head, as if she had just a moment ago been sleeping. She introduced herself as Tina, the captain's daughter, and explained she was working this trip as First Mate, which meant she'd be the one untangling lines and helping with the tackle. Then she looked at Barbara, who was dressed in shorts and a summer blouse, and said, "You're going to freeze like that, ma'am. Want to borrow a sweatshirt?"

Barbara shook her head, although she was already hugging herself and shivering slightly. "It's supposed to get hot later," she said.

The girl laughed. "Not on the water," she said. "Not this morning." She disappeared below deck again and came back up with a ratty gray sweatshirt, which she tossed to Barbara. Barbara put it on and continued hugging herself and shivering.

By the time the sun came up, everyone was fishing. The captain had taken the boat out past Tatoosh Island, onto the Pacific, and within forty-five minutes everyone had pulled at least one salmon on board. The Canadian couple had each caught two big sockeyes in rapid succession, and Tina was kept busy unhooking everyone's catch and getting their lines back in the water. In minutes the deck had grown slippery with fish slime, and the pervasive stink of fish-smell grew so intense it was as much a taste as a smell. The sun had risen on a gray, chilly, misty morning, and the ocean swells regularly lifted and dropped, lifted and dropped *The Raven,* as one after the other the fishers yelled out "Fish on!" and Tina came running with a net or a gaff, depending on the degree of bow in the pole tip.

Barbara was the first to get sick. Then Adam, Adele, and Barrett joined her. The Canadian couple was fine. They stood side by side in the stern of the boat, and it was as if their mass and bulk created a solid, unmoving place in the liquid midst of a rolling, perpetually moving ocean. They kept fishing away, pulling in salmon after salmon, while one by one Barbara, Barrett, Adele, and Adam made trip after trip from the deck to bathroom, from the deck to bathroom. After a while they gave up trying to fish and each descended the short stairway to the cabin below deck, where they lay on benches and cushions, trying to maintain some control over the awful sickness in their stomachs. It was no use. They kept having to carry themselves to the bathroom, where the smell of vomit and diarrhea mingled with the ubiquitous stink of fish.

On one of his trips back from the head, Barrett sat next

to Adele, at her feet, and across from Adam and Barbara. The cabin was a tight, dark place with only two small portholes to bring in light. Benches followed the contour of the boat's hull. They were covered with thin, dirty cushions, and the tops of the benches were hinged and apparently opened up to create storage space. Barbara and Adele were stretched out on the benches, curled up into fetal balls. Barrett was sitting with his head between his legs.

"Barrett," Adam said. "Can you die from seasickness?"

Barrett's voice was harsh. "Damn," he said. "What I'd give for solid ground."

"Jesus," Adam went on. "I'm serious. I really feel like my stomach's bleeding or something. I think I saw blood last time I puked."

Adele said, weakly: "Nobody dies from seasickness, Adam."

"How do you know!" Adam snapped back at her. "Are you an expert or something?"

Adele opened her eyes and lifted her head from the bench. "Adam," she said, firmly. "Your stomach's not bleeding. Once we get on land, you'll be okay."

"Are you sure?" Adam said. He dropped his head down between his legs and clasped his hands over the back of his neck. When Adele didn't answer, he asked again, sounding close to tears: "Honey? Are you sure?"

"I'm sure." Adele looked over her knees, to Barrett, who was sitting up straight now, with his back against the hull. When she caught his eye, she shook her head, as if exasperated.

"Barrett," Adam whined. "Will you go talk to the captain? Maybe he'll take us back in."

Barrett was silent a long moment, then he pulled himself to his feet. "What the hell," he said. "It's worth a try."

"Really," Barbara said, opening her eyes for the first time. "You think he might?"

Barrett made a face, indicating that he doubted it seriously. Then he climbed the stairs to the deck and a metal ladder to the bridge, where he found the captain fiddling with the electronics. He asked him to take them back in, and, as he expected, the captain refused, explaining he'd have to refund the Canadians' money, and that would make the day a loss. Barrett offered to cover the captain's losses, but he just shook his head and looked out over the bridge to the ocean. Barrett returned below deck defeated. Along with the others, he lay around in misery for another hour before the Canadians softened, having anyway caught the boat's limit for salmon, and allowed the captain to take them in. When they finally made it back to the campsite on Cape Flattery, everyone crawled into a tent and immediately fell asleep.

It was late afternoon when Adele opened her eyes. Alongside her, Adam lay stretched out on top of his sleeping bag. He lay on his stomach, naked except for the bright red briefs that clung to him tightly as a tattoo. His body was covered with a sheen of perspiration: a pool of sweat had gathered in the small of his back, and his hair looked as though he had just stepped out of the shower. Adele was also soaked. She ran her hand over her chest and stomach, and sweat ran down her sides in rivulets. She sat up and let herself awaken slowly to the sounds and sensations around her. It was quiet. And it was hot. Very hot. She pulled on a pair of cut-off denims and a T-shirt, and she crawled out of the tent.

The campsite and the surrounding woods seemed eerily

still. There was no breeze, and the heat, even in the shade of the forest, was palpable: she could feel it on her skin like standing close to a fire. The only sound was the constant, faraway murmur of the ocean. It didn't take Adele more than a few moments of standing in the heat to decide she wanted to go for a swim. She retrieved a pair of sneakers from her tent and started down the trail to the shore. When she approached the beach, she found Barrett crouched in the surf. He was sitting on his haunches, wearing a blue bathing suit, looking out over the ocean as water rushed back and forth over his feet and ankles.

At Adele's approach, Barrett turned around and smiled. "You believe this heat?" he asked.

Adele knelt alongside him, immersing her calves and thighs in the water. She threw her torso forward as she pushed her hair up over the back of her neck and submerged her face and hair in the surf, rubbing the cooling water into her scalp and forehead and eyes. She came up shaking her head, getting Barrett wet. "Oh God," she said. "That was good. I think I roasted in the tent."

Barrett laughed and wiped the water away from his face. "Are Adam and Barbara up yet?"

Adele shook her head. "Still cooking," she said. "At least when I left they were."

"Poor Adam," Barrett said. "He thought he was going to die out there."

"He's such a baby." Adele turned around so that she was facing Barrett. She sat in water up to her waist. "Do you mind if I ask you something?"

"Go ahead."

Adele hesitated. She was sitting with her legs stretched out and open in a V, and she swirled the water between her legs with a crooked finger. "I'd better not," she said, and she looked away and then back, as if with that motion she had turned the page in a book and was now reading from a new script. "I got so sick out there," she said, referring to the fishing trip. "For a while, out on the water, it felt like I was blind. Do you know what I mean? It was like I couldn't see because nothing would stay still long enough. Up and down, up and down, drifting, moving. . . . Do you have any idea at all what I'm talking about, Barrett?"

Adele was being cute and Barrett smiled in response. It was an honest smile. "I think I know what you mean. So?"

"So, what?"

"The question," Barrett said. "The question you wanted to ask."

Adele looked down and her expression changed suddenly. Her eyes in an instant grew watery.

Barrett put his hand on Adele's knee. "What is it?"

"Adam and I are not going to last," she said. "I mean, I doubt we'll be together for another month after this vacation."

Barrett looked off, past Adele, his face taking on an appropriate expression, a world-weary look of sadness for the unfortunate ways of this world. Inside him, however, the rate of his heartbeat picked up slightly. His mind was blank, but his blood was moving. "I'm sorry," he said. "I didn't know things were bad between you."

"It's not that things are bad," Adele said. "I doubt Adam has any idea. It's just that . . . he's such a little boy. He's sweet, but it's like being married to a child. You heard him on the boat." She looked up at Barrett, as if wanting confirmation. "He was whimpering, for God's sake. I mean, if someone had taped that exchange in the cabin, it

could have been a ten-year-old boy talking to his mother."
Adele touched Barrett's hand. "Am I inventing all this?"
she said. "Isn't that how it sounded to you?"

Barrett rubbed his eyes with his fingertips, hiding his
face momentarily. Of course Adam was boyish. It was the
way he was. Adele's complaints against Adam threw Barrett back into his own refuse heap of complaints—his
wives' against him and his against his wives—complaints
that had wrecked one marriage after the other. The prob-
lems were many, the details numerous, but after three marriages all Barrett really remembered was the process by
which things fell apart, the faults real and invented that led
to arguments followed by unhappiness followed by sepa-
ration. It wasn't that the specifics, the details of the complaints, had disappeared; it was just that now they seemed
unimportant in comparison to the process of coming
apart, a process he had been through three times already.
So Adam was boyish. That was Adele's complaint. What
was his complaint against Barbara? There were several,
none of which seemed very important at the moment.

Barrett removed his hands from his eyes in time to see
the emotion gathering in Adele's face, building second by
second as he failed to respond. "Of course," he said.
"That's something about Adam. He's like a kid sometimes."

Adele looked up at the cape and closed her eyes for a
long moment. Then she turned to Barrett and stared at him
intently, waiting to read his smallest gesture.

Barrett had been here many times before, at this moment. It was the moment when he had only to touch her
and she would lean toward him and they would embrace.
He could kiss her now. He could touch her. She wanted to
be kissed and touched by him. This was the moment when

it might begin, whatever it would turn out to be: an affair, love, a sexual adventure. He stood up and extended a hand down to Adele. "Let's walk a little," he said.

Adele took his hand and lifted herself from the water. She walked alongside Barrett in her dripping cut-offs and soaked sneakers. Her T-shirt too had gotten wet and it clung to her, the shape of her breasts and the color of her skin almost revealed entirely through the thin fabric.

Barrett looked away, toward the green hills that sloped down to the sand. They were walking toward a place where three boulders formed a semicircle on the beach and three more out in the water completed the circle.

"Can I ask my question now?" Adele said.

"Sure. Go ahead." Barrett answered without looking at her.

"You and Barbara," she said. "Are you going to last? Are you two going to make it?"

Barrett's heart was beating fast. He didn't answer. He looked down at his feet and folded his arms over his chest as if contemplating a response.

They had reached the circle of boulders and Adele stopped and looked around. The boulders formed a small private beach, a place protected from the casual view of others. "I'm going in here," she said, and she pulled off her clothes and waded into a deep tidal pool that was still connected by a flowing stream of water to the ocean.

Barrett had watched her as she tore off her clothes and tossed them in a heap on the sand, his eyes searching out the soft and shadowy places, the slow curves and sloping angles of her skin. He followed her into the tidal pool. When she turned around to face him again, standing waist-deep in water, he stepped close to her, took her hands in his, and said, "No. We're not going to make it."

When he spoke, he heard his voice change, the timbre turning just slightly more resonant, the tone dropping a note. It was his best acting voice and it had emerged out of nowhere, on its own. It surprised him, as did the tears welling in his eyes.

Adele brushed the tears away with wet fingers. "I didn't think so," she said. "You act as though you don't even like each other anymore."

"She doesn't understand me," Barrett said, and he bowed his head and covered his eyes with his hands, and as soon as he did it, the gesture seemed fake to him. He half expected to hear a director yell cut! He pushed on. "I feel empty," he said. "We're married . . . but I feel . . ." He heard himself speaking, but he could hardly believe what he was hearing.

"I know," Adele said, and she embraced Barrett, wrapping her arms around him and holding him tight against her. She repeated: "I know. I know exactly."

Barrett pulled away and held Adele at arm's length. "I have a question for you," he said, allowing a note of urgency into his voice. "The other night, when you went swimming with Adam and Barbara, did you know . . . Did you know I was watching you?"

"From the cape?" she said. "With the binoculars?"

"Yes," Barrett said. "How? How did you know?"

"I didn't. I mean, I didn't know—but I imagined it. I imagined you were up there watching. . . . And it was like I could feel you, I could feel your eyes on me."

"But what made you think . . ."

"It's your eyes. . . . They're hungry. Everyone sees it in you. It's just, like, a hunger about you . . ."

"It's crazy," Barrett said, "because . . . I felt this connection between us then. It was like something real between us. I felt filled up by it. I can't explain, really . . ." He leaned forward, as if he were tired of stumbling for words, and he embraced and kissed Adele, his lips pressing hard against her lips, his tongue pushing into her mouth.

Adele returned the kiss, letting her hands move over his back, clutching and releasing his shoulders—but when his head moved lower, to her breasts, and he tried to pull her down to the water, she resisted. "Not here," she said. "Barrett. Not now." She stepped back from him. They had moved, while kissing, into shallower water, and Barrett was on his knees, looking up at her. She ran her fingers through his wet hair.

Barrett took her hand and pulled her toward him. "Yes," he said. "Here. Now."

Adele shook her head and remained standing. "Someone might come by. Barbara or Adam. . . . They're probably up."

Barrett looked at the sky, at the wavering, late afternoon light. "No one can see us here," he said, and he ran his hand along the length of her thigh. "Adele," he said. He leaned forward and kissed her leg, high, above the knee. "Listen," he said. "There's nothing to life but moments like this. Intense moments like this." He touched his chest. "My heart is racing," he said. "I'm looking at a beautiful woman, and my heart is a drumbeat: it's pounding in my chest." He took Adele's hand and held it over his heart. She came down to her knees in the water. She knelt in front of him, her hand pressed flat against his breast. "We'd regret it forever," he said, "if we let this moment pass." He embraced her and kissed her and turned her body around, moving them both toward shallower water, where he lay on his back and pulled off his swimming trunks, and moved his body under Adele's, threading his legs between her legs. He had, then, only to thrust his thighs up slightly and they were joined. Above him, blocking out the bright yellow circle of the sun, Adele's head was lifted to the sky as if in ecstasy or grief, the heels of her hands pressed against her temples, her fingers buried in her hair. She appeared, from the angle where Barrett looked up at her, to be floating away from the earth, attached to nothing, not him or the ground or the water; and in the pleasure of the moment, Barrett too felt as though he were floating—into a place of pure sensation, rising free of the gritty earth. Then he moved his hips, pushing into the heat of Adele's body, and the seasickness from earlier in the day came back with a rush. He felt as sick as he had at any point on the boat trip.

Barrett tried to hold himself steady to let the sickness pass, but Adele was moving rhythmically, the palms of her hands flat against his chest, pushing him down into the sand and water. He held Adele's wrists, and behind him, from someplace beyond and above the boulders, he heard a sound like a rock might make being kicked in the sand. He wanted to turn around and look, but he was afraid of what he might see. He feared that Barbara and Adam were above them on the beach looking down at them in the water. He closed his eyes and told himself these feelings would pass in a moment if he remained calm. Amazingly, as his mind swirled and his nausea swelled, his body kept properly functioning. Adele appeared to have no idea there was a problem. When he felt her hair brushing his chest, he opened his eyes and found himself looking into a rip in the fabric of the sky, a shifting blaze of energy and light. He threw his forearm up over his eyes, and the motion sent him spinning, as if he were spiraling up and away. With his other hand he grasped blindly for Adele, and when he found her shoulders he pulled himself up and wrapped his arms around her.

"What?" Adele said. "What is it?"

Barrett didn't answer. His eyes were filled with a mosaic of color, blinding him to the solid coastline that might have steadied him; and the blood rushing in his ears made him deaf to the music of water and earth and wind that might have calmed him. He was sick. His body was tumbling through light and space. He held on tight to Adele, as if her body could anchor him.

"Barrett?" Adele said. She wiped away the sweat gathering at his temples. "Barrett," she repeated. "Can you tell me what it is?" And when Barrett didn't answer, when he continued mutely clinging to her, she tried to calm him by saying, again and again, soothingly, "Tell me, Barrett. Tell me. Tell me what it is."

KERI PENTAUK

Is Your Husband Obsessed with On-line Pornography?

Beware, ladies. Though the Times Square adult bookstore is dying, a new form of filth is sweeping across America: the Internet. Have you heard about chat rooms, the IRC, downloaded gifs, and cybersex? You can bet your husband has. Help us put an end to this pernicious trend. Now.

Is your husband an on-line pervert? If you don't know the answer to this question, it's high time you did some investigating, for there exists a deadly sinister side to the Internet phenomenon and your own husband might be an active participant—right under your very nose.

Men account for the vast majority of all Internet users. And as all wives know, men will stray when left to their own devices. Consider the case of Horton, a self-confessed on-line pervert. "I got on the Net a year or so ago and at first I never thought about sex on-line. Now I guess I spend ten or twenty hours a week on-line in that kind of activity." Horton is typical of the new breed: he's a thirty-three-year-old computer professional whose wife Eileen, a busy career woman, is completely unaware of his secret life on-line. Like many men, Horton first became aware of explicit on-line content through one of the many Internet search engines. "I was just surfing around when I typed the word 'sex.' It was amazing how many links showed up." Indeed the proliferation of filth on the Internet is amazing.

Several studies of the major search engines have revealed that the most commonly requested subjects involve vulgar terms like "sex," "tits," and "f**k." In fact, "Michael Jordan" is the only non–sex-related search term to make it into the top ten this year. But there is hope. For those enlightened women who are willing to take on the challenge, the on-line pervert can be reformed.

Behavioral psychologist Dr. Cynthia Hazelwood has just completed a paper with some radical suggestions for controlling male addiction to on-line smut. "It's time for women to take control," she asserts. "Men are fundamentally unsuited for productive social roles without the firm corrective discipline of a female hand. This applies just as well to the Internet as to any other social interaction." In her analysis, Dr. Hazelwood provides a comprehensive assessment of the Internet problem, beginning with the initial step: identifying the culprit for what he is.

Catching the On-Line Pervert

The first step in catching a potential on-line pervert is to watch for unusually obsessive behavior toward the computer. Does he seem to be spending a lot of time in his office or den lately? Does he sneak off surreptitiously or stay up late after you've turned in? These are classic signs of a husband dredging the Internet for filth.

If you suspect that this is the case, interrupt one of his

sessions unexpectedly and examine what's on his screen. If this reveals nothing incriminating, conduct an impromptu audit of the credit-card bill and demand an explanation for any suspicious charges. Several adult locations on the Internet require charges to credit-card accounts. Finally, sit in on one of his Internet sessions and ask specifically to see the "history file of his browser." This file records all recently visited Internet Web sites and will quickly reveal any perverted proclivities.

After you take these steps you may find nothing of concern. But that, unfortunately, is unlikely. A recent survey of 16,000 Internet users (80% of whom were men) reveals what experience with on-line sex they had:

55.9% Downloaded erotic pictures from the Web
48.6% Read sex stories in newsgroups
26.5% Masturbated while on-line
25.7% Masturbated to downloaded material
19.7% Talked dirty in IRC
17.8% Exchanged erotic e-mail

Horton, our self-confessed on-line pervert, admits to all of these and offers the following comments:

Adult Web Sites: "These are usually pretty soft-core or else they charge a fee. *Playboy* has the most popular adult site on the Net. I used to check it out at least once a week."

Internet Newsgroups: "Newsgroups are like bulletin boards where you can read and post text messages. At first, I just found the ones with erotic stories in them. But after some more reaching, I found others with specially coded pictures that you can display on your computer screen. There's a wide range of material and it can get much more hard-core than the Web."

E-mail: "I've had a couple of female pen pals and we exchanged some pretty steamy fantasies."

Internet Relay Chat (IRC): "IRC lets you chat with other people on-line. You type in one window and read their response in another. It can get really explicit. Some people pretty much make out on-line. I suppose it's a bit like those 900 numbers you hear about, like phone sex with a keyboard and a mouse."

If it turns out that your husband is indeed an on-line pervert, you should be ready to deal with him—firmly. And what are the best ways to punish the offender? Again, Dr. Hazelwood has some advice. "It all depends on the degree of transgression," she says. "The punishment should fit both the nature and the magnitude of the offense. I strongly recommend that you act swiftly—and severely."

Punishing Your On-Line Pervert

The best way to determine the severity of your response is to start by getting a written confession from your husband, spelling out exactly which of these activities the culprit has been involved in. This should be handwritten. (The keyboard-addicted on-line pervert hates having to write with an old-fashioned pen, pencil, or crayon.) A suggested template for his confession follows:

"I, <culprit's name>, confess that I am an on-line pervert. In the past <time period> I have indulged in the following filthy and unacceptable behaviors:

266 / KERI PENTAUK

<list offenses from the examples above>

I realize that my actions are reprehensible and respectfully ask that I be severely punished to teach me never to show such disrespect for women again.
Signed,
<culprit>"

Once you have secured this document, Dr. Hazelwood suggests that you use a scoring system to measure the seriousness of his offenses. Assign the following numerical scores to each offense:

Downloaded erotic pictures = 15
Read on-line sex stories = 10
Masturbated while at the computer = 30
Talked dirty in IRC = 25
Exchanged erotic e-mail = 20

Calculate the total and multiply it by the number of months that the culprit has been misusing the Internet. For example, an offender who has been on-line for twelve months, read on-line sex stories, and exchanged erotic e-mail would score 360. Then use your husband's score to determine an appropriate punishment for his offenses, via the guidelines below.

Having established exactly what you are dealing with, you are ready to punish the culprit. Given the degrading nature of the crime it is fitting that whatever punishment you apply should be suitably humiliating. "Do not be lenient in the mistaken belief that he will somehow see the error of his ways and repent," cautions Dr. Hazelwood. "Real behavior adjustment can only be accomplished with a strict and humiliating punishment befitting the transgressions at hand." She proposes the following punishments according to the degree of the offense:

Scores Below 500: Mild Offender

The first part of the punishment is to have the offender write a punishment essay: "I am an on-line pervert and my filthy behavior degrades women. I promise that I will never abuse the Internet for these purposes again and realize that if I do I will be severely punished."

He should complete the same number of punishment sentences as his score in the assessment above (score of 360 = 360 punishment sentences). To further reinforce this part of the punishment, he should be made to write out these lines during time when he would normally be playing with the computer or watching television.

Once he has finished his lines, you can conclude the punishment by making him stand in the corner for at least an hour, to contemplate his wrongdoing. Set an alarm clock or timer to be sure that he spends the full amount of time in the corner.

Scores Between 500 and 1,000: Moderate Offender

Once again, punishment lines are a good way to start. Have the culprit write out the lines as indicated above. But this offender needs more than just corner time to complete his punishment. Dr. Hazelwood proposes what might be called "reinforced lines." He should be taken over your knee and spanked as he recites the lines that he has written out.

"I suggest using a paddle," says Dr. Hazelwood. "Why should you have to sting your own hand to make his bottom sore?" During this procedure, the culprit should be made to recite a line after each stroke of the paddle. As an additional humiliation, he should be made to say "Thank you, ma'am," with each line reading, as well. Twenty to thirty paddle strokes are usually sufficient, but extra strokes should be added for any resistance or bad language used during the punishment.

Do not be reluctant to paddle him as hard as you can. The adult male buttocks are well suited to this kind of punishment and can take dozens of strokes without fear of serious injury. If this reduces him to gasping, crying, and tears, so much the better. On no account should you let him up before he has received the full punishment.

Having soundly spanked the offender, you should give him a lengthy dose of corner time as a final reminder that his behavior will not be tolerated.

Scores Above 1,000: Serious Offender

For the serious offender, you should reserve the most severe, humiliating punishment. "If ever there was a case for 'force majeure,' this is it," advises Dr. Hazelwood. "If every woman in the land takes up arms, we can extinguish once and for all the wildfire of the unchecked male libido."

Start with his punishment lines. Next, the offender is to be humiliated in an entirely "fitting" way. Since he has derived pleasure from images and fantasies that degrade women, he should be made to dress and act like the degraded women he so enjoys. Dress him completely in "sissy stripper" attire and have him apply his own makeup. The results, you may be assured, will be quite comical.

Ideally, you should invite some friends to witness the spectacle; humiliation is dramatically increased by the presence of two or three additional women rather than just yourself. Once he is costumed, make him perform a striptease for you and your guests. Instruct him to dance and wiggle like the strippers and pinup queens he enjoys ogling. Mock him constantly to emphasize his humiliation. Pinch him, spank his bottom, and stuff his bikini panties with dollar bills. Have one of your lady friends record this spectacle with a camera.

Once he is stripped bare, you can commence with the next part of his punishment. If he confessed to masturbating at the computer, he should be made to masturbate— right in front of you and your friends. Far from being an exercise in pleasure, forced public masturbation is an exercise in emasculation—one he will remember with shame every time he puts his hand where it doesn't belong.

It may take him a while to arouse himself under the derisive stares of your friends. Be prepared to wait him out. Taunt and mock him until he does his business. Once he makes his deposit and cleans it up, he'll be ready for the finale—a severe bare-bottomed paddling.

Place a chair in the center of the room and take him over your knee. If there are other women present, each should take a turn in spanking him since they all have, in effect, been degraded by his misogynistic behavior. At each stroke, he should be made to count and express thanks for his punishment. Do not rush this part of the punishment. He should receive between fifty and a hundred hard strokes spaced over a period of twenty to thirty minutes.

Assuming that you have done your work well, he will have a flaming red blush spread across both buttocks and an ego that has been completely deflated. Put him in the corner and take another photo showing his properly punished behind. Display this photo within view of his computer screen—as a future reminder of the penalty for on-line perversion.

Some women may consider this an extreme punishment, but considering the circumstances it is justified. "Women just aren't strict enough these days," laments Dr. Hazelwood. "Our mothers' generation would have spanked these spoiled cyberbrats into shape soon enough and we should do the same!"

Indeed. And once you've punished your husband, you can be sure it will be a long while before he even thinks about going on-line again. But just to be certain, you should revoke his Internet account and install a piece of access-prevention software—such as Net Nanny—on your home computer and his PC at work.

Oh—and as for Horton, our self-confessed on-line pervert? We took the liberty of confronting his wife Eileen with a list of his on-line misdeeds, at their suburban home. Her jaw dropped as she read. "I work sixty hours a week running a business to support this garbage?!" she said, tearing up the papers. "He won't be sitting down at that computer of his for a long, long time—Hor-ton! Get in here!"

Contributors

Michael Bronski is the author of two books of cultural criticism: *Culture Clash: The Making of Gay Sensibility* (1984) and *The Pleasure Principle: Sex, Backlash, and the Struggle for Gay Freedom* (1998). He is also the editor of the anthologies *Flashpoint: Gay Male Sexual Writing* (1997) and *Taking Liberties: Gay Men's Essays on Politics, Culture and Sex* (1997), the latter of which won the 1997 Lambda Literary Award for best anthology. He has written extensively for the gay and mainstream press and has been involved in the Gay Liberation Movement for more than thirty years.

Richard Collins spent half of the 1990s in Romania and Bulgaria, most of the 1980s in London and Louisiana, and his childhood in California and Oregon. His work has appeared in *Exquisite Corpse, Fiction International,* and *Melus.* His book on John Fante is due out from Guernica Editions, Toronto. "The Two Gentlemen of Verona" won the 1996 LIBIDO Erotic Fiction Prize. He lives at the corner of what used to be Rue des Grands Hommes and Rue Poets in the Faubourg Marigny, New Orleans.

Elise D'Haene's first novel is *Licking Our Wounds* (The Permanent Press, 1997). Her short fiction can be found in *HERS* and *HERS 2* (Faber and Faber).

She has written several episodes of Showtime's *Red Shoe Diaries,* an erotic series featuring David Duchovny, as well as several feature films. She lives in Los Angeles with her lover Celeste and their two dogs, Alfie and Gramps.

Edward Falco's most recent publications include the hypertext novel *A Dream with Demons* (Eastgate Systems, 1997), and the short-story collection *Acid* (Notre Dame, 1996). *Acid* won the Sullivan Prize from Notre Dame and was a finalist for the Patterson Prize. He lives in Blacksburg, Virginia, and publishes stories widely in literary journals.

Michael Thomas Ford is the author of more than thirty books, including *The World Out There: Becoming Part of the Lesbian and Gay Community* and *Alec Baldwin Doesn't Love Me and Other Trials of My Queer Life.* His work has been nominated for a Lambda Award and two Firecracker Alternative Book Awards, and his fiction and essays have appeared in collections including *The Best American Erotica 1995* and *1997, Brothers of the Night, Noirotica 3, PoMoSexuals, Queer View Mirror 2,* and *St*rphkrs.*

A. M. Homes is the author of the novels *Jack, In a Country of Mothers, The End of Alice,* and the short-story collection *The Safety of Objects,* and *Appendix A,* an artist's book. She is the recipient of numerous awards, and her work has been translated into eight languages. She teaches in the writing program at Columbia University.

Kevin Killian is a poet, novelist, critic, and playwright. He has written two novels, *Shy* (1989) and *Arctic*

Summer (1997); a book of memoirs, *Bedrooms Have Windows* (1989); a book of stories, *Little Men* (1997); and one of poems, *Argento Series* (1997). With Lewis Ellingham he has written a biography of the U.S. poet Jack Spicer (1925–65) called *Poet Be Like God: Jack Spicer and the San Francisco Renaissance* (Wesleyan University Press, 1998). Killian lives in San Francisco.

Tsaurah Litzky teaches a course on "How to Write Erotic Fiction" at the New School for Social Research in Manhattan. Her work has appeared in *The Best American Erotica, Pink Pages, The Unbearables, Lies and Crimes of the Beats*, and many other publications.

Kelly McQuain, a native of West Virginia, teaches college in Philadelphia. His fiction has appeared in such publications as *Best Gay Erotica 1997, The Philadelphia Inquirer Magazine, The James White Review, Kansas Quarterly/Arkansas Review, The Sycamore Review*, and more. His nonfiction has appeared in the Lambda Book Award–nominated anthology, *Generation Q*, and *Art and Understanding Magazine*.

Mary Anne Mohanraj (http://www.iam.com/ maryanne) has had work in a variety of forums—from staid poetry journals to science fiction anthologies to porn magazines. Recently she published her first book, *Torn Shapes of Desire: Internet Erotica*. She is founder and moderator of the Internet Erotica Writers' Workshop.

Jack Murnighan lives two lives: by day writing and editing at *Nerve Magazine* (www.nervemag.com), by night finishing a Ph.D. dissertation on medieval allegorical poetry. Raised in Illinois, finished in Europe, he currently lives in Brooklyn, prowling the streets for cheap eats.

Ben Neihart is the author of the novels *Hey, Joe* (Simon & Schuster, 1996) and *Rich Girl* (Weisbach Books/ William Morrow, 1998). His stories have appeared in *The New Yorker, Bomb, Nerve,* and *Mississippi Review Web,* and in the anthology *Love Stories from the New Yorker.*

Keri Pentauk is editor of *WHAP Magazine: Women Who Administer Punishment.* She recently edited the book *Rearing a Husband: The Modern Woman's Old-Fashioned Guide to Marital Bliss,* available from Retro Systems. She lives in Southern California with her well-trained husband.

Marian Phillips lives and works in San Francisco. Her previous publications include a translation of *The Confessions of Wanda von Sacher-Masoch* (Re/Search Publications, 1990).

Donald Rawley, the 1998 Pushcart Prize winner for short fiction, is the author of five books of poetry: *Mecca, Malibu Stories, Steaming, Blending,* and *Silence.* His short-story collection, *Slow Dance on the Fault Line,* was published in the United Kingdom (HarperCollins, 1997) and in the United States (Avon, 1998). His first novel, *The Night Bird Cantata,* debuted last summer in the United States (Avon, 1998). Warner Books is publishing his first collection of essays, *The View from Babylon,* in early 1999. His short fiction has appeared in *Harpers, The New Yorker,* and many other magazines.

Thomas S. Roche's work has appeared in two
previous editions of *The Best American Erotica,* as well as
many other magazines and anthologies. He is currently a
columnist for www.gothic.net. His collection of short
stories, *Dark Matter,* is available from Masquerade Books.
He lives in San Francisco.

John Mason Skipp is a busy L.A. filmmaker
(*Peekaboo*), *New York Times* bestselling novelist (*The
Scream, The Light at the End*), editor (*Mondo Zombie,
Book of the Dead*), and musician/composer (*Damage
Control*). He also has two children and seven other books,
plus innumerable essays, music videos, and short stories.

Robin Sweeney (robsweeney@aol.com) is a Bay
Area writer, editor, and activist. She is the author of several
short stories, and the co-editor with Pat Califia of *The Second Coming.*

Cecilia Tan just can't keep sex out of her work.
She is the author of *Black Feathers: Erotic Dreams,* a collection of her erotic short stories published by Harper-
Collins; *The Velvet Dress,* a cybersex S/M novel published
by Masquerade Books; and numerous articles and essays
on sex and eroticism. She also edits anthologies of erotic
science fiction and fantasy for Circlet Press, Inc., and
teaches erotic writing workshops. She has considered
starting a society for sex writers and publishers who are
too busy to have actual sex.

Anne Tourney's fiction has appeared in *The Best
American Erotica 1994, Paramour,* and the e-zines *Fishnet*

and *Dreams and Dragons.* She is working on a master's degree in library science and writing a mainstream novel. Anne is a lifetime devotee of public transportation.

Edo van Belkom (www.horrornet.com/belkom. htm) is author of more than 120 short stories published in a wide variety of magazines and anthologies, including *Hot Blood 4, Hot Blood 6, Seductive Specters, Demon Sex,* and *Brothers of the Night.* His first novel, *Wyrm Wolf,* was a Bram Stoker Award finalist. Other novels include *Lord Soth* and *Mister Magick.* His first short-story collection, *Death Drives a Semi,* was published in 1998. Under the name Evan Hollander he has written numerous erotic stories for men's magazines, several being collected in the chapbook *Virtual Girls,* published by Boston's Circlet Press.

Reader's Directory

Alyson Publications

Alyson Publications Inc., founded in 1980, publishes books for, by, and about lesbians and gay men. Alyson is committed to publishing "books about our lives." 6922 Hollywood Blvd., Suite 1000, Los Angeles, CA 90028; (213) 860-6065; mail@alyson.com or http://www.alyson. com.

Circlet Press

Circlet Press has been publishing fine erotic science fiction and fantasy anthologies since 1992. From vampires to cybertechnology, their books cover all manner of fantastic and futuristic erotic possibilities. Circlet Press, Dept. BAE98, 1770 Massachusetts Ave., Suite 278, Cambridge, MA 02140; http://www.circlet.com.

Cleis Press

Publishing America's most intelligent and provocative sex-positive books for girlfriends of all genders. P.O. Box 14684, San Francisco, CA 94114; (800) 780-2279; cleis@ aol.com.

Fishnet

Fishnet is a multigendered, multipreferential, World Wide Web sex magazine published in connection with Blowfish, the mail-order adult products catalog. Fishnet has been publishing fiction, reviews, essays, and news features since 1996. Fishnet, c/o Blowfish, 2261 Market St. #284, San Francisco, CA 94114; (415) 252-4340; http://www. fishnetmag.com/.

Libido
The journal of sex and sensibility. Published quarterly by Marianna Beck and Jack Hafferkamp. Subscriptions: $30 per year; single issue, $8. P.O. Box 146721, Chicago, IL 60614.

Masquerade Books
World's leading publisher of straight, gay, lesbian, and S/M erotic literature. Richard Kasak, publisher. Bimonthly *Masquerade Erotic Newsletter* subscriptions are $30 per year; book catalogs are free. 801 Second Ave., New York, NY 10017.

Nerve Publishing
Launched on June 26, 1997, the day the Communications Decency Act was toppled, *Nerve* (www.nervemag.com) is a magazine of exceptional photographs and writing about sex and gender. *Nerve* publishes contributions every week from writers such as Norman Mailer, Sallie Tisdale, Rick Moody, Lucy Grealy, and Robert Olen Butler, as well as photographs from Andres Serrano, Sylvia Plachy, and others. The book *Nerve: Literate Smut* is due out from Broadway Books this fall.

Paramour
Luscious, cream-filled pansexual magazine featuring short fiction, poetry, photography, illustration, and reviews by emerging writers and artists. Amelia Copeland, pub-

lisher/editor. Published quarterly; subscriptions are $18 per year, samples are $4.95. P.O. Box 949, Cambridge, MA 02140-0008.

The Permanent Press

The Permanent Press of Sag Harbor, New York, is best known for publishing artfully written fiction, both erotic and otherwise, gaining more than fifty literary honors for their authors. Among their books is the complete literary output of Marco Vassi, perhaps the most accomplished erotic writer of his generation. 4120 Noyac Road, Sag Harbor, NY 11963.

WHAP! Magazine: Women Who Administer Punishment

Badly behaving beau? Spank him, advise the editors of *WHAP! Magazine: The Modern Woman's Guidebook to Marital Bliss.* These authoritarian women use disciplinary methods of the 1950s on their self-indulgent men. Devilishly apt punishments include mouth-soapings to cure sarcasm and enemas for on-line perverts. Naughty hubbies beware! Send $7.95 for sample issue to Retro Systems, P.O. Box 69491, Los Angeles, CA 90069; (310) 854-1043 for credit-card orders, or e-mail retrosys@wenet.net or http://www.whapmag.com.

Credits

Reader Survey

1. *What are your favorite stories in this year's collection?*

2. *Have you read previous years' editions of* The Best American Erotica? *(1993, 1994, 1995, 1996, 1997)*

3. *If yes, do you have any favorite stories from those previous collections?*

4. *Do you have any recommendations for next year's* The Best American Erotica? *(Nominated stories must have been published in the United States, in any form, during the 1999 calendar year.)*

5. *How did you get this book?*
   ___ *independent bookstore*   ___ *chain bookstore*
   ___ *mail-order company*   ___ *other type of store*
   ___ *sex/erotica shop*   ___ *borrowed it from a friend*

6. *How old are you?*

7. Male, Female, Other?

8. Where do you live?
    ___ West Coast   ___ South
    ___ Midwest   ___ Other
    ___ East Coast

9. What made you interested in BAE 1999?
    ___ enjoyed other BAE collections
    ___ editor's reputation
    ___ authors' reputations
    ___ enjoy "Best of" type
    ___ word-of-mouth recommendation
    ___ anthologies in general
    ___ read book review

10. Any other suggestions? Feedback?

Please return this survey or any other BAE-related corre-
spondence to: Susie Bright, BAE Feedback, 309 Cedar
Street, #3D, Santa Cruz, CA 95060, or you can e-mail me
at BAEfeedback@susiebright.com.

Thanks so much.